Roberdeau Buchanan

Genealogy of the Roberdeau family

Including a biography of General Daniel Roberdeau

Roberdeau Buchanan

Genealogy of the Roberdeau family
Including a biography of General Daniel Roberdeau

ISBN/EAN: 9783337197773

Printed in Europe, USA, Canada, Australia, Japan

Cover: Foto ©Raphael Reischuk / pixelio.de

More available books at **www.hansebooks.com**

OF THE

ROBERDEAU FAMILY,

INCLUDING A BIOGRAPHY OF

GENERAL DANIEL ROBERDEAU,

OF THE REVOLUTIONARY ARMY, AND THE CONTINENTAL CONGRESS;
AND SIGNER OF THE ARTICLES OF CONFEDERATION.

By ROBERDEAU BUCHANAN.

PRINTED FOR PRIVATE DISTRIBUTION.

• • •

WASHINGTON:
JOSEPH L. PEARSON, PRINTER.
1876.

To the Memory

OF

GENERAL DANIEL ROBERDEAU,

OF THE

REVOLUTIONARY ARMY AND THE CONTINENTAL CONGRESS,

AND TO

COLONEL ISAAC ROBERDEAU,

OF THE

UNITED STATES ARMY, AND CHIEF OF THE TOPOGRAPHICAL
ENGINEER BUREAU,

This Book

IS AFFECTIONATELY INSCRIBED BY THEIR DESCENDANT,

THE AUTHOR.

PREFACE.

A word may not be out of place in respect to the reasons for publishing a book on family history. The principal of these reasons is that the writer, having in his possession very many facts in relation to our ancestors, and knowing there to be among the members of the family an universal desire for such information, considers it a duty he owes to others to impart his knowledge to them, especially considering that these facts will not only be more valued by each succeeding generation, but will become, also, more difficult to be obtained.

The writer has from boyhood been interested in this subject, and this book is the work of leisure hours. Robert Cunyngham's manuscript of the family, written in or before 1740, being the neucleus around which the rest has collected. Many facts having accumulated from time to time, the writer, in 1872, began more thoroughly to search for information, and in June, addressed a circular letter to such members of the family as he then knew of. And by this means the descendants have all been ascertained by a correspondence with each branch or family.

The publication was at that time looked forward to only as a contingent possibility. But the replies to the circular and to other letters being far more encouraging than the writer had hoped, he now offers the work to the family. But *two hundred* copies have been printed, and are offered at a price that will merely cover the cost. The original design, that the work should be kept in the family, is adhered to, no copies being offered for public sale, but a few have, however, been placed in some of the public libraries.

The latter and main portion of the book is the genealogy of the family. Of this the biographies of General Roberdeau, Colonel D. C. Clymer, and the genealogical charts, &c., have been compiled from historical works, aided by family records.

The remainder has been written almost wholly from information received from members of the family, or from other manuscript records, none of which has before appeared in print, save two or three individual facts or biographies.

And here the writer takes the opportunity to recommend the reader to study the system upon which it is written, being that now usually adopted by genealogists. The whole family is classified into generations, and with but one exception, arranged in strict order of primogeniture. The numbering, 1, 2, 3, 4, &c., running through this portion of the book, shows that those names opposite to which it is placed, appear first, as children, and, are repeated further on in the book, as parents. By following these numbers the reader may trace his pedigree upwards, or his descendants downward.

(Just before the main genealogy is a short one of Robert Cunyngham's descendants abroad, arranged upon another system, which is rather the clearest and best for a *few* names, but impracticable when there are many names or long biographies; the other, must then be resorted to.)

The writer regrets that more extended biographies of some members of the family have not been furnished, but each correspondent in this matter having properly suited his own pleasure, the writer has inserted just the facts received by him, and as nearly as possible in the same wording. Some few omissions yet remain unsupplied by correspondents that it is not deemed advisable longer to wait for. Some few discrepancies of names and dates have been observed in the matter furnished by different persons, but none of much moment. Where they could not be reconciled or corrected, the writer has given that which seemed most probably correct; hence may appear some apparent errors.

Each line has been followed down until it ended in unmarried persons or young children. There is thus hardly a possibility of any one having been omitted, unless it be that of some infant who died young. So that in respect to names, the book may be considered as *complete*.

The writer has endeavored throughout to record the details and dates of facts and events, for those are the soonest lost and most difficult to be recovered, while the general fact may be still well known.

The name CUNYNGHAM is spelled variously. In Robert Cunyngham's manuscript it is thus spelled, which is, consequently, the proper orthography of our branch of that large family. Old writers were not particular as to their spelling of proper names; hence one cause of the varieties observable in these days. In making extracts from old writers the name is here quoted sometimes literally, and sometimes changed to conform to the old manuscript.

It is difficult in a genealogy to give satisfaction to all. Nearly every head of a family has been heard from, and in some cases two or three members, all of whom, with three exceptions, have expressed themselves in favor of this publication; some very enthusiastically. These three have, notwithstanding, kindly given the writer all the information asked for, and none have really objected.

To all those of the family who have so kindly furnished material, the writer returns his sincere thanks. Also to Wm. H. Whitmore, Esq., of Boston, for advice and the benefit of his valuable experience in this subject; and to Albert H. Hoyt, Esq., of Boston, for similar favors. Also to the librarians and assistants in the following libraries: The New England Historical and Genealogical Society, Harvard University, Boston Public Library, Boston Athenæum, Charlestown Public Library, Philadelphia Historical Society, Philadelphia City Library, The Congressional Library at Washington, and to Monsieur J. Taschereau, Director-General of the National Library at Paris. To many others, too numerous to mention, the writer is also indebted for many favors.

The writer asks the indulgence of the family for any omissions that may have been made, and hopes that careful and prolonged search for facts, in his efforts to do justice to the subject and give satisfaction to all, may compensate for lack of other qualifications. And he trusts that the expectations of the family regarding this book have not been set so high as to cause disappointment. It may at least serve to preserve for our children, facts that are interesting to ourselves.

Any errors or inadvertencies that may be observed the writer will be glad to be informed of.

WASHINGTON, D. C., *May*, 1876.

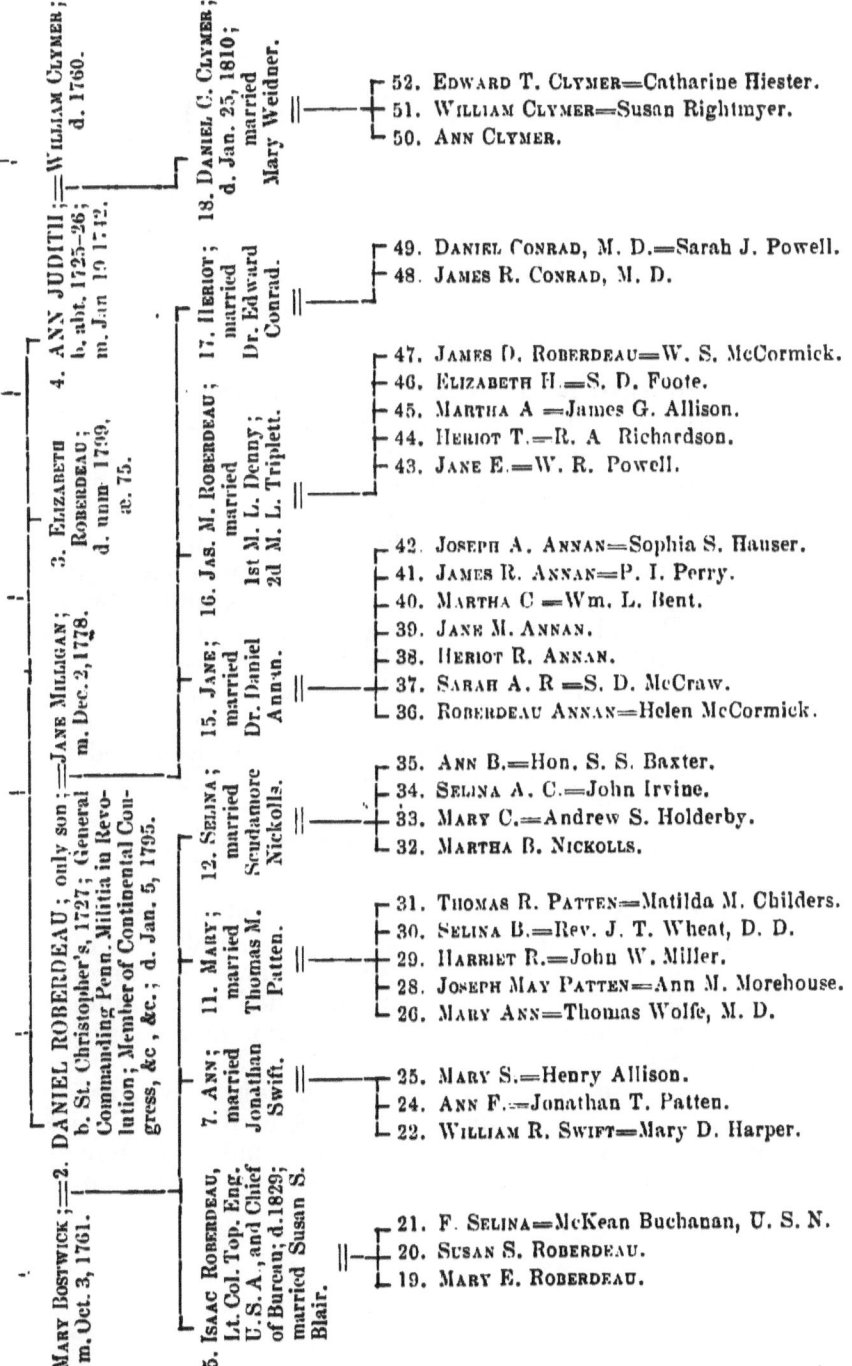

WILLIAM CLYMER; d. 1760.

MARY BOSTWICK ;=2. DANIEL ROBERDEAU; only son ;=JANE MULLIGAN; m. Oct. 3, 1761.   b. St. Christopher's, 1727; (General   m. Dec. 2, 1778.
                                            Commanding Penn. Militia in Revo-
                                            lution; Member of Continental Con-
                                            gress, &c., &c.; d. Jan. 5, 1795.

3. ELIZABETH ROBERDEAU; d. unm 1799, æ. 75.

4. ANN JUDITH; b. abt. 1725–26; m. Jan 19 1742.

18. DANIEL C. CLYMER; d. Jan. 25, 1810; married Mary Weidner.

52. EDWARD T. CLYMER=Catharine Hiester.
51. WILLIAM CLYMER=Susan Rightmyer.
50. ANN CLYMER.

17. HERIOT; married Dr. Edward Conrad.

49. DANIEL CONRAD, M. D.=Sarah J. Powell.
48. JAMES R. CONRAD, M. D.

16. JAS. M. ROBERDEAU; married 1st M. L. Denny; 2d M. L. Triplett.

47. JAMES D. ROBERDEAU=W. S. McCormick.
46. ELIZABETH H.=S. D. Foote.
45. MARTHA A.=James G. Allison.
44. HERIOT T.=R. A Richardson.
43. JANE E.=W. R. Powell.

15. JANE; married Dr. Daniel Annan.

42. JOSEPH A. ANNAN=Sophia S. Hauser.
41. JAMES R. ANNAN=P. I. Perry.
40. MARTHA C.=Wm. L. Bent.
39. JANE M. ANNAN.
38. HERIOT R. ANNAN.
37. SARAH A. R.=S. D. McCraw.
36. ROBERDEAU ANNAN=Helen McCormick.

12. SELINA; married Scudamore Nickolls.

35. ANN B.=Hon. S. S. Baxter.
34. SELINA A. C.=John Irvine.
33. MARY C.=Andrew S. Holderby.
32. MARTHA B. NICKOLLS.

11. MARY; married Thomas M. Patten.

31. THOMAS R. PATTEN=Matilda M. Childers.
30. SELINA B.=Rev. J. T. Wheat, D. D.
29. HARRIET R.=John W. Miller.
28. JOSEPH MAY PATTEN=Ann M. Morehouse.
26. MARY ANN=Thomas Wolfe, M. D.

7. ANN; married Jonathan Swift.

25. MARY S.=Henry Allison.
24. ANN F.=Jonathan T. Patten.
22. WILLIAM R. SWIFT=Mary D. Harper.

5. ISAAC ROBERDEAU, Lt. Col. Top. Eng. U. S. A., and Chief of Bureau; d.1829; married Susan S. Blair.

21. F. SELINA=McKean Buchanan, U. S. N.
20. SUSAN S. ROBERDEAU.
19. MARY E. ROBERDEAU.

GENEALOGY

OF THE

ROBERDEAU FAMILY.

—•—

PART I.—HISTORICAL.

—•—

The family of ROBERDEAU, in this country is of French origin, the first of whom we know of, being Isaac Roberdeau, a Huguenot, who fled from Rochelle, France, on the revocation of the Edict of Nantes, and took refuge on the Island of St. Christopher's, one of the British West Indies, in 1685. Here he married Mary Cunyngham, of that place, the descendant of an ancient and noble Scotch family. She, after her husband's death, came to Philadelphia with her children, and is the progenitor of all of these two families in this country.

As our knowledge of the Roberdeau family begins where that of the Cunyngham ends, the chronology and connection between the two will be better preserved by considering the latter family first:

THE FAMILY OF CUNYNGHAM.

THIS FAMILY, in Scotland, first came into notice in the year 1057, by its progenitor having conferred upon him the old Saxon title of nobility, that of Thane of Cunyngham ; and the family thereafter continued to maintain a high social position, as may be seen from their marriage connections.

The annexed chart, or tree of the family, will assist the reader in understanding the lines of descent of the Cunyngham and Roberdeau families, and also give a clear view of the several branches of the latter family

GENEALOGY

OF THE

ROBERDEAU FAMILY.

PART I.—HISTORICAL.

The family of ROBERDEAU, in this country is of French
origin, the first of whom we know of, being Isaac Roberdeau, a Huguenot, who fled from Rochelle, France, on
the revocation of the Edict of Nantes, and took refuge
on the Island of St. Christopher's, one of the British
West Indies, in 1685. Here he married Mary Cunyngham, of that place, the descendant of an ancient and
noble Scotch family. She, after her husband's death,
came to Philadelphia with her children, and is the progenitor of all of these two families in this country.

As our knowledge of the Roberdeau family begins
where that of the Cunyngham ends, the chronology and
connection between the two will be better preserved by
considering the latter family first:

THE FAMILY OF CUNYNGHAM.

THIS FAMILY, in Scotland, first came into notice in the
year 1057, by its progenitor having conferred upon him
the old Saxon title of nobility, that of Thane of Cunyngham; and the family thereafter continued to maintain a
high social position, as may be seen from their marriage
connections.

The annexed chart, or tree of the family, will assist
the reader in understanding the lines of descent of the
Cunyngham and Roberdeau families, and also give a
clear view of the several branches of the latter family

down to the fourth generation, many of whom are now living. The chart was mainly compiled from *Douglass' Peerage of Scotland, Burke's Peerage of England,* and *Stuart's History of the Stewart Family,* well known to be authentic publications; and from the family records.

The history of the CUNYNGHAM family has been compiled by one of our ancestors, Robert Cunyngham, about the year 1740, or earlier; and the old manuscript, in his own handwriting, has been handed down in our family for five generations. Many of the facts contained therein have been collected and published by later writers. And if this genealogy were intended for the public, it would be sufficient merely to refer the reader to those publications; but as the old manuscript is of itself interesting as a valuable heirloom, it is therefore given entire and with no change, save the many abbreviations are written in full; the numerous capitals, so much in use in the last century, have been suppressed; and the leading names given in capitals, to conform to the style usually adopted by genealogists. The quaint spelling has, however, been preserved strictly; even where it differs from modern writers, especially in the spelling of proper names, as may be seen by a comparison with the foot-notes. The manuscript being comparatively brief, compared to some of the above-mentioned publications, it is thought that additional facts from them, inserted as foot-notes, would be acceptable to the reader, some of those works being exceedingly scarce.

Robert Cunyngham's manuscript is as follows:

GENOLOGIE OF THE RIGHT HONORABLE THE EARL OF GLENCAIRN'S FAMILY.[1]

FREDERICK VAN BASSEN, a Norwegian, wrote a manuscript (now in the Lawyers' Library at Edinburgh) of the rise of some families, amongst whom is that of the Cunynghams,[2] whose progenitor he calls MALCOME, the son of FRISKINE, who assisted Prince Malcome, afterwards king, surnamed Caumore, to escape from Macbeth's tyranny; who being hotly pursued by usurper's

---

[1] The following foot-notes are taken, unless otherwise stated, from *Douglas' Peerage of Scotland,* Edinburg, 1768, which gives a more full account of the family than Robert Cunyngham's manuscript.

[2] This noble family is of very great antiquity in the west of Scotland.—[Here follows the account as given in the text.] We shall deduce the descent of this illustrious family by authentic documents.

men, did hide the Prince by forking hay above him. And after the Prince's happy accession to the crown, *Anno Domini* 1057, he rewarded his preserver Malcome with the Thanedom (should be Baillziery) of Cunyngham, from which his posterity did afterward take their surname.

He gave him a hay-fork for his arms, and *Over fork over*, for his motto, which he was saying when the usurper's men came to him.

2d. WERNEBALD[3] possessed the lands Kilmars, in Cunyngham, in A. D. 1066.

3d. ROBERT,[4] the son of Wernebald, gave his village of Cunyngham and Kirk of Kilmars, with half a carrucal of land belonging to the said Kirk, to the Abbacy of Kelso. He gave also the lands of Glencerguardland in the merus, to the Abbacy of Arbroth, with consent of his wife Richinda, daughter and heiress of Humphrey Barkley, of Guerntilly.

4th. ROBERT,[5] the son of Robert, the son of Wernebald, ratifies the grant made by his father to the Abbey of Kelso, which is also continued by Richard Morvil, constable to the King of Scots, A. D. 1126.

5th. STEPHEN DE CUNYNGHAM[6] married Maud Morvill, daughter to Richard, the Constable. He is one of the fifteen

---

[3] The lands and barony were located in the bailcary of Cunynghame, and shire of Ayr, which hath been one of the chief titles of the family ever since; and of him, all the Cunynghams in Scotland are descended. He left two sons. Robert and Galfridus. The latter is witness to a charter by King Malcolm IV., of a donation to the Abbacy of Scoon, between 1153 and 1165, in which last year King Malcolm died. Robert Cunyngham also mentions this in an appended note on a succeeding page.

[4] He is also witness to an old charter of Richard de Morville, constable of Scotland, *anno* 1162.

[5] The first we find designated *dominus*. These donations are also confirmed by Ingelram, Bishop of Glasgow, in or before 1174, in which year the bishop died. Sir Robert left three children, Robert, William, and James. [The date in the text should probably be 1162.]

[6] Here occurs a difference between these two writers which can be best explained by placing the names side by side:

ROBERT CUNYNGHAM's MS.		DOUGLASS' PEERAGE.
5. STEPHEN, m. Maud Morville.	v.	ROBERT.
6. RICHARD, witness to charter of Lord of Galloway.	vi. HERVIE, obtains Kilmaurs.	RICHARD, witness to charter of Lord of Galloway. 2d son.
7. FERGUS.	vii. SIR WILLIAM.	GALFRIDUS. 2d son.
8. HERVIE gets charter of lands of Kilmaurs.		
9. EDWARD.	viii. EDWARD.	

The difference is seen to be more a misplacement of names than a contradiction. *Nisbet's Heraldry*, 1722, agrees with Robert Cunyngham, and *Burke's* hostages given to King Henry the 2d, of England, for King William of Scotland's liberation, A. D. 1174, ten years after he was taken prisoner at the battle of Anwick.

6th. RICHARD CUNYNGHAM,[7] witness to a charter granted by Allan, Lord of Galloway, to Heu Crawford, the Earl of Loudon's predecessor.

7th. FERGUS CUNYNGHAM,[8] is mentioned in the Register of Paisley.

8th. HERVIE CUNYNGHAM,[9] gets a charter of the lands of Kilmars from King Alexander the 3d, A. D. 1264.

9th. EDWARD,[10] the son of Hervie, mortifies the lands of Grange, in Kilmarnock Parish, in the Abbey of Kilwinig.

10th. GILMORE,[11] the son of Hervie, renounces the league with France and swears allegiance to King Edward, of England, A. D. 1296; had SIR ROBERT and JAMES, who gets lands of Hessendane; from whom Bettan, Barnes, and Siket are descended.

11th. SIR ROBERT,[12] gets a charter of the lands of Lambroughton, from King Robert the 1st, in the 13th year of his reign, A. D. 1319.

Peerage with Douglass' arrangement. In the ninth generation all four agree. There is a difference of spelling often noticed in the old writers, caused by translating names from one language to another. Thus, Galfridus and Fergus are same. Also in the ninth generation, Gilmore and Gilbert. Other examples may be given: Giles and Egedia; James, Jacob and Ichabod.—(See upon this subject *Buchanan of Auchmar's Essay, &c.*, Glasgow, 1723, American reprint, 1849, p. 24.)

[7] Douglass gives Hervie the heir, whom he says was a brave warrior and behaved gallantly at the battle of Large, 1263. Married —— Riddell, heiress of Glengarnock. Got a charter of the lands of Kilmaurs, 1264. Of Richard, whom he styles second son, he gives the same account as in the text above.

[8] SIR WILLIAM, of whom there are many documents; mentioned in the determination of a dispute between the Abbots of Melrose and Kelso, 1269, and in a charter Malcolm, Earl of Lennox, *circa* 1275. Galfridus (Fergus) is named as second son by Douglass.

[9] See above. Written Henry by some writers.

[10] From here, the two accounts agree. Edward died before 1290, his younger son Richard, is ancestor of the Cunynghams of Polmais.

[11] Probably a clerical error: should be Gilmore, son of *Edward*. Written GILBERT, by Douglass, and also by Robert Cunyngham himself, in a note appended to a succeeding page. Witness to a charter of Malcolm, Earl of Lennox, together with James, Lord High Steward of Scotland. He was one of the *magnates Scotiæ* chosen upon the part of Robert Bruce, Lord of Annandale, in the competition for the crown between him and Baliol, *anno* 1292. Donald, a third son of Gilbert, is mentioned; written *David* by Robert Cunyngham on a subsequent page.

[12] Had large possessions in the south and west of Scotland. Swears allegiance to King Edward I., of England, 1296, but afterwards joined Robert

12th. SIR WILLIAM,[13] was Earl of Carrict, in right of his wife, Lady Helen Bruce, sister and heiress to Thomas, Earl of Carrict; had SIR WILLIAM and THOMAS, predecessor to Caprington.

13th. SIR WILLIAM,[14] married Eilasabeth, daughter and heiress of Sir Robert Denison, of that Ilk; had ROBERT and WILLIAM, predecessor to Cuninghamheid.

14th. ROBERT,[15] gets a charter of the lands of Kilmars from Robert, Duke of Albany, Governor of Scotland, on his father

---

Bruce. (Note.—The list of those who were compelled to swear allegiance to Edward I., when he overran Scotland, is called the Ragman Roll; to sign which, "few of any tolerable repute neither durst nor did decline," and it is now regarded as indisputable authority of the antiquity and standing of the families of those whose ancestors signed it.) Sir Robert left two sons, Sir William and Sir Andrew, and died about 1330.

[13] Douglass asserts that it was not the Countess of Carrick, but a former wife, who was the mother of Sir William's children. But Burke, who is high authority upon such matters, goes into quite an argument against Douglass and other writers to prove that she was. He says that the principal argument is: that if Lady Helen Bruce were the mother, the earldom of Carrick would have descended to her sons; but as it reverted to the crown, therefore she had no heirs. In refutation of this, Burke quotes the old charter, that the earldom was limited to heirs *male*, and although Lady Helen possessed it, the later charter of 1362, conferring it then upon her husband, was singularly incomplete in that clause which, in other titles, entails them upon heirs. So that this title could not, by the latter charter, descend to his or her heirs, and, therefore, upon the death of Lady Helen, reverted to the crown. This incompleteness, coupled with the fact that the old charter limited the title to heirs *male*, shows that in conferring it upon Sir William, they doubted the propriety of the act, and intended that at the death of his wife it should not pass to her heirs, being a female, but revert to the crown.—(*Peerage*, ed. 1853, *Family of Sir Th. M. Cuningham, Bart.*)

It may be stated here that the title of the Earl of Carrick was the chief title of the Bruce family before they succeeded to the crown. Lady Helen was the grand-niece of the "renouned Bruce of Bannockburn."

Sir William had four sons: Robert, one of the noble Scotch heirs sent for King David's ransom, and dies before his father; William, the heir; Thomas; and Andrew; Sir William died before 1384.

[14] He was a brave and gallant knight, and out of the 40,000 francs distributed by the King of France to the nobles of his faithful allies, Sir William received 500. He founded the collegiate church of Kilmaurs, and largely endowed it with a provost and eight prebends; *anno* 1403.—(*Douglass*.) He also, "for the health of his soul, and for the souls of all his ancestors"—as the old charters usually express it—gave in pure alms to the monks of the Abbey of Kilwinning, the lands of Grange.—(*Crawford's History of Renfrewshire*, 1710.) By his wife, Elizabeth Dennistoun, he got a vast estate, viz., the baronies of Glencairn, Finlayston, Kilmarnock, Redhall, Collington, &c., and by whom he had three sons; Henry, the youngest, distinguished himself at the battle of the Beauge, where the Scots obtained a glorious victory over the English, in 1421. Sir William died in 1418.

[15] SIR ROBERT was appointed one of the hostages for the ransom of King James I., who conferred the honor of knighthood on him at his coronation, 1424. He was also one of the judges that sat upon the trial of Murdock, Duke

Sir William's resignation, A. D. 1413; he married Janet, daughter to Alexander, Lord Montgomerie, the Earl of Eglinton's predecessor; had ALEXANDER and SIR WILLIAM, of Waterston.

15th. ALEXAND,[16] disposes the heritable office of Bailzie of Cuningham to his uncle, Alexander, Lord Montgomerie; he was made *Lord Kilmars*, by King James 2d, December, 1454; and *Earl of Glenclairn*, by King James 3d, May 25th, 1466. He married Lady Margaret Hepburn, daughter to the Earl of Bothwell; had—

> ROBERT; and
> WILLIAM, Laird of Craigends.[17]

16th. ROBERT THE 2ND EARL, married Elizabeth Lindsay, daughter to Lord Lindsay of Byers, the Earl of Crawford's predecessor; and had—

17th. CUTHBERT THE 3RD EARL, Lord High Treasurer of Scotland; he married Lady Marion Douglass, daughter to the Earl of Angus, predecessor to the Duke of Douglass; had: WILLIAM, and LADY MARION, married to Lord Lisle.

18th. WILLIAM THE 4TH EARL, married Margaret Campbell, heiress of Stephenson; had: ALEXANDER; ANDREW, Laird of Coreschill; HEU, Laird Carlung; and LADY ELISABETH, married to Cunninghamheid.

19th. ALEXANDER THE 5TH EARL, married Lady Jean Hamilton, daughter to the Earl of Arran, Duke of Chastellherault, in France, predecessor to Duke Hamilton; had: WILLIAM, and LADY MARGARET, married to Craigy.

His second wife was Jean Cunningham, daughter to the Laird of Caprington; and had: ALEXANDER, Laird Montgreen; and

---

of Albany, for treason, in 1425.—(See *Crawford's Renfrewshire*, for an account of this trial.) Together with Lord Montgomery, he got a joint commission for the government of Kintyre, Knapdale, &c.

[16] SIR ALEXANDER was a man of extraordinary parts, in great favor with King James II., who created him a Lord of Parliament, by the title of Lord Cunyngham, of Kilmaurs. He afterwards received a charter under the great seal of several lands. And being in no less favor with King James III., was appointed one of the lords of his privy council. He was a faithful and loyal subject, standing loyally by King James in all his vicissitudes of fortune; for which, and in consideration of his many good and faithful services, he was further dignified, May 28, 1488 (not 1466), with the title of Earl of Glencairn, to him and his heirs, forever. His wife was the daughter of Patrick Hepburn, Lord of Hailes, whose son (not the father) was created Earl of Bothwell. He left four sons, the two younger being Alexander and Edward. The earl, fighting gallantly at the battle of Bannockburn, fell with his royal master, King James, on the eleventh of June, 1488.

[17] The family of Roberdeau being descended from the second son of Alexander, first Earl of Glencairn, who will be again recurred to a few pages hence, further extracts from Douglass will be omitted.

LADY JANE, married to the Earl of Argyle, and after him, to Sir William Colquhoun of Luss.

20th. WILLIAM 6TH EARL, married Janet Gordon, daughter to the Laird of Lochinvar, the Viscount of Kenmure's predecesssor; had: JAMES; JOHN, Laird of Ross; and four daughters:—

    1st. LADY JANE, married Haldane of Glencairn; after his death, Kilpatrick of Closburn; and after his death, Ferguson of Craigdaroch.
    2nd. LADY MARGARET, married the Laird of Maclaine.
    3rd. LADY ELISABETH, married Crawford of Auchinames; after his death, the Laird of Craigends.
    4th. LADY SUSAN, married Napier of Kilmahen.

21st. JAMES THE 7TH EARL, was Lord Treasurer, married Margaret Campbell, daughter to Laird Glenarchy, predecessor to the Earl of Bredalbin; had: WILLIAM; JOHN, Laird Cambuskeith, and six daughters:—

    1st. LADY JANE, contracted to the Earl of Cassills, marrying another, she died that day.
    2nd. LADY KATHERINE, married Sir Jas. Cuningham of Glengarnock.
    3rd. LADY MARGARET, married Lord Evendale; after his death, Maxwell of Calderwood.
    4th. LADY ANN, married the Marquis of Hamilton and was mother to Duke James and Duke William.
    5th. SUSAN, Lady Hatton.
    6th. MARY, Lady Kilbernie.

22nd. WILLIAM THE 8TH EARL, married Lady Janet Carr, daughter to the Earl, now Marquis of Lothian; had: WILLIAM, COLONEL ROBERT, and five daughters:—

    1st. LADY MARGARET, Stewart of Mirg [?]
    2nd. LADY ELIZABETH, married Beaton of Creigh; after his death, Chisholm of Crumlie.
    3rd. LADY JEAN, married the Laird of Blair.
    4th. LADY ANN, never married.
    5th. LADY MARION, married the Earl of Finlater; and after his death, Fraser of Philorth, Lord Saltoun's predecessor.

23rd. WILLIAM THE 9TH EARL, Lord High Chancelor, married Lady Jean Ogilvie, daughter to the Earl of Finlator; had—

    WILLIAM, Lord Kilmars, died unmarried.
    JAMES, Lord Kilmars, married Lady Elizabeth, daughter to Duke William Hamilton; he died without child.
    ALEXANDER; and
    JOHN. His daughters:—
    1st. LADY JEAN, married the Earl of Kilmarnock.
    2nd. LADY MARY, married the Lord of Bargauey.
    3rd. LADY ELIZABETH, married Hamilton of Orbistoun.
    4th. LADY ANN.

24th. ALEXANDER THE 10TH EARL, was the Chancellor, third son; he married Nicholas, daughter of Sir Louis Stewart, of Kirkhill, a Lord of Session; had: MARGARET, Countess of Lauderdale.

25th. JOHN THE 11TH EARL, succeeded his brother; he married Lady Mary Erskine, daughter to the Earl of Mar, and had—

25th. WILLIAM THE 12TH EARL, married Lady Henrietta Stewart, daughter to the Earl of Galloway; had: WILLIAM; JOHN, an officer in the Dutch service; ALEXANDER, who died a lieutenant at Porto Bello after it was taken by Admiral Vernon; and JAMES, also dead. The daughters :—

> 1st. LADY MARGARET, married Nichol Graham, of Garthmore, Esq.
> 2d. LADY HENRIETTA, married John Campbell, Esq., a Commissioner of the Custom, and eldest son of Daniel Campbell, of Shanfield, Esq.
> 3d. ———

26th. WILLIAM THE 13TH EARL,[18] not yet married, October the 20th, 1740.

---

[18] To continue the account from a later edition of Douglass by John P. Wood, 1813:

WILLIAM, the thirteenth Earl, succeeded his father, 1734; was made governor of Dumbarton Castle, and obtained the rank of major-general in the army. He married, 1747, eldest daughter and heiress of Hugh Macguire, of Drumdon, in Ayrshire. He died, 1775, leaving six children. The oldest daughter married Sir Alexander Don, Bart.

JAMES, 14TH EARL, succeeded his father, and sold the ancient family estate of Kilmaurs to the Marchioness of Titchfield in 1786. He was a lover of the arts and a patron of the poet Burns, who showed his grief for his benefactor in his beautiful "Lament for James, Earl of Glencairn," ending,—

> "But I'll remember thee, Glencairn,
> And a' that thou hast done for me."

A previous earl, probably Cuthbert, has also been honored by being introduced into one of the poems of his distinguished countryman, Sir Walter Scott, where King James V. is saying—

> "I staunch'd thy father's death-feud stern,
> With stout De Vaux and grey Glencairn."
> *Lady of the Lake, Canto VI.*, 27.

He is again mentioned in Marmion (v. 26) as one of the commanders of the Scottish army. James died unmarried, June 30, 1791, and was succeeded by his brother,—

JOHN, 15TH EARL, born May, 1750, an officer of dragoons, who afterwards took orders. He married Lady Elizabeth Erskine, second daughter of Henry David, Earl of Buchan, and died at Coats, September 24, 1796. Having no children the honors became extinct. The castle of Finlayston, the principal residence of the family, devolved upon Robert Graham, Esq., of Gartmore.

The title was claimed by Sir Adam Ferguson, of Kilkerran, Baronet; by Sir Walter Montgomery Cunyngham, as male heir; and by Lady Harriet Don, sister of the last earl.

Sir Adam Ferguson's claim was decided by the House of Lords, July 14, 1797. The claimant has shown himself to be the heir-general of Alexander, [fifth] Earl of Glencairn, who died in 1670, but hath not made out the right of such heir-general to the dignity of Earl of Glencairn. Sir Walter Mont-

CADETS OF GLENCLAIRN'S FAMILY.	Their Cadets.
1st. GLENGARNOCK was the eldest and greatest branch of this family.	Shulloch, Drumwhattle, Auchtermachen, Caddell, Quarilston, Nevton, &c.
2d. HESSENDANE.	Bolton, Barnes, Siket.
3d. AUCHINHARVIE.	Buquhan.
4th. POLMEIS.	
5th. POLQUERN.	Milncraig.
6th. BONITON.	
7th. MARQUIS OF CANGEE, } In France. 8th. COUNT CUNINGHAM, }	
9th. CAPRINGTON.	Leasan, Lochermoss, Collinan, Enterkin.
10th. CUNINGHAMHEID.	
11th. WATERSTON.	
12th. CRAGIENDS, 2d son, the first earl.	Robertland, Kerncurran, Askinyeard, &c.
13th. CORSEHILL.	
14th. CARLUNG.	
15th. MONTGREENAN.	
16th. ROSS.	
17th. CAMBUSKEITH.	

GLENGARNOCK was the eldest and great branch of this family.

---

gomery Cunyngham had produced no evidences. Lady Harriet Don had not produced sufficient grounds in support of her claim.

Thus the earldom still remains extinct for want of heirs.

Chief seats of the Earl of Glencairn: At Kilmaurs, in Cuninghame, and Finlayston, in Renfrewshire, on the banks of the river Clyde.

Crawford's Renfrewshire says: "Three miles towards the west, from Erskine, upon the coast, on a rising ground, is situate the castle of Finlaystoun, the seat of the Earl of Glencairn, well planted. The house is a noble and great building round a court." It is described in *Murray's Handbook of Scotland*, and located on his map of Scotland.

ARMS: *Argent, a shake-fork sable; supporters, two rabbits proper; crest, an unicorn's head couped; motto, over fork over.*

GALFRIDUS[19] is witness to King Malcome the 4th, charter of foundation to the Abbacy of Scoone.

SIR GILBERT is called to Berwick by King Edward, of England, to hear the claims of Baliol and Bruce for the crown.

DAVID, his son, renounces the league with France and swears allegiance to the King of England.

GENEALOGIE OF THE LAIRD OF CRAIGEND'S FAMILY.[20]

16th. 1ST WILLIAM CUNYNGHAM, THE 1ST LAIRD OF CRAIG-ENDS,[21] was the 16th from Friskine, father of Malcome, who

---

[19] These appear to be appended by Robert Cunyngham as though omitted in their proper places; the former refers to the son of Wennebald, in the second generation of the family, and the latter to Gilmore, or Gilbert, in the tenth.

[20] The following foot-notes are from George Crawford's *History of the Shire of Renfrew*, 1710, continued by William Semple down to the year 1782; printed in Paisley, Scotland, 1782. (The only copy the writer has seen is in the library of the New England Historical and Genealogical Society, Boston.)

[21] Lower upon the bank of the river Grise stands the house of Craigends, adorned with pleasant orchards and gardens, the seat of an ancient family of the surname of Cunyngham, a cadet of the noble family of Glencairn, lineally descended from William Cunyngham, one of the younger sons of Alexander, first Earl of Glencairn, who obtained from his father the lands of Craigends, *anno* 1477.—(Carta Penes, Will. Cunyngham de Craigends.) He was one of the arbiters betwixt the Abbot of Paisley and the burgh of Renfrew, *anno* 1488.—(Chartulary of Paisley.) He married Elizabeth Stewart, daughter and coheiress of Sir Walter Stewart, of Arthurlie, who was of the Stewarts of Darnley, by whom he obtained the lands of Arthurlie. By reason of this marriage the family of Craigends carry the coat of the Stewart, viz., *Or, a fess checquie, azure and argent,* quartered with their paternal bearing, which is, *Argent, a shake-fork sable.* Walter Stewart, of Arthurlie, obtained from King James III., *anno* 1452, a charter of the lands of Wester Patrick. By Elizabeth Stewart, his daughter and heir, these lands came to William Cunyngham, of Craigends. By the said Elizabeth, his wife, he had issue, William his son and heir. He secondly took to wife dame Marion Auchinleck, daughter and coheiress of Sir John Auchinleck, of that Ilk, an ancient family in Kyle, and dowager of Campbell of Loudon, by which marriage he obtained the barony of Auchinleck, *anno* 1499, and to his heirs, male, bearing the name and arms of Auchinleck. But the conveyance being without the consent of the king, who was superior, the barony of Auchinleck fell into the king's hands by recognition.

A few words in addition, as to this marriage with Elizabeth Stewart. By the spelling it will not at once be recognized as that illustrious family, one of whose members then filled the throne of Scotland, and afterwards that of England. The head of the family held the hereditary office of Lord High Steward, a position next in rank to the king; hence, when surnames came into use, they naturally took that of *Stewart,* from their office. In its corrupted form of *Stuart* the name is better known, from the unfortunate Queen of Scots, whose husband was of the Darnley family here mentioned.—See the large chart of the family; copied there from Andrew Stuart's *History of the Stewart Family,* London, 1798. The only copy the writer has seen being in the Philadelphia City Library.

saved Prince Malcome (afterward King Malcome 3d, surnamd Canmore) when Macbeth had murderd King Duncan, or Donaldus 7th; he was the second son of Alexander, 1st Earl of Glenclairn, by Lady Mary Hepburn, daughter to the Earl of Bothwell; he married Elizabeth Stewart, heiress of Arthurly; had: WILLIAM. His second wife was Marion, daughter of Sir John Auchinleck, of that Ilk, by whom he had: DAVID, Lord of Robertland.

17th. WILLIAM, 2D LAIRD OF CRAIGENDS,[22] married Gilles Campbell, daughter to the Laird, now Earl of Loudon, by whom he had—

> GABRIEL;
> WILLIAM, Laird of Kencurran; and 11 daughters:—
> 1st. STEWART, of Castlemilk;
> 2d. WHITFORD, that Ilk;
> 3d. WALLACE, Elderstie;
> 4th. ———, Dairhome;
> 5th. CRAWFORD, Auchinames, elder;
> 6th. CRAWFORD, Auchinames, younger;
> 7th. PORTERFIELD, Duchald;
> 8th. MAXWELL, Nevark;
> 9th. ———, Stanley;
> 10th. FERGUSON, Craigdarrock;
> 11th. CRAWFORD, Crawfordland.

18th. GABRIEL THE 3D,[23] married Margaret Livingston, daughter to Kilsyth, by Lady Margaret Graham, daughter to the Earl of Monteith; had—

> WILLIAM; and
> JAMES, of Ashenyeards.

19th. WILLIAM THE 4TH, married Elizabeth Cuningham, daughter to Cuninghamheid; and had—

---

[22] The lands of Carncurran were acquired from John, Lord Lyle, in 1544, by Giles, (also written Egedia,) Lady Craigends, daughter of Sir John Campbell, of Killock, a younger son of Sir Colin Campbell, of Loudon, and disposed to the said William, her son. William, 2d Laird, also had a third son, Robert, ancestor of the Cunynghams of Bedland, Auchenharvie, and Southbhook.

[23] Margaret Livingston was the eldest daughter of William Livingston of Kilsyth. Her mother was Mary, daughter of Sir Duncan Forrester, of Garden; her brother married Christian, daughter of the Earl of Menteith.—(*Douglass.*) Besides the two sons, Gabriel had a daughter, Janet, married to Sir Patrick Houston, of that Ilk, with issue; and another married to Andrew Sterling, of Portnallan and Leon. Gabriel Cunyngham being at the battle of Pinkie, in the year 1547, was there slain.

The Roberdeau family being descended from James of Ashenyeard, further notes to the Laird of Craigend's family will be dispensed with. The family of Craigends is, however, in Crawford's History, carried to a later date than in Robert Cunyngham's manuscript.

20th. ALEXANDER THE 5TH, married Lady Elizabeth Cuningham, daughter to the Earl of Glencairn; and had—

21st. WILLIAM THE 6TH, married Elizabeth Stewart, daughter to the Laird of Castlemilk; and had—

22d. WILLIAM THE 7TH, married Elizabeth Napier, daughter
to Lord Napier; had: ALEXANDER; WILLIAM of Butesbon;
JOHN; and two daughters:—

JEAN, married Maxwell of Dargavell;
ELIZABETH, married Schaw of Bargarron; and after his death, Brisbane
of Selviland.

23d. ALEXANDER THE 8TH, married his cousin Janet, daughter to William Cuningham, Keeper of the Signet; had: WIL-
LIAM, and five daughters:—

1. ELIZABETH, married Holstoun of Johnstoun;
2. REBEKAH, married Hamilton of Grange;
3. JEAN, married Alexander of Blackhouse;
4. MARION, married Porterfield of Fullwood;
5. ANN, died unmarried.

24th. WILLIAM THE 9TH, married the relict of Sir William
Cuningham of Cuninghamheid, who died without child by
him; she was daughter to the Viscount Ruthven; his second
wife was Christian, daughter to Sir John Colquhoun of Luss;
had: ALEXANDER; WILLIAM; JAMES; and four daughters:—

1. LILIAS, married Wallace of Kairhill;
2. JANET, died unmarried;
3. MAGDALENA, Mr. Campbell of Netherplace;
4. ELIZABETH, married Porterfield of Haplaud.

25th. ALEXANDER THE 10TH LAIRD of Craigends, married
Ann, daughter of Sir John Houstoun of that Ilk, Bart.; had:
WILLIAM; ALEXANDER, who died a child; and four daugh-
ters:—

1. CHRISTIAN;
2. MARGARET;
3. LILLIAS;
4. JOANNA.

His second wife is Katherine Campbell, daughter to Robert
Campbell, merchant in Edinburg, and relict of Provost Aird of
Glasgow; October 20th, 1740.[24]

---

[24] Arms of Cunyngham of Craigends;—*Quarterly: First and fourth argent, a
shake-fork sable, for* CUNYNGHAM; *Second and third or, a fess cheque, azure
and argent, for* STEWART. CREST, *an unicorn's head couped, argent, horned and
maned or, and gorged with a collar cheque, argent and azure.* MOTTO, *So fork
forward:* as in our ancient and modern books of blazons.—(*Nisbet, System of
Heraldry, Edinburg, 1722.*)

19th. JAMES CUNYNGHAM OF ASHENYEARD;[25] second son of Grabriel, third Laird of Craigends, by Margaret Livingstone, daughter to Kilsyth; whose mother was Lady Mary Grahme, daughter to the Earl of Monteith: he is the fourth generation from Alexander, first Earl of Glencairn; and nineteenth from Friskine the father of Malcome who preserved King Malcome Canmore from Macbeth's tyranny, by forking hay upon him. He married Margaret Fleming, daughter to the Laird of Barrochan, and had with others—

20th. WILLIAM CUNYNGHAM, his second son, a writer to the King's Signet, and came to be keeper thereof; he married Rebekah Muirland, daughter to the Laird of Lenhouse; had—

> RICHARD;
> WILLIAM; and
> JANET, married to Alexander, eighth of Craigends.

21st. RICHARD CUNYNGHAM purchased the barony of Glengarnock; he raised, mounted, armd, payd, and commanded a trooop of one hundred horsemen, and went into England under Duke James Hamilton, the 8th July, 1648, with design to restore King Charles to his throne, but were defeated in August, at Preston.

Duke Hamilton was beheaded for his loyalty; and Richard was obliged to do penance in the Kirk of Kilbernie. Mr. Russell the minister used him favorably, allowd him to be in his seat, said: Glengarnock, you was concernd in what is called the wicked engagement; you went into England in an hostile manner, under Duke Hamilton; you did little gude there, and are sorry for it; to which he replied he was; the penitent and minister were sorry so little gude was done for the king. That penance did not hinder him from raising in like manner another troop of one hundred horsemen, with which he entered England under King Charles 2d and were defeated at Worcester by Oliver Cromwell, the third September, 1651.

These services and a considerable sum of money lent, had no return at the Restoration; which I hope will be a warning for his posterity, to serve their king when he governs according to law, with their persons, but no further.

He married Elizabeth, daughter to James Heriot of Trabroun, jeweller to King Charles 1st, and niece to George Heriot, jeweller to King James 6th and King Charles 1st; who, by his last will and testament, gave the greatest part of his estate to build and

---

[25] An account of this family may be found in the "System of Heraldry," by Alexander Nisbet, Edinburg, 1722; where, also, there is a resume of all the foregoing pedigree. The arms of the Ashenyeard branch, are given, as those of CUNYNGHAM OF CRAIGENDS, with a crescent for difference; CREST, an unicorn's head couped, argent; maned and horned or. MOTTO, Virtute et labore.

endow his hospital at Edinburgh. The marriage contract was made at the place of Robertland, the third day of October, 1654. The children were—

1. RICHARD,	born	October 20, 1655.
2. DAVID,	"	November 14, 1656.
3. WILLIAM,	"	January 17, 1658.
4. ELIZABETH,	"	April —, 1659.
5. ANNA,	"	March 12, 1661.
6. WILLIAM,	"	May, 29, 1662.
7. EVERILDA,	"	June 1, 1664.
8. ALEXANDER,	"	June 13, 1665.
9. JAMES,	"	October 1, 1666.
10. THE SEVENTH SON,	"	December 30, 1667.
11. ROBERT,	"	March 24, 1669.
12. PATRICK,	"	July 24, 1670.

Richard Cunyngham of Glengarnock died there, October the 27, 1670; Elizabeth, his wife, died March, 1672; they are buried in Glengarnock isle, in Kilbernie kirk.

The barony of Glengarnock, was after his death, in the minority of his son Richard,[26] sold to Patrick Crawford of Kilbernie, by Alexander the eighth Laird of Craigends, for about sixteen years' purchase. Richard the son, soon after he came of age went to Craigends. His tutor told him he was not satisfied with the sale and would have his lands, the law being so. Craigends writ to Kilbernie to fix the time when they should go to him; when they got there, Kilbernie had, with his own and Glengarnock's tenants, destroyd the house, garden, planting, and everything that could be destroyed.

As for the rich house furniture, most of it was sold by roup to Craigends tennants, who bought them for him.

And for the plate; I Robert, the eighth son of Glengarnock, being at Craigends in the year 1685, the Viscount of Ruthven with other gentlemen came to see his sister, then young lady Craigends. At supper I said these silver dishes and plates were my father's, the arms show it, my father's and uncle's being the same;—fork and chequers. My aunt being my father's sister, had the same. And the roses were my mother's arms, being a Heriot. At night my aunt checked me for speaking; said my uncle was a kind uncle; and kept me close in my room while the company was there, that I might not tell more tales.

John Dick, one of my father's tennants, told me that after my father's death, being often sent to Glengarnock to bring things to Craigends; one day fitting a trunk upon his horse, found it open, peep'd into it, saw many rich things of gold; went and told my mother, who locked it, and gave him a piece of gold. He forbid me to tell, saying it would be his ruin.

---

[26] Nisbet's Heraldry, says: This son Richard was designated of Bedland after the lands of Glengarnock were sold to the family of Kilberney, now dignified with the title of Viscount of Garnock.

Soon after, my aunt persuaded me to go to my brother William, at St. Cristopher's, in America ; said it is a fine place, and I would soon be rich. I readily agreed to go, and have great reason to be thankful to my God for it. This brother had been bound to a merchant in Glasgow, broke his apprentiship ; his master having had civilities from my father gave back his apprentice fee, with which and the rest of his little patrimony, linnens were bought, and he went from Glasgow to St. Cristopher's. The ship calling at Dublin, he took what he had ashore, and spent to [his] very bed. If his passage had not been before paid, he might have been sold for it, which was well known to my aunt.

To that brother, I was sent, with a small quantity of linnens, which he soon spent in drinking. God gave me an aversion to drink, and discretion to put myself to a merchant whom I served a year to learn accompting ; after which I had £70 a year from another merchant, most of which my brother had, and great part of what I got, till I had a wife, and five children ; when I gave him one hundred pound, which he carried to North America, returnd after he had spent it. I had done a kind brother's part, and would do no more.

After the revolution, King William sent the Duke of Bolton's regiment of foot to the Leeward Island. I being a gentleman, born of an ancient and noble family, thought it more honorable to be in the army, than in an accompting house, entered a cadet in the regiment, and six days after got a pair of colors. I learnd, and did my duty ; as occasions offerd, I pressed to go upon action, as a sure way to preferment. I soon was made a lieutenant, to the company of grenadiers, and behaved so, that when the regiment was reduced from thirteen companies, to five of one hundred private soldiers in a company, Colonel Nott put me at the head of his company, which I commanded from the 1st of May, 1695, to 23d January, 1698-9, when the regiment was broke. I never did any man injustice, or refused them liberty to work when off duty. The men had a just sense of it, for as I had rented a plantation, and afterwards purchased one, when I had occasion to employ any of them, as I have twenty at a time, they wrought for me at the wages they had from the other planters, and eat their own provisions except what the plantation afforded. I attended my duty and plantation diligently. God blessed my honest industry, by which I have acquired a good estate, for which I have great reason to be thankful.

Ro: CUNYNGHAM.

ROBERT CUNYNGHAM, the eighth son of Richard Cunyngham of Glengarnock, and Elizabeth Heriot his wife : He is the fourth generation from Gabriel the third Laird of Craigends ; the

seventh from Alexander the first Earl of Glencairn; and
the twenty-second from Friskine father of Malcome, who preserved King Malcome Canmore from Macbeth's tyranny; and
was born at Glengarnock, on the 24 day of March, 1669.   He
went young to the Island of St. Cristopher's in America, as before related, and on the 26th day of September, 1693, married
Judith Elizabeth, daughter of Daniel De Bonneson of Morlais
in the province of Bearn in France, and Mary De Barat his
wife, who was sister to Charles De Barat, Seigneur De Labadie,
lieutenant of the most Christian king's armies, and governor of
the citadel of Lisle in Flanders.   Their children :—

1. ELIZABETH,	born	August 14, 1694.
2. RICHARD,	"	February 13, 1696.
3. RICHARD,	"	July 29, 1697.
4. MARY,	"	April 4, 1699.
5. DANIEL,	"	July 19, 1701.
6. CHARLES,	"	October 2, 1702.
7. SUSSAMA,	"	February 29, 1704, Shrove Tuesday.
8. HERIOT, a daughter,	"	February 11, 1705.

THUS FAR, Robert Cunyingham under his own signature, gives an account of his family and descendants.   It
appears to have been written in the year 1740, as the
Earl of Glencairn and the Laird of Craigends' families
are each continued to the twentieth of October of that
year.   But it seems probable that it was originally written in Robert Cunyngham's younger days, for the reasons
that he particularly describes the acts of his boyhood and
youth, saying little or nothing about his later years, or
of his second marriage,   Nor does he mention his
youngest daughter, Jourdine, by his first marriage.

This manuscript, the most valuable of all the family
heir-looms, is in the form of a small book, six and a half
by four inches, containing forty pages very legibly written, and is in a good state of preservation, considering
its age of 136 years.   It has been handed down in the
elder line of the family through five generations, and is
now in the possession of Miss Susan S. Roberdeau.

We do not read of any *clan* in relation to these, our Scottish ancestors.   The reason being that they were from
the Lowlands of Scotland.   The counties of Ayr and
Renfrew, from whence they originated, and lived, being
south of that range of mountains crossing Scotland, of

which Logan, in his Scottish Gaël, says: "The Grampians, that appear an impenetrable barrier, have long been considered the line of separation between the well-known divisions of Highlands and Lowlands." The county of Ayr is divided into three districts—Carrick, Kyle, and Cunninghame. Kilmaurs is in the latter, in which are the ruins of Kilmaurs Castle, now one of the objects of interest to travelers.—(*Eng. Enc.*)

In the Cathedral at Glasgow are many large and elegant memorial windows, every one of which is a study. Among them are some bearing the names and arms of Cunyngham and Craigends, with the motto of the latter branch, "So fork forward."—(*Private Letter.*)

The manuscript in the lawyer's library, quoted above, begins in the year 1357 and ends in 1670.

Heriot's Hospital, above alluded to, "is a noble quadrangle of the Gothic order, and as ornamental to the city as a building, as the manner in which the youths are provided for and educated renders it useful to the community as an institution. The funds have increased so much that it now supports [1831] and educates one hundred and thirty youths annually, and many of them have done honor to their country in different situations." George Heriot, its founder, followed his father's occupation of goldsmith, then peculiarly lucrative and much connected with that of money brokerage. He followed King James I. to the capital, and died in 1624, extremely wealthy for that period. He had no children, and after making full provision for such relatives as might have claims on him, he left the residue of his fortune to establish this hospital. Sir Walter Scott, in *The Fortunes of Nigel*, from which the above extract is taken, has introduced him as one of the principal characters in that novel—"Jingling Geordie," as he was familiarly called by King James, whose habit it was thus to nickname his favorites. Over the entrance of Heriot's Hospital is the coat of arms of the Heriots of Trabonn, being, *Argent; on a fess azure, three cinq foils of the field.* These cinqfoils are the "roses" by which Robert Cunyngham knew his mother's plate after it had been carried to Craigends, and by which he distinguished it from that of his uncle, who bore the "fork and checkers," meaning the shake-fork of Cunyngham quartering the fess cheque of Stewart.

The Island of St. Christopher, where Robert Cunyngham lived the greater part of his life, is one of the most eastern of the West Indies. It is quite small, being only eighteen miles in length, and from one-half to five in width, and yet there is on it a mountain 3,700 feet high, the remains of a decayed volcano. Its population in 1794 was 4,000 whites and 26,000 negroes. It has since much degenerated, its population being now only 23,000. Its exports nearly $700,000 a year. Basse-terre is the capital.

Here Robert Cunyngham passed his life, and by his diligence acquired a very large estate. His lands lay not only in St. Christopher's, but also in Scotland, and, perhaps, some in England. Besides the chief estate, Cayon, in St. Christopher's, he possessed lands and houses in Basse-terre. It is, moreover, said that he owned other property on the island, called the Capstar estate.

In *Nisbet's Heraldry* Robert Cunyngham is mentioned, as follows:

"Robert Cunyngham, a younger brother of Richard, carries the same arms within a bordure for difference, who has purchased a considerable fortune in America, called Cayon, in the island of St. Christopher, by his valor, and by marrying Judith Elizabeth, daughter to Daniel de Boueson, of Martas, in France, and his wife, Mary de Barat, sister to Charles de Barat Sir de la Bodie, Lieutenant-General to the King of France and Governor of the citadel of Lisle, in Flanders, and with her has numerous issue; for whose arms see plate of achievements."

Among the plates may be accordingly found the arms identical with those emblazoned on several pieces of silver formerly belonging to the said Robert Cunyngham, and which have descended to his posterity, some of the pieces being now in possession of Miss Susan S. Roberdeau. An engraving of the arms is here given, where can be seen the peculiar "differences" used in heraldry to distinguish one branch of a family from another.

The paternal arms of the family being the shake-fork, borne by the Earl of Glencairn; the Laird of Craigends' family is sufficiently distinguished from the elder branch, by quartering the Stewart arms, needs no other difference. James Cunyngham of Ashenyeard adds the *crescent* for difference, to distinguish his family from Craigend's; Robert Cunyngham in like manner surrounds the whole arms by a border as his difference from his elder brother.

Robert Cunyngham's arms may then be thus described: QUARTERLY. *First and fourth, argent, a shakefork sable, for* CUNYNGHAM ; *Second and third, or, a fess cheque, azure and argent, for* STEWART : *In pretence, vert, a chevron or, between three garbs (argent), for* [GREENACRE *or* DARBY?] *All within a border engrailed, gules, for difference.* CREST, *an unicorn's head couped, argent, horned and maned or.* MOTTO : *Virtute et labore.*

The arms are shown in the annexed engraving; which is a full-size fac-simile from the tea-caddy mentioned elsewhere as one of the oldest pieces of the Cunyngham silver.

These arms are of right not borne nor quartered by any of the Roberdeau family, for the following reasons : The sons alone, transmit coats of arms; but when there are no sons, the daughters are heraldically co-heiresses, and their children have the right to quarter the arms with those of their father, both then becoming hereditary. A female bearing arms, has no right to either crest or motto, nor can she transmit them to her descendants. *These remarks apply to all coats of arms.* The writer's researches have failed to discover anything in regard to this shield in pretence.

A usual accompaniment to a coat of arms is *livery.* The writer's mother has heard her father say that the livery of the Cunyngham family, is gray coat, pants, and vest, with silver buttons; and collar and cuffs of black velvet; black hat with a silver band. This traditional account agrees in all respects with the rules for the appointment of liveries, as given by an English writer, John E. Cussans, in his *Handbook of Heraldry.* He says of liveries : " The colors of these depend entirely on the tinctures upon his escutcheon. In both, the dominant color should be the same; the subsidiary color of the livery (collar, cuffs, lining, and buttons) should be of the color of the principal charge." He then continues that for an silver shield, since pure white cannot be well used for a coat, some color must be used approaching to it, such as drab. No mention is here made of the case of quartered arms, but it seems evident that only the *paternal* arms should in this case regulate the livery. Thus in Cunyngham, a white shield with a black charge, calls for a gray (or drab) coat; the collar, cuffs, &c., to be black. The proper color of the shield, silver, it is seen is preserved in the buttons, and silver band round the hat.

Besides the children mentioned in the manuscript, Robert Cunyngham had another, still younger—Jourdine. He also, late in life, married a second time, Mary Gaines, by whom he had one child, Susannah, still a child at the time of his death.

Robert Cunyngham made his will in 1743, by which he entailed his estate upon his descendants; specifying very particularly the lines of descent and contingent remainders. He died before the year 1749; for in that year his widow brought suit against the estate, to establish the validity of the will, and obtain payment of an annuity left her.

Besides this annuity, there was a legacy of £2000 left to Mary Roberdeau, and another to Miss Jourdine Cunyngham, who dying unmarried, left a portion of her property including £200 due from Robert Cunyngham's estate, to her niece Miss Elizabeth Roberdeau.

These two legacies *have never been paid*, and still constitute a claim upon the estate, unless barred by lapse of time or some other legal technicality. Their payment could not be enforced, because the will of Robert Cunyngham in which they originate, never could be found.

These claims being imperfectly understood except by one or two persons, and yet generally known throughout the family, as sort of vague " expectations;" (which, by the way, no family seems to be without;) have led the writer to think that a definite account of the whole matter might not be uninteresting to the family, notwithstanding there seems now but little prospect of anything ever being recovered.

ROBERT CUNYNGHAM'S WILL AND LEGACIES.

Although the will of Robert Cunyngham has never been found, though search has repeatedly been made for it in England, in Scotland, and at St. Christopher's, and by several members of the family, yet the evidence that a will was made is undeniable, for it is quoted in the above-mentioned case of Cunyngham vs. Cunyngham, reported in Belt's Supplement to Vesey's Reports.

This case came on the 13th of April, 1749, before the Lord High Chancellor Hardwick. The plaintiff was the widow of Robert Cunyngham, and was entitled to an estate in Scotland and an annuity of £200 per annum under his will, and a deed of gift. By this deed of gift, dated July 17, 1741, Robert Cunyngham, in consideration of the friendship he had for her, made over unto her, by the name of Mary Gaines, all his lands of Craig, in Scotland, and his movable estate therein, particularly described, upon certain conditions. In default of heirs of her daughter Susannah, to revert to his sons, Daniel and Charles.

The will of Robert Cunyngham is in part quoted in this report, but more fully from extracts obtained from the office in London by Edward M. Clymer, Esq., about the year 1847, from which it appears that the will was made October 27, 1748, in which the testator directs that his houses in Basse-terre town, St. Christopher's, should be affixed to his plantation at Cayon ; and this plantation then let to his son, Daniel Cunyngham, at £2.500 a year, he "charged (committed, entrusted) unto William Mc-Dowell, of Castle Semple, in the shire of Renfrew, Esq., Dewey Ottley, of St. Christopher's, Esq., and the defendant, [William] Coleman, [of London,] and their heirs, upon trust, for the payment of his funeral expenses, debts, and legacies therein particularly described."

He then goes on to entail the estate upon his descendants, as follows :

"And upon further trust, that the said defendant, Daniel Cunyngham, for life, with power for him to charge by his will the said plantation with the double of such sums as he had or should receive as his wife's fortune. Remainder after said son Daniel's death to his heirs, male or female, of his body, and the heirs of their bodies; and if .a female should come to inherit, her husband and children to take the said testator's surname and arms, and not to enjoy otherwise ; and in default of such heirs of the said Daniel, remainder to the said testator's daughters, Mary Roberdeau, widow, Heriot Crook, the wife of Clement Crook, of St. Christopher's, Esq., Jourdaina Cunyngham, and Susannah Cunyngham, then and now an infant ; to have the profits of the said plantation and premises during their lives as tenants in common, the same to be kept in good repair, with the stock of negroes; and after their decease :—Remainder to the heirs male of the body of the said testator's daughter, Heriot Crook. Remainder to the heirs male of the body of the said Roberdeau. Remainder to his grandson, Charles William McKennen, and the heirs of his body. Remainder to the heirs

male of the body of the said testator's daughter, Jourdaina
Cunyngham. To *do.* of the testator's daughter, Susannah
Cunyngham. Remainder to *do.* of the *daughters* of the said
Heriot Crook, Mary Roberdeau, Susannah McKennen, Jourdaina Cunyngham, in the order before mentioned. Remainder
to the Earl of Glencairn and his heirs forever. And then,
amongst many legacies particularly set forth in the will, given
to his children, grandchildren, and relations, the said testator gave to the plaintiff, Mary, by the description of his dear
wife, Mary Gaines, which he had thereto [concealed], all his
lands, plate, household linen, and whatsoever he then had or
should leave in Scotland at his death, for her life for her maintenance, and for the maintenance and education of his daughter, Susannah Cunyngham, and the heirs of her body. Remainder to his son Daniel Cunyngham, and his heirs forever. And
further, he bequeathed to his said wife two hundred pounds a
year for her life, to be paid quarterly; and all such money as
Major Dalrymple owed the said testator; and thereby declared
that the said provision was to be in full of her dower, and hoped
she would be therewith well contented; and further gave unto
his dear wife a diamond ring of twenty guineas value."

The defendants did not appear at the original hearing,
the case consequently came again before Lord Hardwick,
July 31, 1750; when it was decreed "that the will should
be established, and the trusts thereof performed.   *   *
*   And out of the rents, profits, and produce of the said
plantation estate, the plaintiff was to be paid her annuity
in future. The testator's creditors, annuitants, and legatees to come in and prove their debts; &c. After the
satisfaction of the testator's debts and funeral expenses,
arrears of the annuities, &c.; the residue of the rents,
profits and produce, to be applied to the payment of the
legacies *pari passu.*   *   *   *   ."

MARY ROBERDEAU'S LEGACY.

This legacy was for £2000, with interest at 5 per
cent., until the whole was paid. The interest was received by her while she resided in Philadelphia, up
to the time of her death, in 1771. In the letter-book
of her son Daniel Roberdeau, are numerous letters
acknowledging the receipt of remittances of rum, sugar,
&c., sent by Daniel Cunyngham, as payment of the
interest. There are also numerous copies of the in-
voices. William Jackson at St. Christopher's appears

to have been the agent, by whom most of these things were sent. There is also here, one letter from Mary Keighley herself, to her brother Daniel Cunyngham, dated June 5, 1769; in reference to the legacy; in which she said the interest was settled down to November 13, 1768, except a small balance due. And then draws for £100, "which," she says, "will be due the 13th of November, 1769."

Upon the death of his mother, who bequeathed the bulk of her property to her son, Daniel Roberdeau addressed the following letters to his uncle Daniel Cunyngham, and to William Coleman, the London trustee, requesting payment of the principal of the legacy :—

DANIEL ROBERDEAU TO DANIEL CUNYNGHAM.

PHILAD'A, *March 30th*, 1771.

DANIEL CUNYNGHAM, Esq.

HON: AND DEAR SIR :—Although overwhelmed with grief, and disposed rather to indulge silent sorrow, it becomes my duty to open the source afresh, and by communicating, make you a partner of my grief. Know then that on the 13th instant —— the task is too irksome, pray be referred to an article of public news enclosed, which I drew up in compliance with custom, and to prevent news-writers inserting at their own discretion. O! the scene was doleful ! I had drank tea with my dear parent on the 11th instant† and left her cheerful and well at about half an hour after six that evening; within three hours after, I was called to be a spectator of a sight I have not the language to express, for I beheld a dying parent, incapable of exchanging one sentiment, or even of speech. The Lord gaveth and the Lord taketh away, blessed be his holy name. —— I shall forward you my dear mother's will which discovers a partiality for me, but not altogether so great as appears on the face of her will, for she made a private reservation in favor of my nephew of £300 curr'ce.

Just before she was seized with the awful fit, she expressed some uneasiness to my sister Elizabeth then only present, at her having done so little for her daughters, which had sufficient weight, exclusive of my own sentiment with respect to the will, which alone would have operated in their favour; therefore I did not hesitate immediately to make the underwritten concession.

I beg my dear uncle will favour the payment of my mother's patrimony immediately ; as the prospect of a high exchange, probably 70 or more ⅌ct., (if I have orders immediately to draw, and the further advantage of 6 ⅌ct. interest on the loan of money here,) will considerably augment the dependence of the legatees of our grandfather's bounty of £2,000 sterl., with the accustomed interest of 5 ⅌ct. thereon until the whole is drawn for; which shall not be delayed longer than I have an answer, which I pray you will be pleased to favour me with, ⅌ packet directed to this port or by the way of New York or Boston.

As our grandfather's will further gives a special charge to Wm. Coleman, Esq'r, of London, and his successors, with respect to this legacy, it will no doubt be satisfactory to you that he be acquainted with the authority vested in me as executor, and the discharge of the legacy; therefore as also at the united request of all the legatees, I have furnished him with proper testimonials, a precaution, also warranted by the uncertainty of your life, which I trust will be long preserved a comfort to yourself, and a blessing to your family and friends.

My sisters, nephew, wife, and self, and I would lend language to my son Isaac and daughter Ann, the only children God has spared me, unite in affectionate salutations to you, our aunt and cousins, on this sorrowful occasion.   I am

Hon: and dear Sir,
Yr. affect. and obt. nephew and servt.*

† Since April last our too large family
for my mother's comfort at her advanced
time of life, separated at her desire, as I
think I have before advised you.

DANIEL ROBERDEAU TO WILLIAM COLEMAN.

PHILDELPHIA, March 30th, 1771.

WM. COLEMAN Esq'r, London.

My grandfather, Robert Cunyngham, Esqr's, will vests a special trust in you and your successor, with respect to the legacies bequeathed to his daughters. On this subject, it becomes duty in me as executor to the last will and testament of my dear mother, Mrs. Mary Keighley, deceased, the legatee known by the name of Mary Roberdeau in the first above-mentioned will, to make myself known to you, with proper testimonials, accompanying this.

My request, in the name of all concerned in my mother's will, is to beseech you to see that the sum bequeathed by our grandfather of £2,000 sterling, with the allowed interest of 5 per cent. until the whole is drawn for, be secured to my drafts, without any deductions of principal, interest, or commission, until so drawn for; and that you be pleased to put things in such forwardness,

---

* From his letter-book, in which the copies of letters are rarely signed.

that without any delay such assurance be given me as no risque may attend the immediate discharge of my duty; as the prospect of a high exchange, probably 70 or more per cent. (if I have the orders immediately to draw, and the further advantage of 6 per cent. interest on the loan of money here,) will considerably augment the dependence of the legatees.

As a merchant, I offer my best offices to you in this quarter of the world. Please to indulge me with an immediate answer by packet the first opportunity, to this port, New York, or Boston.

I am, with respectful salutations of my mother's heirs,

Respected Sir,

Y'r most ob't servant.

To Thomas Field, at Mr. Simmons and Co. stationers, Leadenhall st., London, Daniel Roberdeau writes, under date of April 11, 1771, "I have a faint notion that the trust in question is now lodged in the Lord Chancellor's hands."

From the above, we see that the interest of the legacy was paid up to November 13, 1768. Mrs. Keighley then draws for £100, being one year's interest, due November 13, 1769. This, and the fact that the interest was at five per cent., shows that the principal was £2,000, and that at the latter date none of it had been paid. Mrs. Keighley's death occurred within eighteen months thereafter; and besides the above letters, and a few others of about the same date, it is not known that any efforts have since been made to obtain this legacy.

THE LEGACY OF MISS JOURDINE CUNYNGHAM.

Jourdine, youngest child of Robert Cunyngham by his first wife, was one of the legatees under his will above mentioned. At her death, about the year 1788, she bequeathed £200 to her niece Elizabeth Roberdeau, during whose lifetime the business was conducted through Mr. Edward Tilghman of Philadelphia, by the house of Messrs. Sargent, Chambers & Co. of London, at least so far as the receipt of the interest on the legacy. Elizabeth Roberdeau dying in the year 1799, bequeathed all her estate, save a few mementos, to her nephew, Col. Isaac Roberdeau.

Col. Roberdeau was the eldest male heir of Robert Cunyngham, in the female line; and the male line being then extinct, or believed soon to become so; and con-

3

sequently a great probability of his inheriting the entailed estate, his letters and papers contain as much
about the estate as about the legacy.

He, believing the heirs of Daniel Cunyngham to be extinct, considered himself rightfully the heir of this estate,
as the eldest son of Daniel, who was the "eldest son of
the eldest daughter." And under this impression, made
several unsuccessful attempts in 1802, 1810, 1818, 1825,
&c., to recover the legacy, which he thought would lead
to the inheritance of the whole estate.

In a letter to Albert Davey, &c., Leeds, April 7, 1825,
and full of general interest, he says:

" When in London with my father in 1783, we resided with
Mr. C. P. Hall, at 44 Leadenhall street. That family were then
in mourning for the last of the two sons, Charles or Daniel,—
the brother of Mrs. [Pogson]. Anthony was then in possession
of the estate of his grandfather Robert; he resided on the Continent, and it was said unmarried; had it been otherwise, his
sister, Mrs. H., and my father, his cousin, could scarcely [have]
been ignorant of the fact; his age I know not, but it must have
been greater than that of my father, who was then about 55
years or more. Residing occasionally with Mr. Pogson in Surrey,
I knew Miss Jourdine Cunyngham intimately; that she received
a legacy from the estate is certain, for on one occasion after Mr.
Pogson having received it, I was instrumental in preserving a
large sum from highway robbery in conveying it to Sutton, in
company with Mr. P. at night near to Mitcham; this annuity
must have been at her own disposal, as the £200 sterling is a part
bequeathed to E. Roberdeau. A chief companion of my father
there was the late Mr. John Thornton of Claphouse, who was
his patron and mercantile friend, before the war of the Revolution, which had suspended their intercourse.

" On our arrival in the U. S. I found my aunt E. Roberdeau,
as most elderly maiden ladies are, the biographer and genealogist
of the family; she had seen a copy of the will of entail, and always averred that Anthony Cunyngham was a bachelor; my
father also, although he seldom spoke on this subject, and never
to me, assured Miss R. that it was the case and that he considered himself the heir under the entail. This information was
drawn from those who had known Mr. C. in Europe.

" The family of Robert, as then existing, consisted, besides
Mrs. Hall of London; of Captain Crooke of the Isle of Wight;
and that of Mr. Caines of St. Cristopher's, who had intermarried
with the female line. So that my position would be true if not
changed by some clause in the will; that my family is the eldest in succession, and if such a change be made, I am very sure
that one only could intervene, who may not have male issue now.

"The entail of this will was guarded by trustees and was probably made hereditary, as through them Daniel Cunyngham was non-suited in his attempt to bar the entail—said to have cost him £10,000."

Col. Roberdeau died January 15, 1829, and the strength of his belief in his right to this estate was such, that he made the following disposition in his will regarding it: "I give and devise,...............in equal parts,..........the reversions...........and remainders that now or hereafter may become due to me.........in my name, or that of my family of Cunyngham, to which, as the eldest male branch, I am or may be entitled; to have and to hold ....to the said Susan S. Roberdeau, Mary Elizabeth Roberdeau, Susan Shippen Roberdeau, and Frances Selina Roberdeau........," &c.

Mrs. Roberdeau, soon after his death, had several conversations upon the subject with her friend, Judge Coxe, of Philadelphia, who became convinced of the validity of the claim; and said if it were not for his large family he would himself go to Europe and attend to it. He was of opinion that the recovery of the legacy would lead to the possession of the whole estate.

Col. Roberdeau's daughters have also made some efforts, and, with a view to identification, in 1858 obtained a sworn certificate from Mrs. Catharine Powell, of Alexandria, an old lady then upwards of seventy-five years of age, stating that she knew Gen. Daniel Roberdeau, his son, Col. Isaac Roberdeau, and the three daughters of the latter. The veteran Gen. Swift also gave the following letter, containing much of general interest:

GENEVA, 30th October, 1857.

DEAR MRS. BUCHANAN.

I have your letter of the 28th, and hasten to reply. I knew your father, Major Isaac Roberdeau, for more than thirty years intimately, as the son of General Daniel Roberdeau, of Alexandria. It was through my agency that your father was appointed in the United States Topographical Engineers. I took him to West Point. He served under my command many years. I have often conversed with him on the peculiar antipathy of his father, General Roberdeau, to a cat, and about the Cunyngham claim, and his gift from his Aunt Betsy, and advised him not to neglect those claims. My father, Dr. Swift, was the intimate friend of your grandfather, General Roberdeau, and of your father. He has often told me of the elegant manners of your grandfather, and of his attachment to his son Isaac; and of a remarkable rencounter of your grandfather with a robber on Hounslow* Heath, when the General captured and proved his guilt, and he was hung, &c. I knew General D. Roberdeau's children, Isaac, Ann my aunt, Mary .(Mrs. Patten), Selina (Mrs. Nickolls), and his son Daniel [James M.], by his second wife, his first being the daughter of the Rev. Mr. Bostwick, from whom his daughter was named Mary or Ann, I forget which. I knew you, three daughters of Isaac—Mary, Susan, and Selina— and often heard of your being named from your aunt, who was named for the Countess of Huntington, General Roberdeau's friend. In Philadelphia your grandfather, General Daniel Roberdeau, lived before he lived in Alexandria, and was there elected a member of the Confederated Congress. Some friends of yours or your husband in Philadelphia, should be written to at once to enquire of the old folks and search records ; especially about your grandfather having entertained them as a friend of .Geo. Whitefield. Your father married Susan, the daughter of Rev. Samuel Blair, of Germantown, and granddaughter of old Dr. Shippen, in Philadelphia. Keep this matter alive and delay not one day. Sally unites with me in love to you and Susan, and so do Belle and Willy. You may remember it was through my exertion that your mother recovered the Philadelphia property........................, and it would be queer if this letter should be a means of urging on the claim of your father under the will of his Aunt Betsy Roberdeau. My love to Roberdeau and Susan from—

Your friend,   J. G. SWIFT.

To MRS. SELINA ROBERDEAU BUCHANAN.

CHARLESTOWN, MASS'TTS.

P. S.—When you write to Mr. Buchanan give my love to him and wish him a successful cruise.   J. G. S.

Appended to the above letter is the following attestation of the Secretary of State of the United States :

In compliance with a request made to me, I state that for many years I have been acquainted with General Swift, formerly of the Army of the United States, by whom the accompanying letter, addressed to Mrs. Selina Roberdeau Buchanan, and dated Geneva, October 30, 1857, was written ; and I know him to be a gentleman of high character and honorable principles, and whose statements may be depended upon.

LEWIS CASS.

WASHINGTON CITY, NOVEMBER 9, 1857.

---

*Other accounts say Blackheath, but there is no discrepancy geographically. Both are very near London, Hounslow Heath being 12 miles southwest, and Blackheath 5 miles nearly south. The heath is probably all one, but named differently, lying partly in two counties. Both places are recorded as being infested with highwaymen.

Edward M. Clymer, Esq., as above stated, has also been interested in this matter, and about the years 1844–9 had search made in London for Robert Cunyngham's will, for it was supposed that it would be recorded there in Doctors' Commons; where are enrolled the wills of parties having property within the See of Canterbury, which includes the British West Indies, but without success; from whence it is concluded that it may be recorded in Scotland. A letter from his attorney, Charles F. Tagart, July 3, 1847, gives a rather discouraging view of the case. The writer thinks twenty years' adverse possession would bar our claim. It is not clearly shown that heirs in the male line have failed. The entail may be docked, for "it would have been competent for any tenant intail, with the consent of the next in remainder, say his eldest son on coming of age, to bar the entail by fine or recovery." As to Mary Roberdeau's legacy, he quotes 2 and 3 William 4, c. 27, s. 40, that after 1833 no suit for recovery of a legacy can be brought after twenty years, &c.

Thus rests the matter of these legacies. A recent letter from St. Christopher's, in answer to inquiries of the writer, says: "The estate of Cunyngham, in the parish of St. Mary's, Cayon, is now in the possession of a French family of the name of Faile. The late Mr. Faile was a native of Bordeaux, in France, and was naturalized as a British subject when he purchased the estate. His widow, a son, and two daughters now occupy it, but it is deeply mortgaged."

ROBERT CUNYNGHAM'S DESCENDANTS.

ROBERT CUNYNGHAM to whom we now return, has given an account of his own life, as already quoted. He died between the years 1743–9, leaving issue by Judith Elizabeth :—

I.   ELIZABETH, born August 14, 1694.

II.   RICHARD, born February 13, 1696.

III.   RICHARD, born July 29, 1697. These three eldest children died early in life.

IV.   MARY, born April 4, 1699, becoming eldest child; married ISAAC ROBERDEAU of Rochelle. Of her and her descendants presently.

V. DANIEL, born July 19, 1701, the fourth son, at the death of his father inherited the estate under the will of entail. Before his death he instituted a suit to bar the entail, contrary to the advice of his sister Mary, then eldest child; in which he failed,—said to have cost him £10,000. He married in England and died between the years 1772 and 1781. Mrs. Cunyngham, (presumed to be the wife of Daniel,) died on the island of St. Christopher, where the family resided, March 1, 1786, of decline, aged 87 years. Their issue :—

1. ROBERT, the eldest son died before 1766.
2. ANTHONY, born probably about the year 1722, became possessed of the estate under the entail, on the death of his father. The impression of his family was, that he did not marry. It appears to be certain that he was a bachelor in the year 1783, at which time he resided either in the south of France, or in Germany, probably the latter. It was also believed that some imprudence in play, to which he was addicted, led to this course, as he was not known to have lived, at any period, either in England or on the island of St. Christopher: nor have we any satisfactory account of his history, or that of the estate since the death of his father, even to the present time.—(*Isaac Roberdeau's MS.*, about 1828.) As he did not marry in early life, it is probable he continued single; or if he did afterwards marry, it is still less probable that he had children. The history of his life is involved in much obscurity. —(*Ibid.*) Daniel Roberdeau, under date of March 5, 1766, thus writes to Daniel Cunyngham about Anthony: "And has the Lord not only bereaved you of your eldest, but of both your sons?" And subsequently, March 22, 1768: "I find with joy, that the account of my cousin Anthony's death was all a mistake; and that he was at the time of your writing, abroad for his improvement. May he be long continued a blessing to his aged parents!" From whence it appears that Anthony was then the only living son.
3. ELIZABETH PHILADELPHIA, who married CHARLES PEARCE, of Upton, near London, who being unfortunate in business, sold that estate, and became connected with the East India Company; and was in the direction of the establishment at No. 49 Leadenhall street, London, in 1783. By the death of a relative, he had previously by act of Parliament annexed the name of HALL to that of Pearce, and probably continued in the situation he held until his death, which occurred before the year 1797, leaving his widow "in circumstances very circumscribed." By this marriage, there were two sons only, and several daughters :—

    i.   DANIEL PEARCE.
    ii.   CHARLES PEARCE. Both died previously to 1783, the last surviving being at the time of his death heir-presumptive to his uncle Anthony, then in possession of the estate.
    iii. ELIZABETH PHILADELPHIA, eldest daughter, married Beddingfield Pogson, who in 1783 resided at Sutton, near Mitcham, in Surrey, ten or twelve miles from London. On the death of her brothers, she became heir-presumptive to Anthony Cunyngham. Her husband died before 1797, leaving her and her children in reduced circumstances, probably indeed, dependent upon her mother. She had nine children, names unknown, alive in 1797.
    iv. HARRIET, born about 1760.
    v., vi. TWO OTHER daughters.
    Four daughters were alive in 1797.

VI. CHARLES, born October 2, 1702, the fifth son of Robert Cunyngham, died "many years ago" (as Col. Roberdeau says about 1825), certainly before 1783, and *without issue*, as at that time, his grand-nephew Charles or Daniel Pearce, was heir-presumptive to his nephew Anthony. Indeed it seems to the writer, evident that he died before his father, for although he is named in the deed of gift to Mary Gaines in 1741, yet is not mentioned in the will dated 1743, as one of the contingent remainders.

VII. SUSSAMA or SUSANNAH, born February 29, 1704; married ———— McKENNEN; died before 1743, leaving issue:—

1.   CHARLES WILLIAM McKENNEN.
2, &c. ONE OR MORE daughters.

VIII. HERIOT, born February 11, 1705; married CLEMENT CROOKE, of St. Christopher's, and had:—

1. CHARLES C. CROOKE, styled Captain, of the Isle of Wight. He married, and his wife died in 1795, leaving issue:—
    i.   A DAUGHTER in England, alive in 1797.
    ii.   A SON in Jamaica, alive in 1797.
    iii., iv., v., vi. FOUR CHILDREN, died before 1797.
2. A DAUGHTER, born in 1728; married ———— MOSSMAN, and died in 1798, or later, of cancer in her hip. Whether issue is unknown.
3. A DAUGHTER, married CHARLES CAINES, of St. Christopher's; died in 1794, and her husband, also, about the same time, leaving issue unknown.
4. A DAUGHTER, born in 1736; married ———— WYLIE, of the Bahamas; a widow in 1797, having issue:—
    i.   WILLIAM WYLIE, eldest son, Chief Justice at that place.
    ii., iii., &c. Other children.
5. Probably a son, Richard Crooke, of St. Croix.

IX. JOURDINE, (Jordine, or Jordiana,) youngest daughter of Robert Cunyngham by his first wife, and not mentioned by him in his genealogy, which was, therefore, probably originally written before her birth. Born probably about 1706-7. She did not marry, and resided with her grandniece, Mrs. B. Pogson, near London, and died under her roof in 1788, leaving £200 to her niece, Elizabeth, daughter of her sister, Mary Roberdeau. Her will is recorded in London.

Robert Cunyngham, late in life, between the years 1741–3, married a second time, MARY GAINES, by whom he had one child—

X. SUSANNAH, an infant when her father made his will, in 1743. Of her the writer knows nothing further.

Mrs. Knight, a cousin of Daniel Roberdeau, the writer is unable to identify.

PART II.—BIOGRAPHICAL.

FIRST GENERATION.

DAUGHTER OF ROBERT CUNYNGHAM, ESQ., OF THE ISLAND OF ST. CHRISTOPHER, W. I.

1. MARY (CUNYNGHAM) ROBERDEAU and lastly KEIGHLEY.—Born on her father's plantation Cayon, at St. Cristopher's, April 4, 1699. She was the eldest daughter, and by the death of her elder brothers and sister at an early age, became eldest child. She married, probably about the year 1723, Isaac Roberdeau, "a gentleman of family and fortune," (so says Colonel Roberdeau's manuscripts,) "a native of Rochelle in France, who, with many others, left their native country upon the revocation of the Edict of Nantes,* and took refuge on the Island of St. Cristopher, in the year 1685." Her husband must have been a young man when he left France, and well advanced in life when she married him, about thirty-eight years after.

Of the pedigree of Isaac Roberdeau, in France, the writer has attempted but little search, owing to distance and the difficulties in procuring information. In an old work, *Indicateur du grandé Armorial Général de France, par Charles D'Hozier,* 1696 ; *Publis par M. Louis Paris ; Paris,* 1765, there is this reference : " Roberdeau Par. [Paris?] 1, 1375." Much inquiry then showed that the work of which this was the index, was a manuscript in the Imperial Library at Paris, and after a fruitless correspondence to ascertain what was there recorded, in hopes of discovering something of our French ancestry, a friend traveling in Europe kindly visited the Library and obtained the following, being all that was on record:

---

* Promulgated at Nantes, in 1598, by Henry IV., for the toleration of Protestants ; revoked in 1685.

"A. D. 1677. Louis Roberdeau, Maître Chirurgien, juré à Paris. *Porte de gueules, à un chevron d'argent, accompagné en chef de deux Y adossés, et en pointe de trois étoiles de même malordonnées."*

What relation, if any, the above is to our progenitor, does not appear; the arms show him to have been of a different branch of the family.

By her husband, Isaac Roberdeau, Mary Cunyngham had three children,—Elizabeth, Ann Judith, and Daniel. After her husband's death, and during the infancy of their son, she removed, with her children, to Philadelphia, in North America, where she became the progenitor of numerous descendants, of whom the two principal branches are Roberdeau and Clymer.

While residing in Philadelphia, Mrs. Roberdeau, after 1743, at which time she is spoken of in her father's will as Mary Roberdeau, widow, was married a second time to a gentleman by the name of Keighley (spelled variously.)† But by him she had no children, and appears to have been again left a widow not long afterwards, for in a deed recorded in Philadelphia, of July 1, 1749, she is described as a widow at that time. Anything further relating to Mr. Keighley, I have been unable to discover.

Upon the death of her father, Robert Cunyngham, Mrs. Keighley received a legacy of £2,000, a large sum in those days. By his will, also, she, with her sisters, constituted one of the joint remainders, as tenants in common, of his large estate. And in default thereof, her heirs male and female succeeded as a further remainder. The interest of this legacy she received regularly from her brother Daniel, who came into possession of the estate, but no part of the principal has ever been paid.

Mrs. Keighley lived in Philadelphia, with her son, until within a year of her death, which occurred March 13, 1771, at the advanced age of seventy-two. Her will, dated December 27, 1764, is on record in Philadelphia; in which she leaves £500 to each of her two daughters, Elizabeth Roberdeau and Ann Clymer; to her son Dan-

---

*TRANSLATION.—A. D. 1677. Louis Roberdeau, Head Surgeon, sworn at Paris. Carries: *gules, a chevron argent, between two Y addorsed in chief, and three stars in base; one and two; all of the same.*

† In the body of her will, given Keily and Keiley: and signed Keighley. Her son in his letter-book, Keighley, but usually Kighley.

iel Roberdeau, she leaves £1,000, and constitutes him
residuary legatee and sole executor. Just before her
death, she made a private reservation of £300 in favor
of her grandson Daniel C. Clymer, as appears by Daniel
Roberdeau's letter on a previous page.

Mrs. Keighley seems to have been a proficient with her
needle. She has worn silk dresses made of the silk that
she herself spun from the cocoons of her own silk-worms.
There is also preserved in Mrs. Holderby's family a white
satin quilt worked by her, a very beautiful piece of work,
which must be now very old. Mrs. Holderby also has
probably the oldest relic in the family, the French Bible
used by our Huguenot ancestors during the time of their
persecution in France. It must be very nearly, if not
over, two hundred years old.

The old silver, with her father's arms, brought by Mrs.
Keighley from St. Christopher's, has been mentioned on
a preceding page. Besides spoons and smaller articles,
there are three larger ones, bearing the arms in full; the
tea-caddy, a sugar-dish, of very graceful hexagonal shape,
and a half-pint mug or can with the date 1699, scratched
on the bottom. Besides these, there was a salver with
the arms, mentioned in Miss Elizabeth Roberdeau's will,
whose possessor is unknown to the writer.

THE ROBERDEAU COAT OF ARMS:

*Sable, a chevron or, between two annulets in fess, and a
tower in base, argent; on a chief of the last, a cross-crosslet
gules;* CREST, *a demi deer-hound, rampant reguardant, (proper,) collared sable, charged with a cross (argent).* MOTTO,
Ne cede malis.

An engraving of the arms is given in the frontispiece,
from the plate of Colonel Isaac Roberdeau, the style
showing it to have been probably the work of Callendar,
between 1790 and 1810, and is truly French, the "tower"
being a common charge in that country and seldom or
never seen in England. The shape of the shield, although
it implies nothing, is that known as the old Norman.

Mrs. Mary Keighley's children, all by her first husband,
Isaac Roberdeau, of Rochelle, are:—

    3. i. ELIZABETH, b. 1724; unmarried.
    4. ii. ANN JUDITH, b. ——; (Mrs. Clymer.)
    2. iii. DANIEL,   b. 1727; of whom as follows:—

SECOND GENERATION.

CHILDREN OF MARY (CUNYNGHAM) AND ISAAC ROBERDEAU, OF ROCHELLE, FRANCE. [1.]

2. DANIEL ROBERDEAU.—Being the only son, properly takes precedence of his sisters, although they were his seniors in years, and, therefore, with his descendants, will be so placed in this genealogy. This is the usual method of some genealogists, particularly the English, to place the names of all sons before those of the daughters. He was born, as already stated, on the island of St. Christopher, one of the British West Indies, in the year 1727. Of his early years we have no account. His after-life, however, shows that he received a good education, and it is believed that he studied, for a time at least, in England. During his minority, as we have already seen, his widowed mother removed with her family to Philadelphia, in North America, "where, after having finished his education," his son Isaac writes, "he qualified himself for mercantile business, and became a merchant of respectability in that city." His letter-book, which will be mentioned more particularly hereafter, shows that he was largely engaged in importing, and had correspondents in London, Lisbon, Madeira, Bermuda, in Ireland, in several of the West Indies, Jamaica, Barbadoes, St. Croix, St. Kitts, Nevis, &c., a large correspondence for times when a letter was six weeks or two months in crossing the Atlantic. His merchandise seems to have consisted chiefly of rum, wines, West India produce, &c., and it is interesting to note the prices at which he bought and sold: Choice Madeira, £65 per pipe; bread, 16 shillings a barrel; rum, 3s. 4d.; cotton, 18d. per lb.; best Muscovado sugar, 54s. a barrel; flour, 14s. 6d. to 18s., or $3.62 to $4.50 a barrel. Thus it is seen that a hundred years ago one dollar would buy three or four times as much as at present.

The earliest mention the writer has found of Daniel Roberdeau, is in 1749, when, at the age of twenty-two, his name appears in a list of subscribers for an assembly to be given in Philadelphia. The subscription was £8, and among the names, occur many whose families were well known then and now in the social circles of that city; and some who were afterwards distinguished in the history of the country. Among the names are, Alexander Hamilton, Daniel Roberdeau, Joseph Shippen, Thomas Willing, etc. (*Watson's Annals of Phila.*, I., 284.)

A few years after this, we find Daniel Roberdeau a member of the "Mystic tie," the evidence being a paper now framed and hanging in a conspicuous place in the Masonic Hall in Philadelphia. The import is as follows, and constitutes the earliest documentary record of our ancestor in this country:

"PHILADELPHIA, *March* 13, 1754.

"Whereas, at a meeting of the Grand and First Lodges, on Thursday the 12th day of March, 1752, a committee was then appointed and fully authorized to look out for a suitable lot, whereon to erect a building for the accommodation of said Lodges, Philadelphia Assembly, and other uses. The undersigned subscribe the several sums:" . . . etc.

Following which, are the names of thirty or forty subscribers, and among them we read:

"For Mr. John Mather, Jr., Daniel Roberdeau, £15; Benjamin Franklin, £20; James Wallace, £15; David McIlvane, £15; Wm. Franklin, £15; S. M., Daniel Roberdeau, £15; I. S., Samuel Mifflin, £20; Thomas Cadwallader, £15; Thomas Hart, £15;" &c., &c., &c. All the records of the First Lodge having been destroyed during the revolution, but little can now be ascertained on this subject.

The *Philadelphia Sunday Dispatch* of July 12, 1874, contains an early history of Masonry in that state. This piece is chapter ccclxxxi., of a series of articles on the history of Philadelphia by Thompson Westcott. We read here that the Masonic Hall, located in Lodge Alley, was purchased by deed dated April 1, 1754. The lot was vested in William Plumsted, T. Bond, Hugh Davey, Edward Shippen, Samuel Mifflin, John Swift, Daniel Roberdeau, John Wallace, and William Franklin. The hall was erected by subscriptions to shares of stock. On the 6th of September, 1785, the Assembly of Pennsylvania passed an act authorizing the sale of this hall, the act reciting that it belonged to the Grand and First Lodges. The lot was accordingly sold in 1792 to the First Universalist Church.

In Daniel Roberdeau's old receipt books, mentioned more generally in a succeeding page, we read:

April 18, 1755, a receipt for £11, 4, 8, "in full for sundry jobs done at the lodge on account of the assembly," and again, June 11, 1755, £1, 14, 5½ "in full, a balance due the lodge," &c., probably his annual subscription.

It is gratifying to find that the cares of mercantile life and the anxieties of the early days of the Revolution, did not prevent Daniel Roberdeau from devoting some of his time and means to charitable objects. We find his name enrolled as one of the twelve managers of the Pennsylvania Hospital on Eighth street; he acted as such for twelve years, from 1756 to 1758, and from 1766 to 1776, being elected annually. Benjamin Franklin was by the managers of the first year above, elected their president. Also among the list of contributors, we read:

1754,	Daniel Roberdeau,	£10	0	0
1756,	do.	13	0	0
1769,	do.	2	10	8
1772,	do.	4	10	0
		£30	0	8

At the centennial celebration in 1851, the address of Dr. Geo. B. Wood's contained the following:

" It would give me great pleasure, were time allowed, to refer to the various individuals who were most active in the early concerns of the hospital, and most liberal in its support; to speak in addition to those already mentioned, of the Joneses, the Griffitts, the Foxes, the Roberdeaus, the Richardsons, the Mifflins, the Lewises, the Whartons, the Morrises, the Logans, and others who acted as managers in the provincial times; the Shippens, the Evanses, the Morgans, the Moores, who acted as physicians and surgeons, . . . But I must forego the satisfaction of further personal details."

At what time Daniel Roberdeau began his political life is uncertain, but about this time he was one of the *wardens* of the City of Philadelphia, which office he held while he was also in the assembly. The duties of the office appear to have been the oversight of various matters connected with the city, such as the ferries, markets, pumps, &c., &c.

PENNSYLVANIA ASSEMBLY.*

In the proceedings of June 28, 1756. In obedience to a writ to the sheriff from the speaker, dated June 15, 1756, for a new election to fill three vacancies, a return being made, Thomas Leech and Daniel Roberdeau were chosen representatives from the county of Philadelphia, and William Masters from the city.

The sessions of the assembly commenced annually on the 15th of October, and continued throughout the year, adjourning from time to time to a fixed day, unless sooner called together by the governor. No measures of great importance immediately followed Mr. Roberdeau's election; he was, however, several times appointed one of two to wait on the governor, to carry a bill for his signature, or to see the great seal attached to an act, etc.; for it was then customary for the house to appoint two members to deliver to the governor any communication they might have to send; and during his continuance in the house, Mr. Roberdeau was frequently appointed in this capacity, and almost invariably was the spokesman, being the first named of the two.

In August of this year, a new governor arrived in the colony, the Hon. William Denny, and on the 23d, Daniel Roberdeau, Benjamin Franklin, and five others are appointed to prepare an address of welcome. The address is exceedingly short, saying merely they will "endeavor to make it easy and comfortable to himself." The humor in these few words reads very like some of Franklin's witty speeches.

Early the next month Mr. Roberdeau was one of a committee of eleven, including the speaker and Dr. Franklin, to prepare a bill granting £60,000 "for the King's use." To this bill the governor objected, and now revived a dispute that had raged for fifty years, and was terminated only by the change of government brought about by the Revolution. The immense tract of land granted by the sovereign to William Penn, constituting him and his heirs proprietors of Pennsylvania, and part

---

* "Votes and Proceedings of the Penn. House of Reps., published by authority."

of New Jersey, was now held by his sons as actual proprietors; they appointed the governor with the royal
assent; but the people had the right to elect their representatives in assembly, with whom rested the right to
grant money. Every year certain sums were voted "to
the King's use" for the support of the province, pay of
the army, etc.; now engaged in an Indian war. The
money being raised by a tax on property, and this tax
was the bone of contention. The assembly always insisted on taxing the proprietory estates, and the governor
resisted, replying that his "instructions" would not
allow him to assent to the bill. The assembly would
then refuse to grant any money. The governor in turn
threatened them with dire calamities if they did not;
and so the dispute raged from year to year. Parton
draws a pitiful picture of the governor's position. He
had to please the proprietaries, who could deprive him of
office; the assembly, who could withhold his salary; and
the King, who could cut his head off! No wonder they
desired to make it "easy and comfortable" to the new
governor.

Such was the general ground of refusal to the present
bill. And after much debate, the house resolved that
the governor's objections are arbitrary and unconstitu-
tional; but nevertheless waived their rights, and appointed a committee of eight, of whom Mr. Roberdeau is
first named, and Dr. Franklin second, to prepare a bill
in accordance with the governor's instructions. To this
he then assented.

A glance at the proceedings of the house will show
that Mr. Roberdeau was one of the most prominent
members in this matter; but how far he aided in preparing the bills, or the part he took in debate, cannot
now be known. The discussion lasted several days.

The next term, October 14, 1756, Mr. Roberdeau is
again reëlected, and placed on the standing committee
on accounts; also on the following special committees:
To revise the militia law; to prepare an answer to the
governor's objections to it; and in February, 1757, on a
committee to prepare and present an address to the Earl
of Loudon, Commander-in-chief of His Majesty's forces
in North America.

March 2, 1758, Mr. Roberdeau laid before the house
the report of the Pennsylvania Hospital. He was at this
time, as before related, one of its managers.

September 12. A message from the governor notifies
the house of a grand meeting to be held at Easton, to
arrange an extensive and durable peace with the Indians,
to which the governors of New Jersey, Maryland, and
Virginia, and Sir William Johnson are invited. Whereupon the house appointed Messrs. Norris, Fox, Hughes,
Roberdeau, Galloway, Masters, Strickland, and Gibbons
to be a committee to attend the treaty. An account of
this meeting and of the various speeches may be found
in the Pennsylvania Colonial Records, Provincial Council,
vol. VIII., p. 175. The meeting was held on the 8th of
October, 1758, at which were present Governor Denny;
six members of the Governor's Council; the above committee of the House of Representatives; magistrates of
Philadelphia; deputy Indian agent, and Indians of the
Mohawk, Oneida, Seneca, Tuscarora, Mohican, and Delaware Nations, with their interpreters.

December 21, 1758. Resolved, that every member who
shall be absent from the house longer than half an hour
after the bell ceases to ring in the fore- and afternoon,
shall be subject to a fine of one shilling for every such
delinquency.

We may note here the interesting fact that the bell
above referred to is the same which afterwards became
historic. It was cast in England; and broke the first
time it was rung. It was, therefore, recast in this country,
with the prophetic inscription from Leviticus, " Proclaim
liberty throughout all the land, unto all the inhabitants
thereof," which was fulfilled twenty-three years afterwards, when the bell gave the first intimation of the
passage of the Declaration of Independence.

Mr. Roberdeau, after having been five times elected
to the Assembly, declines the honor of another election
in the following letter, which appears in the *Pennsylvania
Gazette* of September 25, 1760 :

To the Freeholders and Electors of the County and
City of Philadelphia.

Gentlemen :

The public marks of your esteem in choosing me for several
successive years past one of your representatives in Assembly,
will ever meet with my most grateful acknowledgment; but
finding that a longer continuance in that station would be very

inconvenient to me, I must beg leave to request that you will be pleased, at the ensuing election, to make choice of some other person in my stead.

> I am, GENTLEMEN,
> Your much obliged and most
> Obedient humble servant,
> DANIEL ROBERDEAU.

Notwithstanding this letter, Mr. Roberdeau was again honored, for the sixth time, by his constituents at the coming election as their choice, and so served for another year in the Assembly. He was also again placed on the standing Committee on Finances, as well as on several minor committees. At the close of this term, in September, 1761, he retired to private life and returned to his mercantile pursuits.

HIS MARRIAGE, PRIVATE LIFE, BUSINESS, ANECDOTES, &C.

Mr. Roberdeau now had other responsibilities, for on the third of October, 1761, he married Mary, daughter of the Rev. David Bostwick, D. D., a pious minister of the Presbyterian church in New York. At the time of his marriage his age was thirty-four; that of his wife is uncertain. We, however, do know that she was very young. Her sister-in-law, Miss Elizabeth Roberdeau, used to treat her as a child—send her about the house on petty errands, etc. Her mother being married in 1739, Mary could not have been over twenty-one when married. Mr. Roberdeau's Bible register gives the record of her death and age—"February 15, 1777, aged 3-," the important figure being partially obliterated. It is most probably a 6, making her age at the time of marriage twenty years.

Mrs. Roberdeau's ancestry is here given in the form of a chart, as the clearest way of showing it. For further information of the various individuals and their families, reference may be had to *Savage's Genealog. Dict., &c., &c.; Cothren's Hist. of Ancient Woodbury; McDonald's Hist. 1st Presb. Ch., Jamaica, L. I.; Thompson's Long Island, and Sprague's Am. Presb. Pulpit, &c.,* from which it has been compiled. (See next page.)

During the next few years Mr. Roberdeau devoted himself to his family and his mercantile pursuits. Knowing his earlier years but imperfectly, we cannot say when he

4

ANCESTRY OF MARY BOSTWICK, WHO MARRIED
GEN. DANIEL ROBERDEAU.

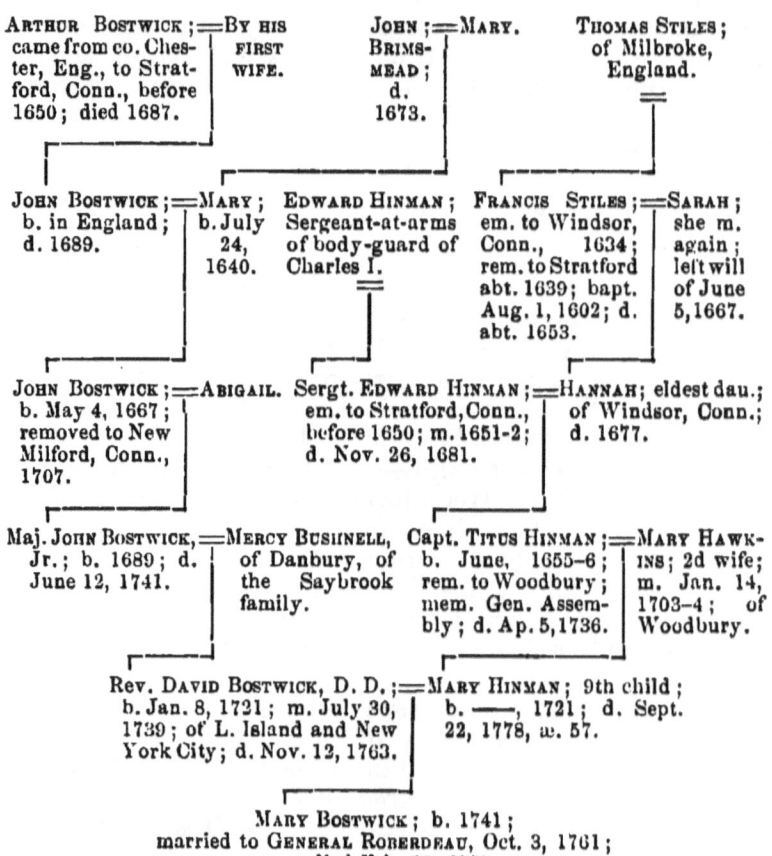

ARTHUR BOSTWICK ;══BY HIS
came from co. Ches-   FIRST
ter, Eng., to Strat-   WIFE.
ford, Conn., before
1650; died 1687.

JOHN ;══MARY.
BRIMS-
MEAD ;
d.
1673.

THOMAS STILES ;
of Milbroke,
England.
══

JOHN BOSTWICK ;══MARY ;
b. in England ;   b. July
d. 1689.   24,
                  1640.

EDWARD HINMAN ;
Sergeant-at-arms
of body-guard of
Charles I.
══

FRANCIS STILES ;══SARAH ;
em. to Windsor,   she m.
Conn.,   1634 ; again ;
rem. to Stratford left will
abt. 1639 ; bapt. of June
Aug. 1, 1602 ; d. 5,1667.
abt. 1653.

JOHN BOSTWICK ;══ABIGAIL.
b. May 4, 1667 ;
removed to New
Milford, Conn.,
1707.

Sergt. EDWARD HINMAN ;══HANNAH ; eldest dau. ;
em. to Stratford, Conn.,   of Windsor, Conn. ;
before 1650 ; m. 1651-2 ; d. 1677.
d. Nov. 26, 1681.

Maj. JOHN BOSTWICK,══MERCY BUSHNELL,
Jr. ; b. 1689 ; d.   of Danbury, of
June 12, 1741.   the Saybrook
                     family.

Capt. TITUS HINMAN ;══MARY HAWK-
b. June, 1655-6 ;   INS ; 2d wife ;
rem. to Woodbury ;   m. Jan. 14,
mem. Gen. Assem-   1703-4 ;   of
bly ; d. Ap. 5,1736. Woodbury.

Rev. DAVID BOSTWICK, D. D. ;══MARY HINMAN ; 9th child ;
b. Jan. 8, 1721 ; m. July 30,   b. ——, 1721 ; d. Sept.
1739 ; of L. Island and New   22, 1778, æ. 57.
York City ; d. Nov. 12, 1763.

MARY BOSTWICK ; b. 1741 ;
married to GENERAL ROBERDEAU, Oct. 3, 1761 ;
died Feb. 15, 1777.

entered into business for himself, or with whom he may have been previously connected. His receipt books, kindly placed at the disposal of the writer by different persons, show the magnitude of his business. These books cover a long period of time, as follows:

The first, December 7, 1754, to May 28, 1761.

The second, November 28, 1761, to May 26, 1767.

The third, April 27, 1767, to September 24, 1790.

The latter does not cover the whole of this period. From December, 1767, to December, 1774, and from July, 1776, to March 1780, there are but few or no entries.

The amounts receipted for add up as follows:

1754, part of Dec. only.....	£ 172	1761, except June to Nov..	£ 848
1755.........	529	·1762..............................	14,678
1756..............................	2,447	1763........	9,645
1757........	10,977	1764..............................	6,257
1758..............................	8,147	1765..............................	1,470
1759	11,099	1766..............................	4,241
1760..............................	6,161	1767..............................	3,098

Total.......................................£79,769

Equivalent in those days to about $386,081.

Or at present, in currency, the larger sum of $1,158,000. an average of nearly $90,000 a year, which appears to have been a very large and prosperous business that he carried on. These receipts are mostly for merchandise, but some entries are for household expenses, rent, etc. During the later years the receipts give no true idea of the valuation, from the depreciation of money during the Revolution. During this time, also, there are but few mercantile receipts, and many relating to the army, and other incidents of the war. Some of the receipts are as follows:

In 1760, £1,040 was invested in "stocks." His house rent about £53 a year; subsequently, another house for about £40. In 1756 are several payments for camp equipage, guns, bayonets, &c.; wherein he is styled "Captain," intimating that he then belonged to the militia. (In the *Penn. Colonial Records*, vii., 76, is the incidental remark, "Mr. Thomas Willing, late a lieutenant in Captain Roberdeau's company.") One payment in 1757, is "£800 in full payment for Snow Marymack, sold to him by the marshal in pursuance of a decree of the court of admiralty of Pennsylvania, and signed Edward Shippen, Jr." (a vessel with two masts like a brig, and a third small mast near the stern). Then follow some entries for men's wages, pilotage, &c., of Snow Boyd; others, for lengthening brig Franklin; refitting ship Nancy, &c. He paid £26 "in full for a chair," a sort of one-horse chaise, carrying two people; and soon after, a black horse, for £17; the next year, two black horses, for £35; and again, another black horse, for £14; he seemed to have a preference for that color! Then, as he rode or walked, occasionally he bought a "pair of spatter-dashes," for £1.

In the second book, is a receipt signed by Francis Hopkinson, one of the signers of the Declaration. In July, 1764, a small sum for "freight of Mr. Whitefield's goods;" and in September, "fifteen shillings in full for dressing Mr. Whitefield and Mr. Wright's wigs." Also, many payments for repairs and expenses of various vessels.

In the third book: In the beginning of the Revolution are many payments for the second battalion, of which he was colonel, £52 for colors. In 1780 the high prices from the depreciated currency, show, five cords of wood £125; thirty bushels of rye, £540; 12¾ yards of linen, £255; one barrel of flour, £145 or about 700 *dollars*. In 1783 £6 for "teaching his son and daughter, Molly, to dance."

It is creditable to observe that most of the entries are worded, "in full to date;" some larger bills are "on account."

Daniel Roberdeau dealt chiefly in the produce of the West Indies, from whence he imported largely. Sugar, molasses, wines, flour, bread, pork, &c.; also, including the products of our own country, as his letter-book and receipt-book both show. In the Pennsylvania Gazette, of July 31, 1766, there appeared the following advertisement:

"WEST INDIA Rum and Spirit, also choice old Maderia Wine to be sold by DANIEL ROBERDEAU, at the South End of Second street, near the Bridge. Said Roberdeau has a store to LETT, in Water street, next Door to Mr. Thomas Clifford."

It appears that Daniel Roberdeau also dealt in lumber; for in some lines, written by tories of those days, and quoted on a subsequent page, the annotations refer to him as a "board merchant;" and in *Watson's Annals of Philadelphia*, I., 451, speaking of the Lutheran churches in the city: "Their next built church was the large church in Fourth street, corner of Cherry street, built there in 1772. The site which they took up had been the board yard of General Roberdeau. While the British occupied Philadelphia, they took out the pews of this church and used it as a hospital."

We next meet with Mr. Roberdeau's name on the books of the Second Presbyterian Church, in Philadelphia, as follows:

Nov. 14th, 1765. "The session met; present, Rev. John Murray, Moderator; John Williams, Gunning Bedford, Elders; Wm. Falconer, Robert Eastburn, Deacons. And taking into consideration the necessity of an additional number of church officers, the following gentlemen were nominated: Messrs. John Rodman, John Rhea, Daniel Roberdeau, Robert Cather, John McCala, and Hugh McCulloch, for elders [and several others for deacons], who all agreed to serve in said offices except John Rodman, who declined for the present; and after due notice had been given to the congregation on several preceding Sabbaths, they were set apart to their respective offices, according to the usage of profession, on the —— day of August following, by the Rev. John Murray, the stated pastor of the congregation. Concluded with prayer."

Mr. Roberdeau's name accordingly appears on the records as present at the meetings as an elder, until 1771.

Daniel Roberdeau's letter-book above referred to, was kindly sent to the writer by one of the family, and has been of inestimable service in preparing this biography. Its size is seven by twelve inches, containing 338 pages of letters, dated from July 6, 1764, to October 29, 1771; all well written, as may be seen from the numerous extracts here given. The style is easy, flowing, and forcible, showing the writer to have been a man of cultivation and refinement. There are erasures with the pen, here and there, as also interlineations, implying care in the choice of words.

Among the letters are several to Benjamin Franklin, Joseph Reed, afterwards very prominent in civil life, Rev. John Witherspoon, President of Princeton College, Rev. John Rodgers, John Fothergill; also to his relatives, Daniel Cunyngham, Mrs. Heriot Crooke, Miss Jourdina Cunyngham; also one from Mrs. Keighley to her brother Daniel Cunyngham. Most of the correspondence, is however, commercial.

In one of the letters to Daniel Cunyngham, there is mentioned a severe loss Mr. Roberdeau had lately sustained in business. "Although I am like to lose about £850 in the affair, [nearly $17,000 of our present currency,] yet I have emerged with honor from an ocean of debt, which was my greatest distress."

The cause of this loss appears to be that in part payment for a schooner he ordered to be built for a certain Messrs. Meyler and Hall, Mr. Roberdeau by their order drew for a portion of the cost, a draft for £600, on one Hutchinson Mure, which was refused payment; Mure having no money in his hands belonging to that firm. Costs were then added, making the amount £850. November 9, 1765, he writes to that firm, "I would prefer bread and water in peace, than the whole world of riches and honor, with vexation. I have and still suffer by my repeated disappointments. I have a fortune, but not in cash. Money is so very scarce, that we fear very shortly we shall want a medium of cash." The matter seems to have annoyed him, particularly as he appears to have been the victim of some dishonesty. And what noble sentiments under such trying circumstances!

After the death of his friend, the Rev. Samuel Davis, Daniel Roberdeau appears to have had the charge of his four children, which trust he gave up, in 1768, to the Rev. John Witherspoon on his arrival in the country as the successor of Dr. Davis in the presidency of Princeton College, after Dr. Samuel Blair had declined that honor in favor of Dr. W. But a few months after, Daniel Roberdeau was regularly constituted guardian of William Samuel and John Rodgers Davis, by the Orphans Court, and "agreeable to their election," as he informed their uncle. Dr. Witherspoon must therefore have declined the charge.

The writer has often heard his mother and aunt speak of the large stature and great physical strength of Daniel Roberdeau, which account they had from their father. The tories of the Revolution, who would naturally caricature the most prominent characteristics, spoke of him as a "spectre of portentous show." And again, "with solemn phiz and action slow," which might imply the same, if large bodies move slowly.

Respecting this, we have an interesting anecdote handed down to us. Daniel Roberdeau's *leg* was particularly large, he complained for many years that he never could get stockings large enough to fit him. In those days we must remember that gentlemen wore "small clothes" as they were termed, reaching to the knee with the stockings showing the full form of the leg. Finally a man was found in London who could weave stockings large enough; and in one of his visits to that city, Daniel Roberdeau set out one day to find his weaver. In passing through Holburn street, he noticed a man observing him very attentively, who at last fixing his eyes on his leg, exclaimed, "Dang it! if I did not know the man I weave stockings for was in America, I should say that was he." Roberdeau turned, and found the very man he sought.

Apropos to this tradition, a letter in his letter-book gives the dimensions of his leg, and is as follows:

PHILADELPHIA, *January* 18, 1769.

Messrs. WOOD & TREVANION.

Dear Sirs : . . . .

Wm. Martin, hosier, in the year 1763 sent me by order of Messrs. Augustus & John Boyd a parcel of stockings, agreeable to a linen pattern sent from here, but either through inattention in his workmen, or a fault in the pattern, he missed my size in some of the stockings; to remedy which, I have taken the exact dimensions of my leg and foot, and must beg the favor of you to order Mr. Martin, or any other hosier that you can depend on, to send me by the very first vessel for this port, twelve pair of fine cotton, and six pair of grey worsted hose, which please charge to my account. Any captain coming here will, I doubt not, cheerfully take charge of them. In all America I cannot get stockings made large enough for me, therefore this commission, though in itself very trifling, and needs an apology, yet to me it is very important; therefore I entreat you'll forgive my freedom, and give very particular directions to the hosier, with a copy of such things as relate to the subject; the dimensions are exact, without any allowance for shrinking or stretching, according to the quality of the yarn, concerning which he must exercise his own judgment, which no doubt will direct him, that cotton stockings do not stretch and that worsted stockings do, therefore, according to my judgment, the latter should be rather under size and the former rather over.

. . . . . . Dear Sir,

Your ob. and obliged humbl. serv.

Foot full 10½ inches long.

Small of the leg 11 inches round.

Calf of do. 20 inches round.

Fifteen months after this, Daniel Roberdeau again wrote: "I thank you for your care of the trifling articles of stockings sent me, but no acknowledgment is due the workman, who did not follow your orders, consequently disappointed me in the sizes being too small." I doubt if we can realize the disappointment, when after waiting over a year, to find the stockings too small.

Many of us knew the friendship between Daniel Roberdeau and the celebrated preacher George Whitefield. His eldest son Isaac was christened by him, and in her old Bible, Elizabeth Roberdeau, sister of Daniel, made the following entry: "Bapt. by Geo. Whitefield, September 20," [1763.] The christening water was held at the time in a china *punch-bowl* that was old even then; and has since been used as a christening font, out of which four generations have now been christened. This punch-bowl is one of the oldest of the family heirlooms; it is about ten inches in diameter, and was imported from China to St. Kitts, and stood on the sideboard at Robert Cunyngham's house, always kept full of punch. It is now held by Mrs. F. Selina Buchanan. Probably all of Daniel Roberdeau's children were also christened from it. Our tradition says that Isaac and Selina certainly were, and also gives the history of the latter name coming into the family, since become such a favorite. Had there been a son, he was to have been named "Whitefield," but after George Whitefield's death, and after several daughters had been born, knowing his wishes, this child was named "*Selina*," after his patroness, Selina, Countess of Huntington, relict of Theophilus, 9th Earl. It was greatly owing to this lady that Whitefield became so well known, for she appointed him her chaplain, which thus brought him in contact with the court and the nobility, and by her assistance he built several tabernacles in England.

Daniel Roberdeau was not a *follower* of Whitefield, as has been stated by some writers, but a *friend.* He was a strict Presbyterian, and not a Methodist. After Dr. Whitefield's death, Mr. Roberdeau writes under date of November 24, 1770, to Mr. Robert Keen, London, as follows:

"Since our friend's decease, I have received a letter from Mr. Smith, who accompanied him in his travel, desiring me to send you per first ship, Mr. W's chest and traveling-box, which is

accordingly sent with bill of lading enclosed by this conveyance ; the chest would not contain his wig-box, and a small
ordinary case for liquors, both which I offered to the captain for
his convenience on the passage, but he refused them and they
are not worth the freight, however they will remain safe for
your commands, everything else is sent except a silver can
weighing twelve ounces twelve pennyweights of silver, which
was left in use in my family; a half-worn pair of buckskin
gloves, his cane with a pinchbeck head ; besides these two, his
sauce-pans, a tin dish, a pint tea-kittle, which the chest could
not contain, and of no value.   The can, gloves, and cane, I am
willing to pay for, and you have my authority to draw for the
same.   I had a silversmith's opinion who weighed the can, that
it was not worth more than the silver, being very long in use
and old fashioned, but I value it much higher than the richest
plate, therefore I hope I shall not be censured for detaining it,
with the gloves and cane as keepsakes."

The wig-box was formerly in the possession of Mr.
James M. Roberdeau, but its whereabouts now is unknown.   This silver can has descended in the Conrad
branch of the family, and was lately given by Dr. Daniel
Conrad to Mrs. M. C. Bent, who now holds it.

An edition of Watts' Psalms and Hymns, published by
Longman, in London, 1759, with the inscription on the
fly-leaf, "the gift of Rev'd Mr. Geo. Whitefield to Daniel
Roberdeau, 1764," is now in the possession of one of his
grandsons.

Miss S. S. Roberdeau has also another memento of this
celebrated man, a medal which was struck in England
and sent to Mr. Roberdeau soon after Dr. Whitefield's
death.   The medal is of gold or heavily gilt, one and
one-half inches in diameter.   On the obverse, a relief
likeness surrounded with the words "The Rev. George
Whitefield, A. M."   On the reverse, the inscription—

"TO THE MEMORY OF
THE REV. GEO. WHITEFIELD, A. M.
Who with reluctant grandeur,
gave, not yielded up
his soul sublime,
At Newbury P., N. America, S. 30, 1770,
in the 65 year of his age.
His conduct is a legacy for all."

Above is a female figure and landscape; and below,
a coat of arms, probably those of Whitefield.

When Mr. Roberdeau came to this country, he was
undoubtedly a man of considerable wealth, part of which

he may have inherited from his father, who was also a
man of fortune. Some of it was his capital in merchandise. His letter-book mentions a plantation in St. Christopher's, called Pelham's River Plantation. We also
read that in February, 1769, this estate had just been
cleared of a mortgage, and that he owned it early as
1752, when he was but twenty-five years of age. This
plantation which he states at 150 acres, and formerly 204
acres, was let for £280 per annum, but as the lease was
to expire in January, 1771, he desired to sell the same
for £7,000, but adds that he is a great stranger to the
value of lands in the island.

In February, 1770, he entrusts the matter to three of
his friends, Dr. Benjamin Franklin, Dr. John Fothergill,
and Charles Pearce, his cousin, writing to them jointly
and separately. Dr. Franklin was at this time the agent
of the State of Pennsylvania, in London, and had already
attained his high rank as a philosopher. To him, Mr.
Roberdeau now entrusted this large transaction, if he
"could condescend to look down from affairs of the
highest public concern, to an affair of the highest private
concern of an unworthy friend." These gentlemen were
unable to effect a sale, although the first price for which
the estate was offered had been reduced; and at last Mr.
Roberdeau determined to go himself to London, in May,
1771, and is successful in effecting a sale to John Boyd,
who lately held the mortgage, for the sum of £4,500, and
very fortunately, for the land was already darkened by
the shadow of the coming revolution. This transaction
we called "large," for if money was four times as valuable then as now, as seen on a previous page, the estate
sold for near $100,000 of our present currency. The
deed was recorded in Philadelphia.

There are several other deeds recorded in Philadelphia,
to which Mr. Roberdeau was a party. One tract of land
containing 124 acres 130 perches, lying on the Delaware
and Schuylkill rivers, he bought of three parties, who
each appeared to have a claim to it, for £100, £200, and
£220, respectively, in 1761.—(Deed II. 15, pages 385,
388, 391.) Four years after, is a deed of partition in
seven parts between as many parties, each of whom
claimed the same, whereby 29½ acres on the Schuylkill
fall to Mr. Roberdeau.—(II. 21, 142.) This latter tract
he sells in 1779 to Mrs. Mary Norris for £33,000.—(I. 10,
338.)

There are three or four other deeds on record here for small transactions.

The letter-book mentions, in December, 1767, a "plantation" three miles from Frankford, where he wished some rafts and lumber left. Frankford is seven miles above Philadelphia, on a creek of the same name, now part of the city.*

These are his possessions—possibly only a portion; of which, in his letter-book, he writes : " I have a fortune, but not in cash." Later in life, he owned houses and lands in Alexandria.

THE REVOLUTION.

Although the Revolutionary War did not begin until 1775, yet the causes which led to it occurred ten years earlier. The chief of these was the odious Stamp Act, the pet theory of Mr. Grenville, then Prime Minister. This act, laying a tax on deeds, notes, &c., took effect on the 1st of November, 1765, which was observed as a day of mourning.

A few days after, Mr. Roberdeau writes : "The merchants have engaged to sell no goods for themselves or any other person, that shall be shipped from England after the 1st of January next. The inhabitants of New York, within these few days, were within an ace of storming the King's fort in that city ; and although it was guarded by regular soldiers, the Governor, on receipt of a manifesto threatening to hang him, was obliged to give up the stamps. What will be the issue I cannot foresee, but I believe from the spirit of the people, there must be a deluge of blood from one end of the continent to the other before they will submit to the Stamp Act." In the latter part of this year the non-importation agreement was entered into by the merchants of the principal seaports. That in Philadelphia, dated October 25, was signed by all the prominent merchants of that city. A lithograph fac-simile of this document is in Independence Hall, Philadelphia, on which Daniel Roberdeau's signature is prominently seen.

To Benjamin Franklin he writes, September 28, 1770, giving as an excuse for not having written earlier " a meeting yesterday at the State-House ; and in consequence of my being employed, with others, as a committee to endeavor to counteract the detestable conduct of some of our merchants the 20th instant in violating the non-importation agreement. But, alas! I fear it is a forlorn hope." This matter was one of the consequences of the Stamp Act. The merchants and others determined that if certain goods were taxed they would not import them. Hence that agreement, that was now broken by some self-interested persons.

An account of this meeting may be found in the *Pennsylvania Gazette* of October 4, in substance as above. John Cadwallader, George Clymer, and others were also of the committee with Daniel Roberdeau " to request merchants and traders to adopt these measures."

The aggressions of England now increased; disputes were frequent between the people and the authorities in Massachusetts and in Rhode Island; the odious *tea* was sent over from England; the port of Boston closed to commerce; then troops arrived, ship after ship, until ten thousand had been collected; at last, in the attempt to destroy some military stores which the Colonies had collected, the skirmishes at Lexington and Concord gave the signal for war, and all who were not already in the field flew to arms. Congress having met six months before this, now began to raise an army. The inhabitants of each State who did not enter the army formed themselves into companies. Committees of safety were constituted, and preparations begun for a formidable war.

In the Army.

The people throughout the Colony who did not enter the reglar army formed themselves into an organization for the defence of the Province, known as the *Associators*. They armed and equipped themselves, chose their own officers, and commenced a systematic course of drilling. In June, 1775, they completed their organization by the formation in the city, of three battalions. Of the second battalion Mr. Roberdeau was elected colonel, with Joseph Reed as lieutenant-colonel, and John Cox and John Bayard as majors. A full list of the field-officers appears in the *Philadelphia Evening Post* of June 24, 1775.

The Associators throughout the State were governed by a Board of Officers and a Board of Privates. Of the former Colonel Roberdeau was elected president.

The Associators, at first voluntary, became afterwards compulsory. Their Code of Rules was approved by the Council of Safety, and soon after enforced by the Assembly, on the 8th of November, in an act enrolling all white males between the ages of sixteen and fifty; and those who would not bear arms should be fined. While this bill was pending, the Quakers, a large and influential body in Pennsylvania, a majority of whom were tories, protested against its passage. To neutralize the effect of this petition, a remonstrance was presented to the Assembly a few days after, on the 31st of October, protesting against the "antiquated and absurd doctrine of passive obedience," and stating that "heretofore no exemption has been made during any previous wars, of fine and taxation. By order of the Board of Officers. (Signed) Daniel Roberdeau, Chairman."

The Associators appear now to have been in active service, for in the proceedings of Congress of January 25, 1776, it was " Resolved, That Colonel Roberdeau be requested to relieve the guard at Trenton, who have charge of General Prescott and Captain Chase, with a trusty guard from his battalion." These two officers, it will be remembered, had been captured by a bold raid into the enemy's line, taken out of bed, and brought safely into the American camp. The Americans had been wanting an officer of that grade to exchange for one of equal rank held by the British.

The Associators having heretofore paid their own expenses, the Board of Privates now petitioned the Assembly for pay for their arms and clothes. This petition is concurred in by another from the Board of Officers, dated February 21, 1776, and signed by Daniel Roberdeau, President, who also asks the Assembly to order drills to take place at least once a week.

In May, 1776, proposals were received by Col. Roberdeau from Mr. Trumbull, for a magazine of provisions for 10,000 men for three months.—(*Penn. Archives*, vol. for 1760–'76.)

On the third of June, Congress ordered a flying camp to be established in the Middle States, of 10,000 men, of which the quota from Pennsylvania was 6,000; and directed the appointment of two brigadier-generals from that State, and one from Maryland.

Whereupon the Assembly was about proceeding to the election of the two brigadier-generals, when a communication was received (June 14) from the Board of Officers of the five battalions of the Associators, protesting against the election, unless the house had the authority of the Associators, "Signed by order, Daniel Roberdeau, President." The cause of this protest appears to be, that the Associators being a voluntary organization, desired to be commanded by officers of their own election.

MEETING OF MAY 20, 1776.

The matter of independence now began to be agitated, which resulted in Philadelphia in a great public meeting, an account of which may be found in a recent work, *The Rise of the Republic,* by the Hon. Richard Frothingham. In giving the state of feeling throughout the country regarding independence, the author says:

"Pennsylvania was fairly alive with the idea of independence. Nowhere had the question been more thoroughly discussed than in its press, and nowhere was the opposition more strongly intrenched, for it had on its side the proprietary government. The tories could point to the instructions of the Assembly as the voice of one-eighth of the inhabitants of America. Warm advocates of independence who desired to retain the charter, agreed in this with the majority of Quakers and the proprietary party. On this well prepared soil fell the resolutions of the fifteenth of May. [Recommending to the Colonies that where no government sufficient to the exigencies of their affairs had been hitherto established; to adopt such government, and that all authority under the Crown should be suppressed; and all powers be under the authority of the people.] The principle it embodies was accepted by the popular party as their rule of action. . . . . The public conviction was embodied in a great public meeting held on the 20th of May, at the State-House, which was called to order by Major John Bayard, a man of singular purity of character, brave and devout; in which Colonel Daniel Roberdeau, a gallant soldier of the Revolution presided, and Thomas McKean, an eminent civilian, took a part. The Resolution of Congress was read, when 'the people, in testimony of their warmest approbation, gave three cheers.' The instructions of the Assembly against independence, of November 9th, were read, when the meeting unanimously resolved that they had the 'dangerous tendency to withdraw this province from that happy union with the other colonies, which we consider both our glory and protection.'"

A protest was then drawn up, addressed to the Assembly, in which after the preamble that the government should be "under the authority of the people"—

. . . . "We, therefore, in this solemn manner, in behalf of ourselves and others, do hereby renounce and protest against the authority of this house for framing a new government. . . . . Signed in behalf of and by direction of the inhabitants of the City and Liberties of Philadelphia, upon due notification met; Philadelphia, May 20, 1776. DANIEL ROBERDEAU, Chairman."

This protest was presented to the Assembly on the 22d, and laid upon the table.

The author of the above book has stated to the writer the importance of this meeting. They were so early in the field, and so decided in their proceedings, that they became an example for the other colonies, and the account of the meeting was published in all the papers in the country. Of the effect of the meeting in the province, he says: "This great demonstration was felt throughout the province. The position it took was responded to by local committees, public meetings, and military battalions. . . . The Assembly so far yielded to the outburst of popular feeling, as on the 8th of June to adopt instructions authorizing the delegates to concur in forming further compacts between the United Colonies, and in promoting the safety and interests of America, reserving to the people the sole right of regulating their internal government." And in a note, adds: "In Marshall's Remembrances (p. 82), it is stated that the great meeting met in the State-House yard, in the rain, at ten o'clock, and continued till twelve, and after the adjournment, the committee of Philadelphia appointed persons to carry the resolves to the counties." Bancroft, in his History of the United States, also refers to this meeting, and to Colonel Roberdeau, its chairman.

PRIVATEERS.

While engaged in the army, now that England had destroyed the commerce of the Colonies, their vessels were converted into privateers. Daniel Roberdeau's receipt-book shows that, April 2, 1776, he paid £100 for one-eighth share in the sloops Congress and Chance, privateers, and a month or two afterwards is a receipt for £400 from him as treasurer of this company.

It appears that these vessels were successful in making some valuable captures, and John Adams, in a letter to his wife, May, 1776, refers to the "valuable prize" taken by the privateer fitted out by Daniel Roberdeau and John Bayard.—(*P. Force's Am. Archives*, 4, VI., 489.) In the receipt-book of Colonel Roberdeau is the following: "Received, July 25, 1776, of Daniel Roberdeau, treasurer to the privateers Congress and Chance, the sum of £6,097, 1s., 3d., which, with five bags of silver coin and plate, is in full of the trust reposed in him. Received by order and in behalf of owners of privateers Congress and Chance," &c.

About this same time (July 17) Colonel Roberdeau purchased a pair of pistols for £12, which may be those he had with him when he captured the highwayman, an account of which is given on a subsequent page, and which his son Isaac says were captured by a privateer early in the war of the Revolution.

Another receipt shows £100 for a share in privateer General Mifflin.

The silver above captured was tendered to Congress, as appears by the following, of June 12, 1776:

"Colonel Roberdeau, in behalf of the owners of the privateers which have taken some prizes, on board of which was a quantity of dollars, to the amount of 22,000, having tendered to Congress the moiety belonging to them in exchange for Continental bills of credit: Resolved that it be accepted."

THE COUNCIL OF SAFETY.

We will now recede a few months. At the beginning of the Revolution, as above stated, there were in the various colonies organizations known as the Councils of Safety, whose duties were, as their name implies, to guard the public safety of their respective colonies.

It was soon after the battle of Bunker Hill had roused the country, that the Pennsylvania Assembly constituted the Council of Safety for that province—on the 30th of June, 1775. Among those composing it were some of the most prominent and influential men in the colony—Henry Wynkoop, Anthony Wayne, Edward Biddle, Thomas Willing, Benjamin Franklin, Daniel Roberdeau, John Cadwallader, Robert Morris, Thomas Wharton, and

others, in all twenty-five, " to be a Committee of Safety
for calling forth such and so many of the Associators
into actual service, when necessity requires, as the said
committee shall judge proper; for paying and supplying
them; to provide for the defence of the province against
insurrection and invasion; for encouraging the manu-
facture of saltpetre, etc. Seven or more constituting a
board for the transaction of business."

The proceedings of the Council of Safety are published
in full in vols. X. and XI. of the *Pennsylvania Colonial
Records*, in 16 volumes, printed officially in 1852. A pe-
rusal of those pages would be interesting to any of our
family, and but a small portion can be quoted here. They
organized July 3, 1775, by the choice of Benjamin Franklin as president.

July 15. Colonels Roberdeau and Cadwallader and
Mr. S. Morris are sent into New Jersey to confer with
the principal inhabitants, to know if they will assist this
Colony in defending the river.

August 3. Colonels Cadwallader, Wayne, and Roberdeau and three others are a committee to draft rules and
regulations for the government of the Associators. The
articles were read and approved August 19.

In October, 1775, another Council of Safety was appointed by the Assembly, most of the former members
being reëlected.

January 12, 1776. Colonel Roberdeau and Mr. Clymer
are a committee to procure copies of petitions, memorials,
&c., addressed to the Throne or to Parliament since 1762,
and the answers to them. The committee reported on the
19th, six in all, to which no answers had been returned.
It was then resolved that these two gentlemen wait upon
Congress with these copies of petitions.

June 28. Colonel Roberdeau, Mr. Clymer, and Mr.
Rittenhouse are a committee to ascertain what fortifications are required at Billingsport, and to make a draft of
the same.

Besides these notices Colonel Roberdeau is repeatedly
mentioned on various occasions: to inspect ordnance;
regarding the purchase of cannon; to procure shot; in
reference to Brigadier-General McDonald and other prisoners; on pikes and entrenching tools; on a barracks
committee; one of a committee to collect saltpetre, (*Even-*

5

ing Post, July 4,) &c., &c.   July 5, 1776, the Declaration
of Independence was read, and from this date Colonel
Roberdeau's name does not appear as present at the
meetings, as he was then in the field, as will be seen below.   Heretofore he was present at almost every meeting, daily, and appears to have entered into his duties in
this sphere with will, giving his whole time to this and
to his battalion.

Elected Brigadier-General.

For the account of this we are indebted to our relative,
Edward M. Clymer, Esq., who kindly placed at the disposal of the writer all the *original* papers.

When Congress directed that two brigadier-generals
should be appointed from Pennsylvania for the Flying
Camp, Colonel Roberdeau, in behalf of the Board of Officers, sent a circular letter to all the Associators throughout the Colony, calling upon them to send delegates to
meet at Lancaster for their election.   The Board of Privates likewise sent a similar letter.

Accordingly two officers and two privates from each
of the fifty-three battalions of the Associators of the Col-
ny met at Lancaster on the 4th day of July, 1776.   Mark
the day.   The acquisition of the title with which Daniel
Roberdeau has descended to posterity is coeval with the
birth of the country he was fighting for.   The meeting
organized by the choice of Colonel George Ross as chairman, and Lieutenant-Colonel Daniel C. Clymer as secretary.

There were present besides the above, Colonels Daniel
Roberdeau, John Patton, W. Montgomery, J. Armstrong,
Mark Bird, Majors Robert Knox, Gabriel Hiester, Cap-
tain Sharp Dulaney, Privates Th. Montgomery, Paul
Cox, and others.

The protests of the Boards of Officers and of Privates
to the Assembly were read.   The circular letters of the
two boards calling the meeting were read.   It was then
decided that each delegate should have one vote, and
"that both brigadier-generals be voted for at the same
time, and the highest in votes to be the commanding officer."   A vote was then taken, with the following—

RESULT:

Whole number of delegates*...............................	228
Number present and votes cast....................	193
Daniel Roberdeau...........................	160
James Ewing.............................	85
Samuel Miles..............................	82
James Patton.............................	24
Curtis Grubb..............................	9
George Ross...............................	9
Thomas McKean...........................	8
Mark Bird.................................	7

"The President immediately declared Daniel Roberdeau First Brigadier-General, and James Ewing Second Brigadier-General." The meeting then gave authority to its president to commission them; and further, gave these officers power to call out into action any number of the Associators, and resolved that the Associators would march under their orders, &c., &c., &c. The journal of the meeting is signed by its president, George Ross, also a signer of the Declaration, and by its secretary, Daniel C. Clymer. The result of the election is published in the papers of the day, and in full in *Rupp's History of Berks and Lebanon counties.*

His battalion addressed to General Roberdeau the following very complimentary letter upon his election, published with the reply in the *Philadelphia Journal* of July 17:

To THE HON. DANIEL ROBERDEAU, ESQ.,
  First Brigadier-General for the Province of Pennsylvania.

SIR: We are desired by the Board of Officers of the Second Battalion to inform you, that they are fully sensible of the great attention and zeal with which you have conducted yourself, whilst in the station of their colonel; not only for the general and important interest of our bleeding country, but for those of the battalion in particular. Nothing but the consideration of your being advanced to a situation in which you can be more extensively useful, could alleviate the regret they feel on the removal of their colonel.

We are instructed, unfeignedly to congratulate you on your election to the distinguished department you now fill; which we have no doubt you will conduct with honor to yourself, and advantage to the cause in which our lives and fortunes

---

* Fifty-seven battalions in the Colony; four not represented here. ·

are so deeply engaged : and permit us to assure you, that the officers and privates of the Second Battalion will always esteem it a particular privilege to be under your commands ; and you may depend upon their zeal and readiness in all occasions to support your authority and execute your orders.

Signed by order, and in behalf of the Battalion :

JOHN BAYARD, *Colonel.*
JONATHAN B. SMITH, *Capt.*
SAMUEL MASSEY, *Lieut.*

PHILADELPHIA, *July* 10, 1776.

To this, General Roberdeau modestly replied ; and speaking of his own want of talent for the position, added : "It is the cause of God . . . who can give efficacy to the feeblest efforts."

At this time, General Washington was in a very critical position in New Jersey ; and on the fifth of July, it was decided in Philadelphia to send all the associated militia of the State to his relief. Accordingly all subsequent mention of General Roberdeau alludes to him as in the field in command of the Pennsylvania forces. John Hancock, President of Congress, also wrote to General Roberdeau, under date of July 14th, directing him to forward to the Jerseys, the whole militia of the Colony.—(*Peter Force's American Archives,* 5th series, I., 326.)

When the urgent need for reinforcements had passed, and the men becoming wearied with the privations of a soldier's life, wanted to return home ; they found fault with their food, complained that their business suffered, &c., &c. To allay this dissatisfaction, General Roberdeau issued a proclamation to the Pennsylvania Associators, and addressing them as Gentlemen, counseled patience ; the surest way to revive their business, was to remain and whip the enemy ; the complaints regarding their provisions should be remedied as soon as possible ; and those who could not bear a little inconvenience at such a time were beneath the regard of himself and every other earnest man.

The address is strongly worded and eloquent, and was so highly approved by the State Convention (House of Representatives) when read before them ; that it was ordered to be printed in the English and German newspapers.—(*Ibid.,* I., 1062, *and* II., 24, *August* 19.)

In the proceedings of the Council of Safety, are frequent mention of supplies sent to General Roberdeau,

&c., &c. July 12. Upon his application, arms were ordered for the armed brigantine Venus. And on the 23d, 100,000 cartridges were forwarded.

In the proceedings of Congress, August 1, a letter of the 30th July from Brigadier-General Mercer, and one of the same date from Brigadier-General Roberdeau, and sundry others, were read: Resolved, That the two first be referred to the Board of War.

The following week General Mercer writes to General Washington, under date of Amboy, 8 a.m., 7 September, 1776: "By some neglect of the messenger, your letter was not received till seven o'clock this morning. General Roberdeau waits on your Excellency to know the result of your determinations, and to inform you of the state of the troops in New Jersey." This letter is published in full in *Sparks' Correspondence of the Revolution*, I., 285.

In the fall of this year, General Roberdeau was seized with an infectious fever that then raged in the camp, from the violence of which he narrowly escaped with life. At this time of his prostration, the Council of Safety nobly came to his relief, and in the month of December "Resolved, That an order be given to John Bray, or any other constable, to impress a close carriage with horses from James Pemberton, John Pemberton, Israel Pemberton, or Samuel Emlen, jr., to remove General Roberdeau to Lancaster." This act of kindness to their former associate shows the high estimation in which he was held by them, and merits our warmest admiration. These persons from whom the carriage was impressed were Quaker tories, and among the most wealthy in the city; and carriages were not then as numerous as at present, there being only eighty-four enumerated in the whole city a year or two previously. These persons, with some others, were arrested the next year for their tory sentiments.

At Lancaster General Roberdeau received the untiring care of his wife, who had probably removed to Lancaster some time previously to avoid the confusion centering in Philadelphia.

"At this moment of debility and weakness, his affliction was augmented by the unexpected death of his wife, from the effects of the same disease, which was doubtless contracted in her attendance upon him during his

illness.   She died at Lancaster, on the 15th of February,
1777, and is interred under the communion table of the
Presbyterian Church in that place.   A change of circumstances, at once so great and so rapid, was sufficient to
have affected permanently a mind less susceptible than
his.   A few months since he was endowed with athletic
powers the most extraordinary, his fortune was ample,
and his family in health and plenty.   He now felt almost
infantile weakness, diminution of property, and to crown
all, the bereavement of a wife whom he loved with a
tender and manly affection, and in her loss to witness the
derangement of a family so lately his pride and comfort.
It may, therefore, be fairly presumed that he never perfectly recovered either his mental or his bodily powers.
From an early period he had embraced the doctrines of
the Christian religion, and became not only a sincere but
an active believer in the gospel of the Christian church.
From this source he afterwards derived all the consola-
tion that was permitted him in this life, and from this
source, also, he drew fortitude which enabled him to
look back without regret to those scenes of domestic
felicity that had now vanished."—(*Isaac Roberdeau's MS.*)

General Roberdeau thus records the death of his wife
in the family Bible, portions of which are now lost by
the leaf being worn away :

"[Mary] Roberdeau departed this life February 15th,
1777, aged 3[6? years, and is buried] with her still-born
daughter, in the Presbyterian [Church ——.]"

THE COMMISSIONERS TO PARIS.

While General Roberdeau was thus prostrated and his
services unavailable to his country, his energy in her
defence prompted him to aid her in another way—by
opening his purse to the urgent needs of Congress.   In
the fall of 1776 Arthur Lee had been appointed Commissioner to Paris, to be joined there later in the year by the
two other Commissioners, Benjamin Franklin and Silas
Deane.   But Congress not having funds for their outfit,
General Roberdeau, with extreme liberality, advanced
from his private fortune the large sum of eighteen thous-
and dollars.   The tradition handed down in several
branches of the family so names the sum.

Of this transaction, the writer has as yet been able to
obtain from the several branches of the family, but little

definite information. **Mrs. Dr. Wheat** wrote from Chapel Hill, N. C., April 12, 1858: "It is well known to many that grandpa did advance eighteen thousand dollars for the Commissioners, Franklin, Lee, and Deane, and some of our cousins older than you and I have seen some papers to that effect, but none of them could I obtain"

Mrs. McCraw, in reply to the writer's inquiries upon this subject, writes as follows (December 14, 1873): "Some years ago I heard cousins Thomas R. Patten and his sister, Mrs. Miller, talking of some such business as that referred to by you, and they seemed quite sanguine on the subject; but whether they had any papers to confirm them in their expectations I cannot affirm, but think they must have heard of or seen something on the subject."

The veteran, General Swift, who has conversed with some of the worthies of the Revolution, and spoken with General Roberdeau when a boy, refers to this matter in a letter of February 15, 1860, quoted in a succeeding page.

But by far the most definite and valuable information comes to us from the Annan family, which says that the fact of this money being advanced by General Roberdeau, was a recorded fact in Washington. Many years ago, Mr. Thomas Mustin, a very old clerk in the Treasury Department, (appointed there by President Monroe, whose relative he was,) made an extract for Mrs. Annan from the books of that department, to this effect: "Paid for interest to Daniel Roberdeau on the amount advanced by him to Franklin, Lee, and Deane, Commissioners to Paris, ... £———." "It is almost certain," adds our informant, "that the *principal* of the sum advanced by my grandsire for the purpose before stated, *has never been paid* by the government. The fire in the Treasury Department, which consumed so many revolutionary papers, has in all probability destroyed every vestige of evidence in regard to the facts I have stated."

This matter seems to have been well known among the older members of the family, but almost lost sight of among the later generations. An incomplete search in the Treasury Department lately, failed to find any papers relating to this subject; the officials saying the fire in the building by the British in 1814, or the later one in 1833, had probably destroyed the papers searched for.

Parton remarks in his Life of Franklin, that during the month of preparation before leaving for France, "he collected all the money he could command at such short notice, between three and four thousand pounds, and lent it to Congress." Does it not seem probable that Franklin might have applied to his friend General Roberdeau at this time?

After the recall of Mr. Deane, John Adams was appointed in his place. His friends urged his acceptance of the mission, and in his "Works," published by his grandson, C. F. Adams, Esq., their letters are given, James Lovel, Elbridge Gerry, President Laurens, R. H. Lee, and also one from General Roberdeau.—(I., 276.)

IN CONGRESS.

Before General Roberdeau had sufficiently recovered his health to resume command in the army, he was destined to serve his country in a high sphere. The General Assembly of Pennsylvania conferred upon him the highest honor within their power to bestow: and elected him a member of the Continental Congress. To this august and dignified body, he was chosen on the fifth of February, 1777; the delegation consisting of the following gentlemen: Benjamin Franklin, Robert Morris, Daniel Roberdeau, Jonathan B. Smith, George Clymer, and James Wilson. Their credentials were presented, and they took their seats on the twelth of March following, in the old State-House, Philadelphia.

General Roberdeau immediately entered upon his duties, and was soon after placed upon the Standing Committee on the Commissary's Department, and the next year on the Board of Treasury, and also on the Marine Committee for the State of Pennsylvania. He was also appointed upon numerous other special committees; his knowledge of mercantile and monetary affairs being available upon the clothier general's department, on the pay-rolls, on purchases, etc.; while his familiarity with military affairs caused his appointment on preserving the health of the troops, on filling up the army, on a conference with General Gates on the general state of affairs, etc. Also one of those to whom all applications of French and other foreign officers were referred. His courteous and dignified manner made him prominent in

more than one occasion of state and ceremony; while
his graceful pen was engaged in writing proclamations
and addresses.

During his whole continuance in Congress, he was also
in frequent correspondence with President Wharton, and
Vice-President Bryan, of the Supreme Executive Council of Pennsylvania, in keeping them informed of the
state of affairs, and receiving important information.
And lastly, the most prominent act of his official life, his
part in connection with, and signing the *Articles of Confederation between the Colonies.*

A few days after General Roberdeau took his seat, he
was appointed on a committee to confer with Generals
Gates and Green, on the general state of affairs.

March 19th. He was appointed one of a Committee on
Foreign Affairs, to whom all applications from foreign
officers should be referred;—a delicate duty, as many
French officers wholly unqualified for command desired
commissions; many of whom being of noble families and
having much influence at court; the committee must
act with great tact, so as to avoid giving offence at the
French Court on the one hand, and for the welfare of
the army on the other. The applications of Lafayette,
De Kalb, and Pulaski were referred to this committee.

May 9th. General Roberdeau was granted leave of
absence for his health; which he had not recovered
when elected to Congress.

The fall of this year (1777) was a gloomy period for
the Colonies; General Howe having gained the battle of
Brandywine took possession of Philadelphia, and Congress after adjourning on the 18th of September hur-
riedly left for Lancaster, and thence after a few days, for
York. In the *Works of John Adams,* by his grandson,
C. F. Adams, we read (I., 267): "Arrived at York, Mr.
Adams found comfortable quarters in the house of General Roberdeau, one of the Pennsylvania delegates, 'an
Israelite indeed,' and he assured his wife that his spirit
was not worse for the loss of Philadelphia."

The loss of the capital, as Philadelphia was called, was
most disheartening, but the drooping spirits of the country revived, when a month later, General Burgoyne surrendered his whole army to General Gates at Saratoga.
The news arriving at York on the 31st of October; General Roberdeau on that day dispatched a long letter to

Vice-President Bryan of the Supreme Executive Council, with copies of the convention of surrender, list of prisoners, &c. This letter and many others are published in the *Pennsylvania Archives*, in twelve volumes, by Samuel Hazard.

A few days previously, General Roberdeau had also written to Vice-President Bryan relative to some dispatches lately received by Congress from General Gates. The letter concludes as follows: "The express gives a verbal account that two spies were discovered, by some Continental troops, round our General Clinton's quarters, habited like unto the British soldiers for the very purpose. . . . A singular anecdote I must not omit: One of the spies when discovered swallowed a silver ball which he was made to disgorge by the immediate application of an emetic; it contained intelligence from the British officer Clinton, who commanded up the neighborhood, to General Burgoyne. These anecdotes will not be published, nor are they to be depended upon; nevertheless, as I believe them, they are offered for your amusement."— (*Pennsylvania Archives* for 1776–7, p. 639.)

THE ARTICLES OF CONFEDERATION.

This matter had been under consideration in Congress for some months, and was debated clause by clause, but unfortunately the views of the framers of this important state paper can be but imperfectly known.

General Roberdeau was in favor of those clauses, that no State be represented by less than two or more than seven representatives; that no person serve as President of Congress more than three years; regarding the disputes between States, that Congress be the last resort, &c.; and in article 9, relative to yea and nay votes. The clause directing that the sum to be paid by each State into the national treasury should be ascertained by the value of *all* property within the State, when under debate was negatived. Bancroft, in his History, thus describes the subsequent action on this clause: This vote "was followed by a motion having for its object to exempt slaves from taxation altogether. On the following day (October 14) eleven States were represented. The four New England voted in the negative. Maryland, Virginia, and the two Carolinas in the affirmative. The decision remained with the central states. Robert Morris, of Pennsylvania, against Roberdeau, and Duer, of New York, against Duane, voted with the South, and so the votes of those States were divided and lost. The decision rested on New Jersey, and she gave it for the complete exemption from taxation of all property in slaves. This is the first important division between the slave-holding States and the States where slavery was of little account."

Finally, after months of debate, the last article was agreed to, on the 13th of November, and General Roberdeau, in his solicitation to send the earliest news, writes to Vice-President Bryan late that evening, as follows, urging him to speedily call together the Assembly for their ratification:

"We have the happiness to inform the State that the Confederation has this evening passed Congress. . . . . The several articles, though agreed to, are not arranged in the order they are to appear. . . . . . Therefore we ardently wish a full representation of the State may be convened to receive them, and that a determination upon them may be speedy, as the ratification, in our opinion, is of importance to the Independence of America."

The letter gives his own unqualified assent to the articles.

On Saturday, the 15th of November, 1777, as the Journals read, "a copy of the Confederation being made out, and sundry amendments made in the diction, without altering the sense, the same was agreed to." The Confederation was then submitted to the several States for their ratification, but it was not until the 9th of July following that a majority of States empowered their delegates to sign it, which was done on that day by the delegates of nine States; Daniel Roberdeau being among those from Pennsylvania, having the honor to affix their names. The other States acceded to it afterwards. The infant country now had a Constitution. This important paper is still preserved among the archives of the State Department, at Washington. It is in one sheet, about ten feet long.

At the close of November a great scarcity of provisions existed in the army, and General Roberdeau was appointed one of a committee to whom the matter was referred. The committee sent expresses to New York and

Connecticut, to the Supreme Council of Pennsylvania, and to the various departments of the army throughout the whole country. A committee of three, of whom General Roberdeau was chairman, was sent to the Assembly of Pennsylvania. To Vice-President Bryan, General Roberdeau writes: "The ruin of the army" is one of the alternatives. Space forbids giving here the details of the measures adopted. The necessity was extreme, and it was not until March that the deficiencies were supplied.

In December, General Roberdeau was again honored by the Assembly with reëlection to his seat in Congress, and on the 15th " Mr. Roberdeau, a delegate from Pennsylvania, laid before Congress credentials of the appointment of delegates from that State, which were read, as follows: . . ." The members certified therein are Benjamin Franklin, Robert Morris, Daniel Roberdeau, Jonathan Bayard Smith, James Smith, of Yorktown, William Clingan, and Joseph Reed, Esqs.

In the middle of January of the next year, 1778, four members were added to the Board of Treasury—Messrs. Clark, Roberdeau, Forbes, and Langworthy. The duties of this board were onerous in the extreme, hardly exceeded, if equaled, by those of the Board of War. Not a day passed but what some matter was referred to, or some report received from these two committees. The former had the oversight of all the finances of the Colonies. Every application from the various paymasters, quartermasters, commissaries, general officers, from the States;—applications innumerable, must be referred to them, the matter carefully considered, and a report made. In fact, the duties of this board were so arduous, together with those of the numerous other committees upon which General Roberdeau was appointed, that at his own request he was relieved by Congress on the 11th of March following.

In July, 1778, Philadelphia being evacuated by the enemy, Congress resumed its sessions there ; and soon after, the commissioners having concluded the treaty with France, a French fleet under Count D'Estaing entered Delaware Bay, bringing the Sieur Gerard, minister plenepotentiary, who was received at Chester by a committee of Congress—Messrs. Hancock, R. H. Lee, Drayton, · Roberdeau, and Duer, and escorted to his lodgings in Market street, amidst a salute of artillery and the joyful acclamations of the inhabitants. The minister was formally received by Congress in August, and the day closed with an entertainment given to him by Congress.

In November, Mr. Roberdeau was added to the Marine Committee for the State of Pennsylvania; this committee having the supervision of all naval affairs.

November 25, 1778, Mr. Roberdeau, Mr. Clingan, and Mr. Searle, three delegates from Pennsylvania, attended, and produced credentials of the delegates of that State, which were read.

The vote of the Assembly is given in the papers of the day, as follows:

ELECTED.		NOT ELECTED.	
Daniel Roberdeau	28	George Gray	20
William Clingan	28	John Wilson	24
John Armstrong	27	John Cadwallader	23
William Shippen, Sr	27	Samuel Miles	24
Edward Biddle	28	Samuel Morris, Jr	23
Samuel Atlee	27	Samuel Howell	24
James Searle	27	John Nixon	23

General Roberdeau's term now drew to a close, after having been three times honored with an election. On the third of March, Mr. Muhlenberg, a delegate from Pennsylvania, attended and produced credentials, by which it appears that Frederick Muhlenberg, Henry Wynkoop, and James McLene, Esqs., were on the 2nd of this month elected delegates in the room of Daniel Roberdeau, Edward Biddle, and William Clingan.

In the Journals of the Assembly of February 22, and of March 1st, it is stated that Daniel Roberdeau's term has expired, and that the two others resigned their seats in Congress. It seems to have been the custom not to elect members for a longer time than two successive years. It was generally so in most or all of the States, although there were exceptions. One notable one is mentioned in the Life of Thomas McKean, that he was the *only member* who served from the Stamp-Act Congress in 1765, to the peace in 1783. In accordance with this tacit rule, it is seen also that Benjamin Franklin and Robert Morris, both his seniors in Congress, were passed over in the preceding election, leaving General Roberdeau then at the head of the delegation. During his term, in addition to the various duties we have enumerated in the foregoing pages, the records of the Supreme Executive Council and

Journals of the General Assembly show that he paid several official visits to those bodies, and was also in communication with them by letter, particularly the latter. Besides these, the Journals of Congress mention many letters received from all parts of the country by him in his official capacity and laid before Congress. He also, with the other delegates, received large drafts of money from Congress to be transmitted to the Council. The Council at one time also request him to name some officers as suitable for commissions in a new regiment about to be formed—a tribute to his military capacity.

From the foregoing pages it may be well seen that General Roberdeau was a very prominent man in his day. He was a good writer, his style being clear and forcible. His great physical strength undoubtedly gave him unusual energy of mind and body. The frequency with which we find his name mentioned in the records of the Assembly, the Council of Safety, and the Journals of Congress, attest the earnestness with which he grasped his duties. And in whatever position we find him, he appears among the leaders. Step by step we have seen him rise until he reached the highest place in the gift of the people. The Continental Congress wielded powers rarely possessed, before or since, by one body. It was supreme, knowing no superior but its own will. In it were vested the executive, the legislative, and the judicial powers of the government. It is singular that a people fighting for liberty should have chosen a government so eminently autocratic. And in these days, when the powers are divided, we little realize the dignity or importance of a member of the Continental Congress.

It may well be noted here that in the whole of General Roberdeau's official life—in the State Assembly, in Congress, and in all the other positions to which he had been called—it is gratifying to be able to say that there has not appeared against him one word of censure or disapproval of the course he pursued. On the contrary, there is evidence of regard for him. Witness the care of the Supreme Council for him in his sickness in the army, and the confidence Congress placed in him in granting leave of absence to work that lead mine, and most notably his steady advance up to one of the most distinguished and honored places in the gift of his State. —(*Journals of Congress and of the Penn. Ho. Reps.; Colonial*

Records, Council of Safety and Sup. Ex. Council; Hazard's Penn. Archives, &c., &c., &c.)

LEAD MINE AND STOCKADE FORT.

Leave of absence was granted to General Roberdeau April 11, 1778, to allow him to superintend the working of a lead mine, from which to procure lead for the army. How it was that *he* became connected with it does not appear, unless it was his ceaseless and untiring exertions in the cause of liberty led him to those scenes where he could be of most service. So, leaving his duties in Congress and the comforts of his own fireside, he braved the hardships and dangers of the backwoods, where he had to erect a fort for protection against the Indians.

But little regarding this fort is now known. The traditions in the family relate simply the fact, so we must look elsewhere for an account of it, and the only record we find is in *Hazard's Pennsylvania Archives*, in twelve volumes of 800 pages each, published by the State, a work which contains, together with his *Colonial Records*, in sixteen volumes, all documents that could be collected relating to the revolutionary history of that State. In the former work are fifty or sixty letters of General Roberdeau's, some of which have been here quoted on previous pages. From these letters, also, Hazard has given a history of this fort, on page 454 of the Appendix.

FORT ROBERDEAU.

From a letter from General Roberdeau, dated Carlisle, April 17, 1778, it appears that he was then on his way to work some lead mines to supply the great scarcity of lead to the public. He was at that time a member of Congress, of whom he asks and afterwards obtains leave of absence for the purpose. He says:

"The confidence the honorable the representatives of our States have placed in me by a late resolve, together with the pressing and indispensable necessity of a speedy supply of lead for the public service, induced me to ask leave of absence of Congress to proceed with workmen to put their business in a proper train; and have reached this place on that errand and have collected men and materials and sent them forward this day, proposing to follow to-morrow. My views have been greatly enlarged since I left York, on the importance of the undertaking and hazard in procuring it, for the public works here are not furnished with an ounce of lead but what is in fixed ammunition. On the other hand, the prevailing opinion of people as I advance into the country, of Indian depredations shortly to commence, might not only deter the workmen I stand in need of, but affright the back settlers from their habitations, and leave the country exposed and naked. To give confidence to one and the other, I have drawn out of the public stores here twenty-five stand of arms and a quantity of gunpowder, and intend to proceed this morning, but was applied to by John Caruthers, Esq., lieutenant of the county, and William Brown, commissary of provisions for the militia, who advised with me on the subject of their respective departments; and by the account they give of the orders from your honorable Board to them as to calling out and supplying the militia, I find the State is guarding against the incursions of the savages. This confirmed me in a preconceived intention of erecting a stockade fort in the immediate neighborhood of the mine I am about to work, if I could stir up the inhabitants to give their labor in furnishing an asylum for their families in case of imminent danger, and prevent the evacuation of the country. Mr. Caruthers convinced me of the necessity of the work for the above purpose, condescendingly offered one company of the militia, which he expected would consist of about forty men, under my command to coöperate in so salutary a business, as it consists with the order of the Council respecting the station, being only a deviation of a very few miles; and that one other company of about the same number should also join me, for the greater expedition, until the pleasure of the Council was known. . . . . Mr. Brown expressed much concern for the scarcity of provisions. I was advised very lately by Judge McKean of a quantity of salted beef in the neighborhood of Harris' Ferry, and before I left York I applied to him by letter to advise me of the quantity and quality, with a design to purchase, as I intended to employ a much greater number of men than are already employed at the lead mines, to carry on the business with vigor. . . . .

"I intend to build such a fort, as with sufficient provisions, under the smile of Providence would enable me to defend it against any number of Indians that might presume to invest it. If I am not prevented by an opportunity of serving the state eminently, by a longer stay in the wilderness, I propose to return to my duties in Congress in about three weeks. Will the Council favor me with the exemption of a number of men, not exceeding twenty if I cannot be supplied by the adjutant-general, who has orders co-extensive with my want of smelters and miners from deserters from the British army, to suffer such to come to this part of the country, contrary to a preceding order? . . . Besides the supplying of provisions to the militia in Bedford, it is very important that the intended stockade should be seasonably furnished with that article. . . . .

"My landing is at Water street in Juniata, but I could, on notice, receive any supplies from Standing Stone.

"I am most respectfully, Sir,
your most ob. and very hum. servt.,

(Signed) "DANIEL ROBERDEAU."

On the 23d of April, he writes from Standing Stone to John Caruthers. . . . . An attack is threatened by thirty Indians who expect re-inforcements of 300 more; other reports not so reliable say 1000 whites and savages. Desires him, therefore, to call out the militia if he has authority to do so. General Roberdeau has only ten Continental soldiers with him.

On the 27th of April, General Roberdeau writes from Sinking Spring Valley to President Wharton, "I am happy to inform you that a very late discovery from a new vein promises the most ample supply, but I am very deficient in workmen. Mr. Glenn is with me to direct the making and burning of bricks, and is come up to build a furnace; by which time I expect to be in such forwardness as to afford an ample supply to the army. Of 40 militia-men, I have at most 7 with me, which retards building a stockade to give confidence to the inhabitants who were all on the wing before I reached this."

But little is known to us about this fort or where it was erected. In a letter from General Potter, dated Penn's Valley, May 19, 1779, three forts are spoken of in this valley, as having together but one lieutenant and fifteen men as a guard. He says: "I cannot help being surprised that there has been no militia sent to this part of Bedford county that joins us, neither to Frankston nor Standing Stone, except a small company of Buchanan's battalion that would not go to Fort Roberdeau."

August 6, 1779, Capt. Cluggage dates a letter from Fort Roberdeau, and says: "This morning I arrived at this point, bringing with me what men I could collect on the way. I think from the accounts of my brother, that the number of the enemy in these parts must be very large," and adds another postscript: "This moment there is twelve men arrived, and with what can be spared from this garrison, I will march immediately to Morrison's Cave."

In another letter, dated at this fort, October 10, 1779, Capt. Cluggage says: "My company has been received, and passed muster, three officers, and forty-three rank and file, one of the latter killed or taken."

We presume, therefore, that this was Fort Roberdeau built on account of the lead mines, and named after him, in Sinking Spring Valley. In an article in the Columbian* Magazine for

---

* See an extract from this Magazine in *Hazard's Register of Pennsylvania*, VIII., 36. Description of Bald Eagle Valley, or Sinking Spring Valley, so called, from "the swallows, which absorb some of the largest streams of the

1778, allusion is made to the attempt to procure lead from the mine in this valley during the Revolution, and says "a large fort of logs was erected and some miners employed, also a considerable quantity of ore procured and some lead made."

Thus does Mr. Hazard record this interesting subject. The tradition in our family states that the expense of erecting this fort was met wholly by General Roberdeau, which is abundantly verified by his letters as published by Hazard, and other evidence.

June 6, 1778, he writes from York, where Congress was in session, to Vice-President Bryan:

. . . . "My account exhibited to the Assembly, when last in Lancaster, refers to a debit, of which I was not then possessed, paid Capt. Piper, who guarded Wm. Todd to Lancaster, for his expenses, which is now before me in a proper entry of £6.11.3.," and hopes the Council will include it in the above account and remit the whole, adding, "my late engagement in the lead works has proved a moth to my circulating cash, and obliged me to make free with a friend in borrowing."

On the 30th of March, 1778, General Roberdeau, with others, petitioned the General Assembly, and reciting that upon the recommendation of Congress, having opened a lead mine, they desire the lands whereon the mine lies, be vested in the petitioners; and the next day the Assembly resolved as follows:

"On considering the petition of the Honorable Daniel Roberdeau and company, for vesting the lands therein mentioned, whereon there is a lead mine, in Frankstoun township, in Bedford county, in the said Daniel Roberdeau and company, to which they lay claim; Resolved, That this house will not determine in whom the title of said lands is; but being of opinion that the utmost encouragement should be given to opening said mine and smelting the ore therein for public benefit, will indemnify the said Daniel Roberdeau and company from any loss they have already sustained or may sustain in opening the said mine and smelting the ore, if they shall immediately proceed upon said work, and diligently and faithfully prosecute the same."

The following appears upon the journals of Congress after General Roberdeau's return from the mine, but I

---

valley, and after carrying them for several miles under ground in a subterranean course, return them upon the surface." An account of the fort, and of these streams, is here given.

can find no report of the Board of War on the subject, or any further mention in Congress:

"June 23, 1778. Ordered: That the Board of War estimate the expense of the fort lately built by Mr. Roberdeau, in Bedford county, in Pennsylvania, and report the same to Congress, with their opinion by whom the same ought to be defrayed."

It does not appear that any remuneration was made to General Roberdeau for his expenses in working this mine and erecting the fort, although it is seen to have been done by the orders of, or at least with the consent of, Congress and the Assembly, both of whom it seems felt themselves in a measure responsible. On the 1st of April, 1779, the Assembly reiterated its resolve of March 31, that General Roberdeau be indemnified; and the matter remained before the house as late as 1781, without settlement, although the journals show that it was repeatedly brought up for consideration.

SECOND MARRIAGE.

But a very few days after General Roberdeau's last election to Congress, he contracted a second marriage with Miss Jane Milligan, of Philadelphia. A notice of the event appearing in the *Pennsylvania Packet*, of December 3d, 1778, as follows:

"Last night, was married, General Roberdeau to Miss Milligan, an agreeable young lady, who has every qualification to felicitate the nuptial state."

From the similarity of the name which she gave her son, born some years after, it is presumed that she was a daughter, or at least a near relative, of James Milligan, of Philadelphia.

This gentleman is frequently mentioned in public affairs of this time, in connection with the finances. He was, in March, 1776, one of the numerous Signers of Bills of Credit; July, 1776, one of three Commissioners to Settle the Accounts of the Northern Department; in March, 1778, spoken of as Commissioner of Claims at the Treasury; Nov., 1778, one of six Commissioners of the Chamber of Accounts; Nov., 1779, Auditor-General to the Treasury; Oct., 1781, Comptroller of the Treasury.

THE MEETING OF MAY 24-25, 1779.

No sooner had General Roberdeau retired to private life, than he was again called before the public, to preside at a meeting of the citizens to devise measures to reduce prices and counteract the operations of monopolizers. The account here given is from the *Pennsylvania Packet*, of May 27, 1779.

At a general meeting of the citizens of Philadelphia and parts adjacent, at the State-House yard in this city, General Daniel Roberdeau was unanimously requested to take the chair, who introduced the business with the following—

ADDRESS.

"*Gentlemen:* Although I feel pain from the situation in which you have been pleased to place me, it is with pleasure I meet you, my fellow-citizens, to consider and determine upon measures for our mutual and public happiness. A beneficent God has hitherto blessed us with success, and carried us through a four years' war, with as few misfortunes as could possibly be expected. We have much to be thankful for; and though many worthy individuals have greatly suffered, yet as a nation, we have but little to complain of.

"The dangers we are now exposed to, arise from evils created among ourselves. I scorn, and I hope every citizens here scorns, the thought of getting rich by sucking the blood of his country; yet, alas! this unnatural, this cruel, this destructive practice, is the greatest cause of our present calamities. The way to make our money good, is to reduce the prices of goods and provisions. It is not the quantity of money which any man gets, but how far that money will go when he comes to lay it out again, that makes him poor or rich.

"The tax that has been laid upon us by monopolizers and forestallers within these six months past—for it may justly be called a tax—amounts to more money than would carry the war on twelve months to come.

"There is at present no law for regulating the prices in the shops and markets, neither is there any law to prevent the regulations being made; and, therefore, the whole rests upon the virtue and common sense of the community. I have no doubt but combinations have been formed for raising the prices of goods and provisions; and therefore, the community in their own defence, have a natural right to counteract such combinations, and to set limits to evils which affect themselves.

"It is impossible, gentlemen, to cure the disease all at once, but it must be begun upon; and as this city appears to be the place in which the disease was first bred, this likewise is the place where the remedy ought to be first applied. Do you, gentlemen, set the example, and I think there is little doubt but others will follow it.

"Within these five or six months, goods and provisions have risen week by week; surely, gentlemen, we can do as much as the monopolizers have done, and bring the prices down again week by week. By this means there will be money to spare to pay taxes with; for at the rate things now are, it takes all the country people's money to go to the shops with, and all the town people's money to go to market with; and the whole community is growing poor under a notion of getting rich.

"Some worthy citizens, who have the success of our glorious cause at heart, have undertaken to form a plan for regularly reducing the prices of goods and provisions, and keeping up the value of money; and this plan, as I understand, is to be laid before you at some future meeting. For my own part, gentlemen, I shall joyfully assist in any judicious measure for the public happiness, and have no doubt but you will do the same.

"It is a surprising thing that the more goods we have had brought into the city, the dearer they have been; and this is one of the evils which it is absolutely necessary to enquire into. But the great point is to begin.

"The paper I hold in my hand contains some resolutions which have been drawn up and agreed to by a committee of citizens, which, with your approbation, I will read. I propose first to read the whole through, and then read it a second time by paragraphs, in order to take your sense thereon.

"The paper being read, after some amendments, was agreed to."

It is substantially as follows: After the preamble that prices have risen as stated in the speech:—Resolved, That a cargo having been imported for Mr. Robert Morris, a committee be appointed to inquire of him and others what part they have acted respecting this cargo; that another committee enquire the prices of provisions since the first of January, and prepare a plan for regularly proceeding in the business of reducing the prices; that they also enquire of those holding public money, in what manner the trust imposed upon them has been executed. The tenth and last resolution was in the following words:

"*Resolved*, That it is the opinion of this meeting that no person who by sufficient testimony can be proved inimical to the interest and independence of the United States, be suffered to remain among us; and that the committees be directed to take measures for carrying this resolution into execution."

On the first committee were Timothy Mallack, (secretary of the Supreme Executive Council,) David Rittenhouse, (so celebrated for his scientific knowledge,) Thomas Paine, Charles W. Peale, (the eminent artist,) and two others. The second committee included the first, and the following in addition: Col. Henry, Paul Cox, Cadwallader Dickinson, and twenty-four others.

At the conclusion,—"The thanks of the meeting were unanimously returned to the chairman for his noble and disinterested manner of conducting the business."

This meeting is spoken of in the life of President Joseph Reed, who, it will be remembered, was an intimate friend of General Roberdeau. His life is written by his grandson, the Hon. William B. Reed, who says: "A large meeting was held in the State-House yard, at which Daniel Roberdeau presided. His speech on taking the chair was highly inflammatory," &c. And adds, in relation to the second committee then appointed, which was permanent, "The institution of this committee is a leading incident in the local history of these times. Its members were numerous, and its sessions nearly permanent. The control it exercised seems to have been absolute and severe." Other towns and even distant States organized similar committees.

An anonymous writer in the *Penn. Packet* of June 5, 1779, gives a very droll picture of the state of affairs at that time; he says, "I had money enough some time ago to buy a hogshead of sugar; I sold it again and got a great deal more money than it cost me; yet what I sold it for, when I went to market it again, would buy but a tierce. I sold that, too, for a great deal of profit, yet the whole of what I sold it for would afterwards buy but a barrel. I have now more money than I ever had, and yet I am not so rich as when I had less. I am sure we shall get poorer and poorer, unless we fall on some method to lower prices, and then the money we have to show will be worth something. I am glad the good work is begun."

Let us now turn to another account of this meeting. We have read what its friends say, it is but fair to listen to its enemies. The following is by one *Stansberry*, a tory, and may be found in full in *Watson's Annals of Philadelphia.*

AN HISTORICAL BALLAD OF THE PROCEEDINGS OF A TOWN MEETING AT PHILA-
DELPHIA, MAY 24–25, 1779.—BY STANSBERRY.

'Twas on the twenty-fourth of May,
A pleasant, warm, sunshiny day,
   Militia folks paraded,
With colors spread, and cannon too,—
Such loud huzzas, and martial view,
   I thought the town invaded.

And now the State-House yard was full,
And orators, so grave and dull,
   Appear'd upon the stage.
But all was riot, noise, disgrace,
And Freedom's sons, o'er all the place,
   In bloody frays engage.

Each vagrant from the whipping-post,
Or stranger stranded on the coast,
   May here reform the State,
And Peter, Mick, and Shad-row Jack,
And Pompey-like McKean in black,
   Decide a people's fate.

. . . .

With solemn phiz and action slow,
Arose the chairman, *Roberdeau*,
   And made the humane motion,
That tories, with their brats and wives,
Should flee, to save their wretched lives,
   From Sodom to Goshen.

He central stood, and all the ground
With people covered, him surround—
   And so it came to pass
That as he spoke with zest upon it,
He turn'd his face to those in front,
   To those behind, his *back*.

This grave offence—his voice was drown'd—
He should have turn'd himself all round
   Like whirligig in socket;
Or, if this did his art surpass,
At least he should have took his end
   And put it in his pocket.

. . . .

The "ballad" is quite long, ridiculing most of the prominent characters of the day. To the chairman he devotes three whole stanzas, but most of the others mentioned are alloted a line or less.

Another tory has exercised his genius in a similar manner. The following is from a recent work by Winthrop Sargent, of Philadelphia, entitled "*Loyalist Poetry of the Revolution:*"

EXTRACTS FROM THE AMERICAN TIMES.—A SATIRE.

Room for a spectre of portentous show !
Make room for triple-headed Roberdeau !
Churchman, dissenter, Methodist appear,
Chairman, and congressman, and brigadier.
Cerberean barker at the Stygian ford,
Where is thy Bible, say, and where thy sword?
Thy Bible—that long since was wisely lost
Because its maxims with thy practice crossed ;
Well, but thy weapon, was it lost in fight?
Hush ! I remem.—'twas to aid thy flight.
Of brass, lead, leather, treble is thy shield,
And treble tremblings seize thee in the field ;
Treble in office and in faith thou art,
And nothing double in thee but thy heart.

Speaking of the citizens arming against taxation, he continues :

Servants were seized, apprentices enroll'd.
Youth guarded not the boy, nor age the old ;
Tag-rag and bob-tail issued on the foe,
Marshal'd by Generals Ewing, Roberdeau.

Still another poem in the same work, taken from *Rivington's Royal Gazette*, of September 18, 1779, is particularly directed against the members of Congress, a portion of which runs as follows :

THE WORD OF CONGRESS.

Come, Mifflin, let me put thee on the stage :
As thou with Britain, war with thee I wage.
Fierce Mifflin foremost in the ranks was found.
Ask you the cause?   He owed ten thousand pound.
Great thanks to Congress and his doughty word,
· He cancell'd debts by flourishing his sword !
Not that he cares for Congress or its voice ;
Broils are his int'rest, tumult is his choice.
But that he wants the necessary skill
A pliant people to inflame at will.
But that his genius yields to Roberdeau
In every act of managing the low.

Whatever else these pieces may show, they at least indicate those whom the tories desired to revile as being the most energetic in the cause of independence. The latter, indeed, ascribes to General Roberdeau great powers with respect to such a man as Governor Mifflin, who was at that time President of Congress.

IN PRIVATE LIFE—IN LONDON—ADVENTURE WITH A
HIGHWAYMAN.

General Roberdeau now retired to the quiet scenes of private life, living in Philadelphia with his family, where he remained during the remainder of the war. Soon after peace was declared, in 1783, he embarked with his son Isaac to visit his relations in London, as appears by a letter of his son, on a previous page. Here they resided with his cousin, Mr. Charles Pearce-Hall, at No. 44 Leadenhall street, and occasionally with Mr. Pogson, in Surrey. General Roberdeau returned about the close of the year, but his son remained three or four years to prosecute his studies.

During this or one of his other visits to London a remarkable incident occurred to General Roberdeau. To the south and southwest of London, Black Heath and Hounslow Heath, now the locality of some of the most sumptuous seats in the vicinity of the metropolis, were then, and had been for years, infested by highwaymen; not singly, but in powerful bands, the terror of all designing to pass that way. Here Wat Tyler's rebellion broke out in 1381; and the next century witnessed the exploits of the famous Jack Cade, in 1450.

Through this vicinity, General Roberdeau having occasion to pass, was attacked by the whole band, who surrounded the carriage, and the leader, opening the door, demanded his watch and money. Quick as thought the general seized the man by the shoulders, threw him down on the floor of the carriage, placed his foot upon him and a pistol to his breast, "If you move an inch I will shoot you," then called to the coachman to whip up and fire right and left. The horses sprung from those holding them, and the band, seeing their leader captive, stood amazed; and General Roberdeau drove into London with the robber's feet hanging out of the carriage. He delivered up his prisoner to the authorities, by whom he was tried and hung for his crimes. General Roberdeau received the reward offered for his capture. This was the last of those successive bands of robbers that for centuries had infested that locality.

The writer in relating this adventure to a Prussian gentleman, some few years ago, was surprised by being informed by him, that he had heard it before, and upon inquiry, was told by this gentleman; that he had been on the spot, and that it was the habit of the villagers "to relate to travelers the story of the American officer who captured the highwayman on that site."

The silver-hilted small-sword, and pistols inlaid with silver which General Roberdeau carried on this occasion, he left to his son Isaac, by whom they were bequeathed to the writer. Col. Roberdeau's will says of them: "They have been the means, under Divine Providence, of securing the safety both of my father and me. The pistols were purchased from on board an American Privateer, early in the war of the Revolution, by whom they had been captured by [from?] the British, and were the companions of my father during the whole of that contest."

The occasion on which these pistols secured Colonel Isaac Roberdeau's safety, is presumed to have been that mentioned on a previous page ; when he says he was instrumental in preserving a large sum of money from highway robbery at night, when riding with Mr. Pogson in Surrey on their way to Mitcham ; which lies beyond Black Heath, through which they must consequently pass.

The sword is that kind known as a small-sword, "then the constant companion of every one who assumed the rank of gentleman," to use Sir Walter Scott's words. This sword was worn by General Roberdeau ever after as his dress sword ; and his son Isaac afterwards had the silver hilt gilded to be worn with his uniform in the army.

The pistols are large, double-barreled, fired by the ancient flint and pan ; the handles are of ebony, richly mounted and inlaid with silver; the other portions are carved to match. They are large, compared with those used at the present day, and heavy, carrying a ball of $\frac{9}{16}$ of an inch in diameter.

REMOVAL TO ALEXANDRIA, VA.—THE CINCINNATI.— ANECDOTES.

After General Roberdeau's return to Philadelphia, he removed his family to Alexandria, Virginia, sometime between March, 1784, and April, 1785, probably early in this latter year. For this step, he doubtless had good reasons ; which being unknown to us, it seems a great mistake of his, in leaving a community where he had so long resided, and with whom he had been so closely identified. He gave up all his associates for a comparatively small town. His removal could not have been for commercial reasons, for it is believed that he did not again engage in business after the Revolution.

Here General Roberdeau had purchased a house in 1776, which he now made his permanent residence. It is still standing, situated on the east side of Water, now Lee street, between Wolfe and Wilkes streets. It is of brick, twenty-eight by forty-two feet, three stories and an attic in height. The rear looks out on the Potomac; and the ground sloping down to the water, was prettily terraced for a garden. General Roberdeau also owned much other land in the vicinity and adjoining. The front door was guarded by an enormous lock, not set into the wood, but screwed on the surface. Our relative, Mrs. Dr. Wheat, writes: "The great key in the front door lock is still in use. I was told, in my childhood, this lock was brought from Rochelle, France; its huge proportions look formidable in these modern times." This old lock is then at least 188 years old!

Within a few months this house has been purchased and modernized. A modern lock replaces the former one, which the present owner kindly gave to the writer. One other memento must not be forgotten. In the upper hall, are some hooks that General Roberdeau had fixed in the ceiling, from which to suspend a swing, for his children's amusement. They are still there.

In this house, General Roberdeau's two younger children were born. In these parlors, his elder daughters were married. Here, also, he entertained the PATER PATRLE. The friendship formed with his distinguished leader, begun in the army, or prehaps earlier, remained unbroken until his death. We can recall the account of his being sent to him by General Mercer, and doubtless there were many other occasions when they met that history does not record.

The following letter is of interest, not only for its contents, but for the writer, so long and familiarly known—the Hon. George Washington Parke Custis, of Arlington. It is in possession of our relative, to whom it is addressed:

ARLINGTON HOUSE, *9th May*, 1849.

DEAR SIR: I have received your letter. I have a perfect recollection of General Roberdeau, and of his welcome to Mt. Vernon by Washington. Roberdeau was a patriot of '76, and a member of the old Congress of the Confederation.

I have no further knowledge of General Roberdeau that can in any wise be interesting or useful to you.

And remain with respect,

Your ob. servt.,

GEORGE W. P. CUSTIS.

To J. R. ANNAN, ESQ., Cumberland, Md.

General Roberdeau's daughter Selina had her wrist broken by the upsetting of the carriage while riding with Mrs. Washington, and being badly set, it never healed perfectly straight.

In connection with this topic, is another letter, published some time ago, and but for its length, would be inserted here. At that time a controversy was being carried on in the newspapers relative to the question whether General Washington used profane language at the battle of Monmouth, as had been alleged. Finally the veteran, General Joseph G. Swift, wrote to Daniel Huntington, Esq., of New York, dated Geneva, May 16, 1855, taking the negative; and in giving his reasons therefor, stated his father's, and his own acquaintance with the revolutionary worthies—Generals Lincoln, Schuyler, Pinckney, Alexander Hamilton, Gilbert Stuart, and others; and in this letter occurs the following passage: "My father was introduced to Washington by General Lincoln in 1784, at Mt. Vernon, and saw General Washington at General Roberdeau's and at Mr. Hooe's, in Alexandria. His remark on Washington's manner and conversation was, that they were far from familiar, though polite, and that there was a grandeur in his aspect." This letter was published in the New York Courier, and copied into most of the other papers of the country.

Another letter from the same distinguished officer, full of interest, is as follows:

GENEVA, 15 *Feby.*, 1860.

DEAR MRS. BUCHANAN: Sally's and my love to you and Susan, and your children, and our respects to Mr. Buchanan.

I wish you to write to me as soon as you get this, all you remember, and tell me all you know about your father. It is my purpose to make a Record, about one honest man at least. Your father told me that his father was a grandson of the Cunyngham family;—that he held large possessions in St. Cristopher's, W. I.,—that he came to Philadelphia in the early days of Whitefield, who lived in his family,—that his first wife was

Mary or Ann Boucher [Bostwick], I forget which, your grand-mother; when he became Brig. Gen. in the army of the U. S., 1776. He was also of the State Assembly, and in 1778 a member of the Congress that formed the Confederacy. Your father and my father were fast friends, calling each other Isaac and Foster, and your grandfather was also a friend of my father; the latter once saw the general's antipathy to a cat; and the general told him the way he captured a highwayman in England, when the general went there to receive some bequest. But hope is it about the $18,000, Dr. Franklin's outfit to France, Charles Abert wants to know about it.—[Original scarcely legible.]—This procrastination that is losing you.—What! nothing but dust? but useful dust, in this dirty state of existence.

Was your mother the granddaughter of Doctor or Judge Shippen? and was Dr. Samuel Blair related to Hugh and Robert of Edinburg?

The first public service of your father was at the instance of General Washington, in the survey and laying out of the city of Washington under Andrew Ellicot in 1798 [1792].—In 1809 I met your father at Germantown, took him to Washington, on engineering duty, accompanied by dear Mary, going a girl to see her aunts and Mrs. Deneal in Alexandria. Your father was kept occasionally, as I had employment to offer him in the Engineer Department, until 1814, when he entered the Topographical Corps, and at my instance went to West Point to instruct in topography, and then to Brooklyn in the United States Engineer Department there, and then to assist on the United States and Great Britain boundary line. In 1817 he went with with me to Georgetown, and lived opposite my residence there until my resignation; and he continued on that duty until his death, on my return from the west in 1828. . . . .

When you have complied with my request, please return therewith *this letter, as I have no transcript of it, and it may be useful to me.*

Your respec. friend,
J. G. SWIFT.

At the close of the war, was formed the well-known Society of the Cincinnati, of which it is believed General Roberdeau was one of the original members. Foote, in his *Sketches in Virginia*, plainly infers as much; and Mrs. Dr. Wheat is under the impression that she has seen General Roberdeau's diploma. His name does not appear among the original members of the Pennsylvania society, and as he resided in Virginia at the time of its formation, it seems probable he was a member in that State. But this latter society was dissolved many years ago, and their funds left to the Washington University at Lexington, but their records cannot now be found. The Hon. Hamilton Fish, President-General of the Society, in answer to the writer's inquiries, in a very courteous note replied that he had "examined the rolls of all the existing State Societies of the Cincinnati, as also those of the extinct societies which he has been able to find, but without finding the name of Daniel Roberdeau." But adds that some of the rolls are very imperfect, and that of Virginia almost absolutely wanting.

GENERAL ROBERDEAU'S ANTIPATHY TO A CAT.

This fact, alluded to in the above letter, was most remarkable. The general had an unaccountable aversion to being anywhere in the vicinity of a *cat*. It was no affectation but an inborn idiosyncrasy. He could not account for it, and tried hard to overcome it, but without the least success. It affected him with a peculiar faintness and difficulty of breathing, increasing to such an extent that it was *involuntary* for him to leave the room. He was *never* mistaken when he said there was a cat in the room, an instance of which occurred once when invited to dine at Chief Justice McKean's. Knowing his antipathy they made careful search and aired the rooms, but the moment General Roberdeau entered he said "There is a cat here." They assured him there was not, for they had taken proper precautions on his account. He replied he *knew* there was a cat there, and retired to another room, while a further search revealed a kitten crowded behind the bookcase! The writer's father has often heard his mother and aunts tell of their girlish tricks played on General Roberdeau, of secreting a cat in the room in which he was sitting, and the general never failed to perceive it instantly. One day in coming down stairs he encountered a cat in his way, and not liking to turn back, drew his sword and stood until the cat made way for him to pass.

This peculiarity does not seem to be inherited among the general's descendants, except in three or four cases it has appeared in a modified form. Mrs. Jane Annan seemed in a limited degree to partake of her father's antipathy, as, also, her daughter, Mrs. McCraw, who, although not affected to the same extent as her grandfather, has a great aversion to them, without being able well to describe her feelings.

Another of the general's children, James, was affected, somewhat like his father, but not so severely; he would appear about to have a spasm if he remained in the presence of a cat; and his friends were obliged to keep them from the room he was in. None of his children inherited this; but it has appeared among his grandchildren of the Powell family, who are "afraid of them."

Miss Mary E. Roberdeau, the eldest daughter of Isaac, partially inherited this antipathy, which here showed itself in another form, occasioning an eruption on the skin, passing off soon after the cause was removed.

Very similarly affected was the writer's sister. Although excessively fond of pets, and cats in particular, it has been noticed that after fondling one, a most terrific cold in the head would suddenly ensue. She would sneeze time after time, her eyes water profusely, and her face become flushed. The violence would subside after putting the cat away, leaving no trace visible the next morning. It has always been considered a modified form of her great-grandfather's antipathy.

It may be worthy of note, thus to record how far, and to what degree, such an antipathy may be hereditary.

The history of this antipathy was once related by a stranger to one of the family without knowing him to be such. Our relative thus relates the occurrence: "About a year ago I made a visit to a friend's house, five miles in the country. The children had some beautiful kittens; I begged one of them for a little girl of my acquaintance; the kitten was put in a small basket, a cloth tied over the top, my host and myself took our seats in the omnibus which was to take us to the city. The kitten commenced crying, and an old man I never saw before, but who was an acquaintance of my friend, commenced talking about cats, and said 'he knew of a person who could not stay in a room with a cat—he lived in Philadelphia, and his name was Roberdeau.' My friend, who knows all about my family, said to the old man, 'the person you are speaking about was the grandfather to this gentleman,' meaning me. The old man did not look to be more than seventy, and I thought could know nothing of Daniel Roberdeau personally, and I had the curiosity to ask him how he got the story. He said when he was a boy he lived in a commercial house in Baltimore, who were correspondents of Daniel Roberdeau, and the peculiarities of Daniel Roberdeau and his family were often the subject of talk in his employer's house. Subsequently, I got my friend to see the old man, Mr. Owings, and ask him if he knew anything else about Daniel Roberdeau. Mr. Owings was full of the subject, and like an old man, fond of gabbling when he can find a listener. Amongst other things, he said Mrs. Daniel Roberdeau was very luxurious in her habits, and required *two* maids to turn her into bed." This was Mrs. Mary Roberdeau to whom he referred.

We cannot pass by the letters of General Swift without a few words of their writer. He was the son of Dr. Foster Swift, and the first graduate of the Military Academy at West Point, in 1802. In 1812 he became chief engineer of the army; and resigned in 1818. The writer remembers with pleasure once having seen General Swift when he called upon the writer's mother, and dined with the family. He also heard him relate the cause of his resignation, but was too young to pay much attention to it. During this visit an incident occurred not to be forgotten by those present. This old gentleman, at the age of 74, asked his daughter to accompany him while he sang My Orra Moor,* "I wish to sing that song here once again in memory of old times, and in front of that picture," said he, pointing to a portrait of Colonel Roberdeau hanging over the piano. While singing, his eyes rested on the likeness of his old and valued friend, and the tears rolled down his cheeks. There was hardly a dry eye in the room.

General Swift, after his resignation, was employed several times in important situations by the government as a civil engineer, in which he had a high reputation. He was a member of several literary societies, and died in 1865, at the age of eighty-two. Besides his friendship with five generations of our family, he was also connected by marriage. His uncle, Jonathan Swift, married General Roberdeau's daughter Ann.

General Roberdeau was of commanding and dignified presence, which he even carried into his own family. With his children, although "a tender and affectionate father," to use the words of one of his sons-in-law, he was

---

*The words are from Addison's Spectator, No. 366.

very strict. His son Isaac once asked for the pope's eye at dinner, a part usually preferred by epicures, when his father made him leave the table, saying that part was for his elders. At another time Isaac contradicted his father! They were walking in the fields, when the general said, "My son, the cows seem to enjoy eating grass so much I should think it would be good for the table, dressed as greens," to which Isaac replied: "Why, father, I do not think we could eat it." But the general not liking this reply, being against his principles of education, said: "Isaac, you should not contradict your father in that way, I will have some for dinner and try it." So he cut some of the choicest grass in the pasture and brought it home. When dinner was served that day, he helped Isaac to the grass; but before he had served all at the table or touched his own plate, Isaac asked, "some more grass, if you please, father." "There! my son, what did I tell you?" Presently the general, anxious to pass judgment upon his new dish, took a good-sized mouthful, but such an insipid mass of strings and fibres he never before put in his mouth. He nearly strangled in swallowing it. "You rascal! why did you not tell me," cried he. How Isaac swallowed a whole plate full he says he never knew.

Isaac at another time also unintentionally got the better of him. He was trying to learn the clarionet, when his father entered the house, and asked, "what is that tooting? If you want to blow that thing you had better go into the stable." Thither Isaac went, but at the first blast all the horses all broke loose and ran. He never afterwards told the story without laughing at his father's disconcerted looks when he saw the horses galloping off.

This reference to the dinner-table recalls to mind an old cellaret that General Roberdeau used. It is a brass-bound tub on a pedestal, with a top and brass handles. There were formerly a punch-bowl and a pair of decanters belonging to it. It is now in possession of Mrs. F. E. Shober.

SEVERE ILLNESS.—REMOVAL TO WINCHESTER.—HIS DEATH.

In the spring of 1794, General Roberdeau was prostrated by a severe fit of sickness. From the few facts that can be gathered from old letters, it seems that his sickness was a disease of the nervous system resulting

7

from some mental shock, such as the trying scenes of the Revolution. The effects may not be visible for many years, and then become apparent. Even at this late day, many have recently died from the same cause, incident to the late unhappy contest. In a letter to his daughter, Ann Swift, of March 4, 1794, he writes upon relegion, then a few words of English politics, and concludes: "I have experienced great debility for a long time past, but blessed be the Source of all my mercies, it had a check yesterday, and this day His providence will do for me all that His goodness shall graciously dictate, and that will suffice. I think to pay Isaac a visit, who solicits it; besides, it may be of use to restore my strength. I expect you here this spring, and possibly shall not be disappointed. I am, my dear Selina's affect. father, DANIEL ROBERDEAU."

During a relapse, General Roberdeau made his will, dated April 29, 1794, but being too weak to sign it, made his mark. A few days after, however, May 1st, he added a codicil, signing it with his own hand, and on the 5th of July, adds another codicil, in which he states that he is perfectly recovered from his recent sickness. The apparent recovery being common in this disease. He was well enough to go down stairs, and undoubtedly also to walk out of doors. At this time he sold his house in Alexandria; disposed of part of his furniture, and advertised the remainder at auction; saying, he proposed moving to New York. His sons-in-law, Thomas Patten and Jonathan Swift, offered a higher price for the house, to keep it in the family, but the deeds had already been signed.

Under date of May 28, 1794, Mr. Thomas Patten, who then lived in Alexandria, writes to his brother-in-law, Isaac Roberdeau, at Lebanon, Penn., there engaged as engineer of canals, etc., as follows:

" Yours of the 5th inst. came duly to hand. It's happy, perhaps, that you have full employment just now, to prevent those unpleasant sensations that no doubt would be the result of reflection; when declining nature is obvious, and exhibits proofs of the amazing constitution that your father has been blessed with, as that alone, I am convinced, has continued him till now. So far from being able to ride to Lebanon, he has not been able to leave his bed for four or five weeks; and should you not be able to leave your employment, perhaps you may never have it in your power to take a last farewell of a tender and affectionate father; a task, however painful, yet is dictated by filial affection."

After this, General Roberdeau removed his family to Winchester; it consisted of his wife and the three younger children; the elder children being married, and living elsewhere. Here he lived but a short time, when he had another attack of sickness, which terminated fatally on the fifth of January, 1795; being then in his sixty-eighth year. Thus passed away, one who had endeared himself to all who knew him; a truly good and devout Christian; conscientious in the faithful performance of whatever duties he had in hand; kind and affectionate to his family, and whose memory is justly revered by his descendants.

His son-in-law, Thomas Patten, thus announces his death, dated Alexandria, January 9, 1795:

"DEAR ISAAC: The fatal die is cast! and our father is no more. Can it be? Yes, that best of fathers, that best of husbands, and that best of men, has paid that debt which no man can be surety for, and now wings his way to that peaceful mansion, where neither moth nor rust corrupt. He died on Monday last, and was buried on Wednesday, and nobody in this town till to-day heard that he was sick. Very accidentally I heard this morning, by a gentleman just from Winchester, that unwelcome news. . . . "

General Roberdeau's remains were interred in the rural burying-ground, of the Presbyterian Church in Winchester. The spot was about fifty feet north of the northwest corner of the church. About ten or fifteen years ago they were removed with most of the other bodies to Mt. Hebron Cemetery, where they now lie, at the extreme further end from the gateway, and near the fence. It is a beautiful, quiet spot, just beyond the busy noises of the town, but its stillness was interrupted during the late contest, when this hallowed spot was a battle-field. The old church, too, felt the strife, being turned into a magazine. The grave* is marked by a horizontal marble slab, raised a little from the ground, bearing the following inscription:

SACRED TO THE MEMORY OF
GENERAL DANIEL ROBERDEAU,
who departed this life,
January 5th, 1795,
Aged 68 years.

*See *Foote's Sketches in Virginia.*

General Roberdeau's will and codicils bequeath a life estate to his wife, and £70 each per annum for the support and education of his three younger children during their minority. The rest of his estate to be equally divided between his seven children—Isaac, Ann, Mary, Selina, Jane, James, and Heriot. Upon the death of his wife and the coming of age of the three latter children, those sums there appropriated are each to be equally divided. His wife, together with Charles Simmons and Alexander Smith, are constituted executors. The will was proved in Winchester, Virginia, May 5, 1795. There is no record of the amount of real estate bequeathed, but the personal property is appraised at £366, 14s.

Conclusion.

It is believed that no likeness of General Roberdeau now exists. It may be there never was one, although Mrs. Dr. Wheat is under the impression that long ago she had seen a profile. Recent search and inquiry has failed to find any trace of a likeness. In person, General Roberdeau was a very large man. Beyond this, we can only conjecture from family likenesses among his descendants.

No biography of General Roberdeau, or even sketch of him beyond a few lines, has heretofore appeared in print. At the request of two gentlemen in Philadelphia sketches of the general have been sent to each of them. One to R. S. Hunter, Esq., "to be presented at the meeting of July 2d, 1876, in Independence Hall, and afterwards deposited in the archives of the National Museum." The other sketch to S. Agnew, Esq., for his History of the Second Presbyterian Church. A third, at the request of a member of the family, was sent to a gentleman in Alexandria, who published an abstract in the Alexandria Sentinel, from which it was copied into Virginia, Tennessee, and North Carolina, and other papers. The manuscript was afterwards returned to the writer at his request.

Mrs. Jane Roberdeau continued to live in Winchester until her death; where also, her children grew up and afterwards married. For a time, however, owing, perhaps to the distance intervening, there was but little intercourse between them and the others of the family.

In the Winchester Times of October 7, 1873, a piece

entitled Annals of Winchester thus alludes to Mrs. Roberdeau, then living in the old house on Market street, long since torn down: "In a stone house opposite old Colonel Maguire's and north of Dr. Balmain's, was Mrs. Roberdeau, widow of General Roberdeau, who had been an officer of the Revolution."

A portrait of Mrs. Roberdeau in her youth hangs in the house of her granddaughter, Mrs. Bent, in Winchester. She is distinctly remembered by some of her grandchildren, one of whom thus writes: "I remember my grandmother well. In her youth she was handsome, I have heard, and can well believe it, for she had beautiful black eyes and fine features up to the time of her death. She was a dignified old Scotch lady, occasionally using a Scotch word, to the amusement of her grandchildren."

Mrs. Jane Roberdeau lived to an advanced age. The number of her years is unknown, but her death occurred fifty-seven years after her marriage. She was buried by the side of her husband; and added to the stone, below the previous inscription, is the following:

" Here also are deposited
the remains of
MRS. JEAN ROBERDEAU
widow of
GEN. DANIEL ROBERDEAU
who departed this life
Sept. 3, 1835."

GENERAL ROBERDEAU'S CHILDREN.

By his first wife, Mary Bostwick; all born in Philadelphia. (From his Bible register, portions of which are worn away, but restored in brackets.)

Daniel Roberdeau married to Miss Polly Bostwick, Oct. 3, 17[61.]

5. i.		Their son ISAAC, born September 11, 1763; on Sunday morn[ing.]
6. ii.	Died Oct. 13, 1769.	Their daughter MARY, born August 24, 1765; Saturday p. m., 8.—
7. iii.		Their daughter ANN, born December 3, 1767, Thursday p. m.—
8. iv.	Died Sept. 14, 1770.	Their son DAVID BOSTWICK, born August 22, 1770, Wednesday p.m.
9. v.	Died.	Their daughter [illegible], born August—, 1771.
10. vi.	Died.	Their daughter PHILADELPHIA, born July, 1772.
11. vii.		Their daughter MARY, born May 6, 1774, at 8 o'clock.
12. viii.		Their daughter SELINA, born November 9, 1775.
13. ix.		[Mrs. Mary] Roberdeau departed this life Feby. 15th, 1777, aged 3[6 years, and is buried] with her still-born daughter in the Presbyterian [Church at Lancaster, Penn.]

By his second wife, Jane Milligan (collected from various sources):

14. x. JEANY, born in Philadelphia, July 17, 1781; died very soon after.
15. xi. JANE, born in Philadelphia, January 22, 1783.
16. xii. JAMES MILLIGAN, born in Alexandria, April 12, 1785.
17. xiii. HERIOT, born in Alexandria, in 1788.

3. ELIZABETH ROBERDEAU.—Eldest child of Mary Cunyngham and Isaac Roberdeau, was born in the Island of St. Christopher, in 1724, and with the family came to Philadelphia, where she spent the remainder of her life. She owned some land in Philadelphia; deeds being there on record in her name. She attended the Second Presbyterian Church. A petition from many members of this church, dated October 21, 1788, is addressed to the pastor, Rev. Ashbel Green, approving of music, and requesting that an anthem be regularly given out at the Sunday evening lectures; it is signed by Elizabeth Roberdeau among others. Her residence, in 1793, is noted as being "in Cherry alley, between Fifth and Sixth." This so-called "alley" is a *street* 40 feet in width; now called Cherry *street*.

Miss Elizabeth Roberdeau, as already seen, was the recipient of a legacy of £200 from her aunt, Miss Jourdine Cunyngham, about the year 1788. She was undoubtedly much interested in matters relating to the estate of Robert Cunyngham, as well as the family generally; for her nephew, Isaac, calls her the "biographer and genealogist of the family." It is a matter of regret that some of her knowledge should not have been committed to writing, and so preserved to the family.

Elizabeth Roberdeau never married, and died in Philadelphia. The church record thus notices her funeral: "March 31, 1799, Miss Elizabeth Roberdeau, 75 years." She was buried in the grave-yard of the Second Presbyterian Church, in Arch street, above 5th; but in 1867, the march of improvements necessitating the removal of this burying-ground, the bodies were transferred to Mount Vernon Cemetery, near Philadelphia. Her *name* does not appear in the list of removals, as the inscription on the grave-stone may be illegible, many being so noted in the records; but all were carefully set up again after removal.

Miss Roberdeau bequeathed all her property to her nephew, Isaac, save a few mementos to his daughters.

The will is dated April 1, 1796, and is recorded in Philadelphia. She died possessed of many old heirlooms that were brought from St. Christopher's—an old looking-glass; some of the Cunyngham silver with the arms of that family upon it, already described. Her Bible, of very early date, printed in England, contains many records of births, marriages, and deaths of the older members of the family.

4. ANN JUDITH (ROBERDEAU) CLYMER.— Second daughter of Mary (Cunyngham) and Isaac Roberdeau, of Rochelle, was born on the Island of St. Christopher, in the year 1725 or '6; and removed with the rest of the family to Philadelphia; where she was married, January 19, 1742, as appears by the records of Christ Church, to William Clymer, of that city.

Of the Clymer family: The first of the name was Richard Clymer, who came from Bristol, England, in 1705, and settled in Philadelphia, where he was a shipping merchant and ship-builder. His mother's name was Catharine. He also had a brother, William, a member of the Assembly, who was buried April 26, 1740; dying without issue, as we may infer from his will, in which he left *inter alia*, £100 to Christ Church, the interest to be paid annually to twelve widow women of the church. Richard Clymer's wife is unknown, and she probably died before him. He was the father of several children, viz: Christopher, whose son, George, was a signer of the Declaration of Independence; William, above mentioned; Margaret, who died unmarried; Sarah, baptized in Christ Church, September 20, 1713; and perhaps others. Richard Clymer died August 18, 1734, his will being dated July 8th, 1734. Only two of his children left descendants.

The descendants of Christopher Clymer are given in the Genealogy of the *Lloyd and Carpenter Families*, by C. Perrin Smith, 1870.

William Clymer, above mentioned, was a captain in the English Navy, commanding the frigate Penzance during the reign of George II., and was lost at sea, leaving a will, dated October 16, 1760. Ann, his wife, died on the old estate near Morgantown, Berks county, in April or May, 1782, leaving but one child:—

18. Daniel Cunyngham, born in Philadelphia, April 6, 1748.

THIRD GENERATION.

———•◦•———

CHILDREN OF GENERAL DANIEL ROBERDEAU. [2.]

5. ISAAC ROBERDEAU.—Born in Philadelphia, September 11, 1763. His early education was received in this country, and after finishing his classical studies, accompanied his father to the West Indies, visiting the old estates of the Cunyngham family at St. Christopher's, which visit he afterwards remembered with much pleasure. From thence, proceeding to London, they resided with his father's cousins, Mrs. Pearce-Hall and Mrs. Beddingfield Pogson. While there, in 1783, Isaac profited by the greater advantages for learning that the Old World afforded, and continued his studies. After spending four years in England he returned to America, turned his attention to civil engineering, and soon began the practice of that profession.

His first public service was in 1791, at the instance of General Washington, as assistant engineer to Major L'Enfant and Colonel Ellicott in the planning and laying out of the City of Washington.

In November of that year Daniel Carroll, a cousin of one of the Commissioners, for some unknown reason, attempted to disarrange the engineers' plans by building a great brick house, which he called Duddington, directly upon the site selected for the Capitol. Major L'Enfant gave Mr. Roberdeau orders to tear it down, but the latter being stopped by a magistrate's warrant, Major L'Enfant organized a gang of laborers and before morning leveled the whole edifice to the ground.

The Commissioners were furious, and took the part of Mr. Carroll. Whereupon began a series of quarrels between the Commissioners and those whom they employed, that terminated only with the office of Commissioner. Carroll proposed to sue L'Enfant, but was quieted only when the Commissioners rebuilt his house, but on another spot—on New Jersey avenue between E and F streets southeast, where it still remains, a grim old relic, surrounded by a high brick wall and a park of forest trees.

In January another quarrel arose. It seems Major L'Enfant withdrew twenty-five men from the city work and placed them in the stone quarries under Mr. Roberdeau. This displeased the Commissioners, who immediately wrote (January 9th) to Mr. Roberdeau, dismissing him from their employ. He replied the next day, recommending the necessity of employing men at the quarries, and stating that unless barracks are erected in the city for men, there would be great delay when spring opens, &c., &c. The Commissioners replied the same day by reappointing him, and telling him to proceed in the work as he suggests. To this Mr. Roberdeau wrote that he cannot comply with their request, his orders from Major L'Enfant being positive. "Until by him I am discharged, from whose authority soever he holds his rank, in this business, I should not think myself justified in neglecting his orders as my superior. . . . I have received no orders from the Major to proceed in that part of the city. . . . I had no directions from Mr. Ellicott concerning the surveys of the Territory of Columbia, excepting that part of the Eastern Branch. . . . It would be interfering in customs, to which I have no claim, until Major Ellicott shall desire it. I have the honor to be," &c.

Upon receipt of this letter the Commissioners again dismissed him from their employ, although Mr. Roberdeau was undoubtedly right in the matter, for these reasons : Major L'Enfant and Colonel Ellicott were each acting in a different sphere—the former made the drawings, the latter the surveys. Mr. Roberdeau being at this time under Major L'Enfant, could with no propriety undertake the work entrusted to the latter without his sanction. Nor could he neglect that to which Major L'Enfant had assigned him. The Commissioners were evidently wrong in communicating directly with Mr. Roberdeau ; for in all like positions, where there are several grades of authority, orders must be transmitted down through successive grades, else no one could know how his subordinates were employed.

Here, then, we have the root of the whole difficulty— Major L'Enfant *would not* be dictated to. He whom pos-

terity now regards as "the most intellectual of all the
party," and "whose plan is gradually indicating itself as
the magnificent distances fill up with buildings," whom
Washington himself selected, and regarded "as better
qualified than any one who had come within his knowledge in this country, or, indeed, of any other"—he would
allow no interference with his plans, and was himself dismissed for "insubordination" two months afterwards.
Fortunate, indeed, is it that he was retained even that
long. "As L'Enfant made the city it remains, with little
or no alteration."*

Notwithstanding the Commissioners' two letters to Mr.
Roberdeau, of the 9th and 10th of January, they with
much vacilation allowed him to remain in their employ
for some time subsequently, and after he left the work
they wrote to Colonel Ellicott, March 14, that they were
willing to employ him.

The Commissioners quarreled with everybody. Ellicott was dismissed soon after this, as also his assistants,
Briggs, B. Ellicott, and J. Ellicott. At a later period
the architects of the Capitol—Hallett, Hadfield, Hoban—
followed one another, to say nothing of the innumerable
dismissals among inferiors. Even an ex-Commissioner
was charged with "indecent language and conduct,"
which "they attribute to a derangement of mind."—(*Letter of June* 10, 1795.) Most of the letters of the Commissioners evince considerable heat on their part.†

In Mr. Roberdeau's manuscript papers the only allusion to this affair is as follows:

A disagreement arose between the Commissioners of the City
of Washington and the engineers and surveyors appointed to the
execution of the work, which occasioned the resignation of all
of them. To this circumstance may be properly attributed, all
the disasters which subsequently occurred, both as they regard
the position and architecture of the public buildings, as to the
insuperable difficulties into which the public property was
thereby thrown.

Mr. Roberdeau's friendship with Major L'Enfant and
Colonel Ellicott continued through their lives.

While engaged upon this Washington work, Mr. Roberdeau was at times occupied in making the plans of the

---

* See *Washington Outside and Inside*, by G. A. Townsend; also, *The
Federal City*, in course of publication, by S. D. Wyeth, who communicated
to the writer some of the facts here given.

† See, also, the Commissioners' journal, letter-books, and official papers.

city. On one occasion his favorite cat, whose accustomed place was on his shoulder while he was at work, after lazily watching the movement of his pen, made a sudden spring, before she could be prevented, to the middle of the drawing then nearly completed and still wet from his pen! Mr. Roberdeau, whose mild temper would not allow him to punish the innocent offender, gently lifted the cat down to the floor, with a remark similar to that of Sir Isaac Newton's: "There pussy, you know not what you have done." And without a further word began another drawing.

Mr. Roberdeau, after leaving this work, went to his father's house in Alexandria, and thence, in the fall of the year, to Philadelphia, where he lived with his aunt, Miss Elizabeth Roberdeau, at No. 49 Cherry alley, now Cherry street.

On the seventh of November, of the same year, 1792, he was married to Susan Shippen, eldest child of the Rev. Samuel Blair, D. D., of Germantown, near Philadelphia.

ANCESTRY OF SUSAN SHIPPEN BLAIR.

The ancestry of Mrs. Susan Roberdeau is here given in the form of a chart. Dr. Samuel Blair, Sr., her grandfather, was one of the instructors at the "Log College." in Pennsylvania, and among his pupils were some who were afterwards the brightest lights of the Presbyterian pulpit. John Rogers, James Finley, Rev. Samuel Davies, President of Princeton College; and others. Dr. Blair, Jr., his son, "was considered the most accomplished and promising young minister in the Presbyterian church." In *Sprague's American Presbyterian Pulpit* is related this incident in his life: "He seems to have been a young man of fine talents, and more than ordinary acquirements. In proof of the justice of this remark, it may be added here, that in 1767, after Dr. Witherspoon had declined the first call of the trustees of the College of New Jersey [Princeton] to the presidency of that institution, young Blair, though not over twenty-six years of age, was elected to that office, with, as we have reason to believe, entire unanimity. But when the intelligence came from Scotland that owing to a change of circumstances, Dr. Witherspoon would probably accept the call if it were renewed, Mr. Blair imme-

ANCESTRY OF SUSAN S. BLAIR, WHO MARRIED COL. ISAAC ROBERDEAU.

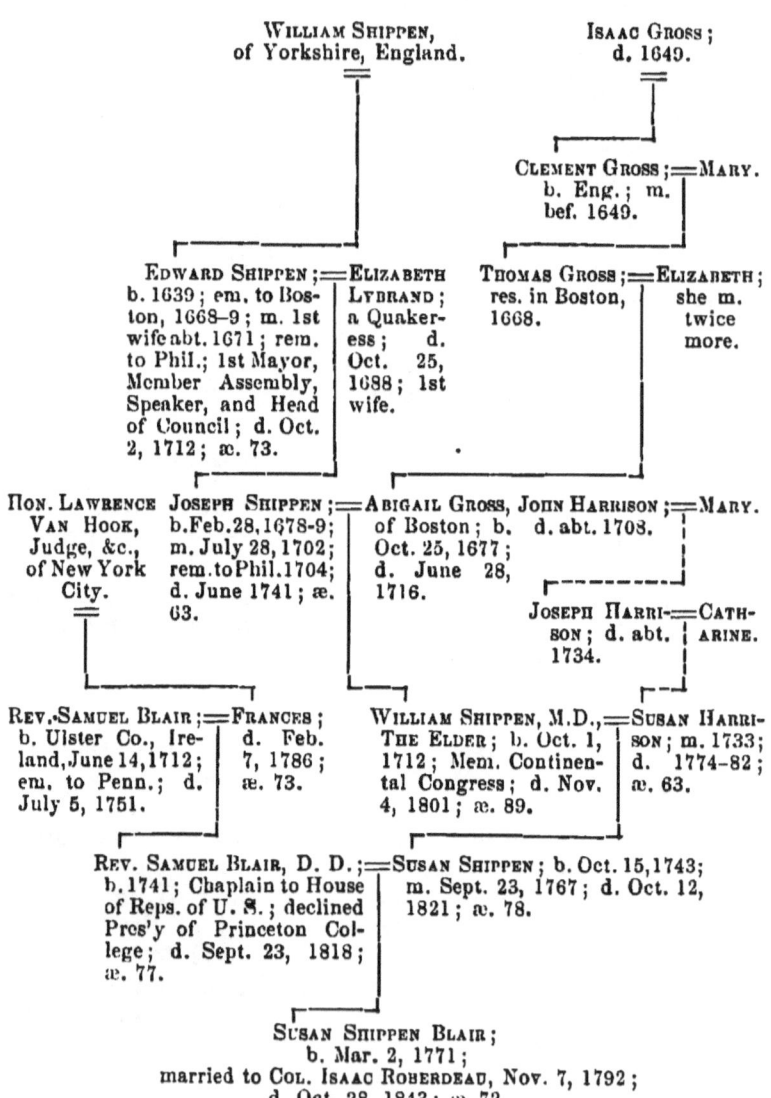

WILLIAM SHIPPEN, of Yorkshire, England.

ISAAC GROSS; d. 1649.

CLEMENT GROSS; b. Eng.; m. bef. 1649. ══ MARY.

EDWARD SHIPPEN; b. 1639; em. to Boston, 1668–9; m. 1st wife abt. 1671; rem. to Phil.; 1st Mayor, Member Assembly, Speaker, and Head of Council; d. Oct. 2, 1712; æ. 73. ══ ELIZABETH LYBRAND; a Quakeress; d. Oct. 25, 1688; 1st wife.

THOMAS GROSS; res. in Boston, 1668. ══ ELIZABETH; she m. twice more.

HON. LAWRENCE VAN HOOK, Judge, &c., of New York City. ══

JOSEPH SHIPPEN; b. Feb. 28, 1678-9; m. July 28, 1702; rem. to Phil. 1704; d. June 1741; æ. 63. ══ ABIGAIL GROSS, of Boston; b. Oct. 25, 1677; d. June 28, 1716.

JOHN HARRISON; d. abt. 1703. ══ MARY.

JOSEPH HARRISON; d. abt. 1734. ══ CATHARINE.

REV. SAMUEL BLAIR; b. Ulster Co., Ireland, June 14, 1712; em. to Penn.; d. July 5, 1751. ══ FRANCES; d. Feb. 7, 1786; æ. 73.

WILLIAM SHIPPEN, M.D., THE ELDER; b. Oct. 1, 1712; Mem. Continental Congress; d. Nov. 4, 1801; æ. 89. ══ SUSAN HARRISON; m. 1733; d. 1774-82; æ. 63.

REV. SAMUEL BLAIR, D. D.; b. 1741; Chaplain to House of Reps. of U. S.; declined Pres'y of Princeton College; d. Sept. 23, 1818; æ. 77. ══ SUSAN SHIPPEN; b. Oct. 15, 1743; m. Sept. 23, 1767; d. Oct. 12, 1821; æ. 78.

SUSAN SHIPPEN BLAIR; b. Mar. 2, 1771; married to COL. ISAAC ROBERDEAU, Nov. 7, 1792; d. Oct. 28, 1843; æ. 72.

diately declined the invitation, and Dr. Witherspoon
was re-elected. This was regarded at the time as a remarkable instance of self-sacrifice to the public good.
He felt that the interests of the college demanded the
services of a man of matured mind, and eminent qualifications; and therefore gave way with a modesty and
magnaminity worthy of record." Dr. Blair was for two
years assistant pastor of the old South Church in Boston,
and chaplain to a brigade of artillery in the Revolution.
(Journals of Congress for May 17, 1780.) He was also
Chaplain to the House of Representatives of the United
States in 1790–2. He was honored by several literary
societies, receiving the degree of A. M. from both Princeton and from Harvard Colleges, and D. D. from the University of Pennsylvania. He was also a member of the
American Philosophical Society.—(*Sprague's American
Presbyterian Pulpit; The Log College, by A. Alexander.*)

The genealogy of the Shippen family was published
in 1855 by Thomas Balch, Esq., entitled "*Letters and
papers relating to the provincial history of Pennsylvania,*"
soon to be republished. The latter edition will include
the descendants of Dr. William Shippen, the elder, to
the present time, all of whom were omitted in the former
edition. Dr. William Shippen, the elder, was a physician of eminence in Philadelphia,—one of the founders,
and trustee of Princeton College; a trustee of the College of Pennsylvania; Vice-President of the Philosophical Society; and in his old age a member of the Continental Congress, and colleague of General Roberdeau.
His son, Dr. William Shippen, the younger, was also a
very eminent physician, and founder of the Philadelphia
Medical School.—(*Thacher's Medical Biog.; Lossing's
Field-Book of the Revolution.*)

To resume: Mr. Roberdeau continues, in his manuscript above quoted:

Immediately after my marriage, I was appointed agent for the
board of directors of canals and turnpikes in the State of Pennsylvania; the duties of which I performed until the arrival of
the engineer, Mr. William Weston, from Gainsborough on
Trent, in England; who had been sent for under a large salary
to take charge of the canals and other works of internal improvement in that State. This gentleman, with the approbation of the directors, appointed me his assistant, in which capacity I served and conducted the canal intended to connect the

waters of the Schuylkill with the Susquehanna, to his perfect
approbation; until the failure of funds of all these companies in
1796 occasioned the relinquishment of the works and the return
of Mr. Weston to his native land.

This canal extended from the Susquehanna, below
Harrisburg, to the Schuylkill, at Reading, a length of
seventy miles, and is now known as the Union Canal.
Mr. Weston's reports frequently mention Mr. Roberdeau.
Upon his arrival Mr. Weston found over 600 men at
work, a portion of them being engaged in making their
own bricks, which could not be procured elsewhere. This
canal was not completed till 1827, enlarged in 1850 at
a cost of two and a half millions, and is now in operation,
the oldest in the State, if not in the country.—(*Hist. Acct.
of Canals*, 1795; *Hist. of R. R. and Canals*, H. V. Poor.)

Mr. Roberdeau then continues :

By this occurrence (the failure of funds) I was again thrown
out of employ in my profession—a profession which was then
little cherished and imperfectly understood, even in the army of
the United States; as most of the officers of engineers engaged
in the Revolutionary War were foreigners, who had, with few
exceptions, returned to their respective countries. And as the
Military Academy at West Point was not established until 1802,
there existed no taste or desire for this kind of literature ; nor
was there a college or seminary of learning where the profession
could be attained, and for many years afterwards but imperfectly, even under the patronage of the government.

During this posture of affairs, Dr. Shippen, the grandfather of
my wife, advised my removing to an estate he possessed in Sussex county, New Jersey, called Oxford Furnace, and entering
into partnership with a person accustomed to that business. As
any plan promising even partial success is preferable to an idle
life, I unfortunately engaged in it [1796] and arked my little
all in the project, which ended entirely in discomfiture.

Mr. Roberdeau elsewhere records that while residing
in Sussex county he " paid taxes, voted at elections,
and was major of brigade under different governors for
seven years." On the 22d of February, 1800, agreeably
to a resolution of Congress addressed to the people of
the United States, he had the honor to deliver an oration
on the death of General Washington but a few months
after his lamented decease. It was soon after published,
the title-page being as follows :

"An oration upon the death of General George Washington, pronounced before the officers of the Second

Brigade, Fourth Division, of the Militia of New Jersey, at Johnsonbury, Sussex county, on the 22d of February, 1800. Published at their request; by Isaac Roberdeau, Major of Brigade." (Philadelphia, 1800.)

This pamphlet is catalogued in the *Washingtoniana*, by Franklin B. Hough, and is dedicated—

" To His Excellency Richard Howell, Esq., Governor, and Captain-General, and Commander-in-Chief in and over the State of New Jersey, &c., &c. . . ."

About this time [1801] Dr. Shippen, the elder, died, leaving a large estate, which was inherited by his son William and his daughter Susan, the mother of my wife. To the latter Oxford fell, and it was by her conveyed to my wife, but greatly encumbered by legacies and incumbrances, that it was afterwards sold to discharge them.* Upon this event I removed to Germantown, and undertook the settlement of the estate, which, after a long time and much labor, was accomplished.

As I had studied the science of arms in early life, in which my profession as an engineer afforded many advantages of improvement, I had made several attempts to enter the army, but this could not be accomplished with a rank suited either to my support or capacity, until the war with Great Britain in 1812 broke out, when an opportunity occurred and I was appointed in the Topographical Engineers, with the rank, pay, and emoluments of a major of cavalry.

Major Roberdeau's commission took rank from the 29th of April, 1813. The Topographical Engineer Corps being just constituted, consisted of four majors and four captains, who were attached to the general staff of the army.

During the war Major Roberdeau's first services were at Fort Mifflin, below Philadelphia, on the Delaware. He was then, at the instance of General Swift, the Chief of the Engineer Corps, sent to West Point to instruct in topography; then to Brooklyn.

Upon the termination of the war but three officers of this corps were retained on the peace establishment, Roberdeau being one of the majors. Congress, however, in recognizing the general staff, provided for the permanent appointment of six topographical engineers and four assistants.

At the conclusion of the war, among other duties, I received an order to report the boundary-line between the British possessions in Canada, and the United States, by the river St. Law-

---

* In 1809, the purchaser being Morris Robeson, grandfather of the present Secretary of the Navy.

rence; which was performed as far as the Great Falls of St.
Mary's, at Lake Superior; which was accomplished.

This survey was of more importance and magnitude
than appears from this modest mention. The treaty of
peace which closed the Revolutionary War had fixed the
boundary between the United States and Canadas *in the
middle of the rivers and lakes*, &c., thus leaving a very
open question as to what was the middle, many islands
thereby being disputed possessions. The Treaty of Ghent,
signed December 24, 1814, which closed the late war,
provided for a settlement of this difficulty, in the 6th and
7th clauses, by a survey to be made. Under this treaty
Colonel Hawkins was the agent on the part of the
United States, and Colonel Roberdeau the engineer detailed to make the survey in the presence of the two
agents.   Sailing-Master Champlin was ordered in the
Porcupine to accompany Colonel Hawkins and Colonel
Roberdeau, Topographical Engineers, who had to exam-
ine the boundary between the United States and Great
Britain.—(*N. E. Hist. and Gen. Reg., XVII.*, 27.)

The survey commenced where the 45th degree of lati-
tude crossed the St. Lawrence, and thence proceeded up
that river, Lake Ontario, Niagara river, Lakes Erie and .
Huron, and as far as the falls at the outlet of Lake Superior, a distance of nearly nine hundred miles.   .

The report of this survey, dated February 15, 1817,
and now in the Engineer Bureau, is quite voluminous,
in which there are frequent interlineations in the peculiar hand of Colonel Roberdeau, also seventeen plans of
different portions of the line, their style showing them to
be also his workmanship, and rarely are drawings of
those days so neatly done.

The country here surveyed, was for the most part a
wilderness, inhabited by Indians, from whom the party
purchased many fine furs and other mementos. Their
wardrobe, too, suffered from their hardships, so that on
their return, on being invited to dine at the President's,
Colonel Roberdeau appeared in a calico shirt. He ex-
cused himself to Mrs. Madison, pleading their hardships,
and with much drollery, saying that they had but twelve
shirts between them; Col. Hawkins had eleven, and he
had one!

, Upon my return from this duty. in 1816, and on the arrival
of General Simon Bernard, from France, as Assistant Engineer,

and the consequent formation of a Board of Engineers, my orders attached me to it, and occasioned the removal of my family to West Point, then the headquarters of the corps, where they remained until August, 1818; when the chief officers of the general staff were ordered to reside in Washington.

I was then ordered to take charge of the formation of a Topographical Bureau, upon the plan adopted and pursued in France by Carnot, which brought my family at this time to the seat of government, where they have remained ever since.

Colonel Roberdeau having organized this bureau, was placed at the head of it, where he remained until his death. In April, 1823, he received the brevet of lieutenant-colonel. In 1826, the Topographical Engineers were made a separate corps, and so remained until within a few years past, when they were again merged in the Engineers.

Between Mr. Calhoun and the family of Colonel Roberdeau, there existed a warm friendship; commencing with their official relations while the former was Secretary of War. Upon his yearly tours of inspection of the various military posts, Colonel Roberdeau generally accompanied him, and kept a private journal of the movements and expenses of the party. The *Columbian Sentinel*, of Boston, September 27, 1820, contains a notice: "The Secretary of War left New Haven on Friday last on his return to Washington, accompanied by Major Roberdeau of the Topographical Engineers, and Mr. Hagner, one of the Auditors of the Treasury."

In 1824, the approaching presidential election occasioned one of the most exciting periods in the political history of the country, Mr. Calhoun being then one of the candidates for the Vice-Presidency. At this time, Colonel Roberdeau was one day present at a public dinner, where one of the guests arose to eulogize Mr. Calhoun's opponent, but the length of his speech, and the dullness of his words, wearied his hearers until their patience was well nigh exhausted. As he concluded, Colonel Roberdeau being called upon to reply, slowly arose, and looking around until he had caught the eyes of all present, gave the toast: "John C. Calhoun; THIS name needs NO comment."

This speech, so unexpected, so great a contrast to the previous, fell upon the ears of his hearers with magical effect, and brought forth from them cheer after cheer,

8

proving, indeed, the truth of the words. The press took
it up and gave it to the country at large. At the election, the choice fell upon Mr. Calhoun with a handsome
majority.

Colonel Roberdeau was also obliged to visit such military posts as came within the jurisdiction of his bureau.
During a visit to Fort Washington, the countersign for the
day (July 12, 1826), was in his honor, given ROBERDEAU.

The artist, Jarvis, was at this time in Washington,
painting the portraits of the Cabinet; and as Colonel
Roberdeau entered his studio one day, he said: "Stand,
Colonel, I will paint your portrait; the minister has disappointed me." The portrait of Colonel Roberdeau,
thus commenced, was afterwards finished by Sully.
With the celebrated Gilbert Stuart, also, the Colonel was
intimate; and in the well-known, full-length portrait of
Washington, with his hand extended, Colonel Roberdeau's hand was his model.

And besides a miniature on ivory, there is another
portrait of Colonel Roberdeau, painted by an amateur,
and intimate friend—Major Williams, then just from
West Point, and assigned to duty in the Colonel's office,
and who subsequently fell fighting gallantly before
Monterey. Major Williams had married Miss Peter,
one of the Custis family, and this portrait, hung at
Arlington with the family portraits of the Custis, Lee,
and Washington families, until the close of the late war,
when it was removed with other things belonging to
Mrs. Lee, and has recently been presented by the daughter of the artist to the Colonel's family.

The Colonel was a great pedestrian, as his profession
as a civil engineer might suggest. While studying in
Europe, he at different times walked through Wales and
the south of France; and at a later period, over a great
part of this country. It could more readily be done in
those days, before railroads were built. His last day's
journey was from Reading to Philadelphia, a distance of
fifty or sixty miles. Once, he was lost in the woods, and
for hours walked without finding a trace of habitation;
and slept that night on the ground, with his knapsack
for a pillow. At dawn, he heard the barking of a dog,
and following the sound, came to a hut, where he found
a guide to point out his way. He ever after experienced
pleasure at hearing a dog bark. He dressed suitably for

walking, with thick woolen stockings, even in summer, buckskin breeches, and his knapsack on his back.

Between the family of President Adams and the Roberdeaus, an intimacy that had existed between their sires and grandsires, was continued in Washington. The Colonel's daughters were frequent guests, for days at a time, at the White House, assisting at the receptions.

At Mr. Adams' inauguration, the Misses Roberdeau were of the presidential party in attending the ball in the evening.

After the families had separated by the removal of the Roberdeaus to Philadelphia, a correspondence was kept up for many years between them. Miss Mary E. Roberdeau having sent Mr. Adams a little memento of her own work, received the following letter from him.

MISS MARY E. ROBERDEAU, PHILADELPHIA.

QUINCY, 23d *October*, 1832.

DEAR MISS ROBERDEAU.

Your very kind note of the 6th inst., accompanied by your very acceptable present of an elegant and useful purse, the work of your own hands, has reached me safely. Accept for them my cordial thanks; and be assured that your gift shall be as perpetual an appendage to my person, as the Red Ribband of the Bath was to that of Sir William Draper. The linen bag, faithful as it was to keep my portable metallic treasures, is discarded; and if the unfortunate sailor's mark of Moll Thompson* should take the place of current coin in my purse, so long as the purse itself shall endure, I shall have that in my pocket, which is better than money,—a token of your friendly regard.

On my last passage through Philadelphia, I missed the pleasure of seeing you; and learnt that you had left the city on the morning of my arrival there. After a short summer here, during which I have often been reminded of the cheering addition to our enjoyments of the last autumn, by your visit, we are again preparing for our flight southward. My son Charles and his family have spent the summer with us, and are to return to Boston as we depart for Washington. My hopes are to reach Philadelphia about three weeks from this day.

With my respectful compliments to your mother and sisters, I remain, dear Miss Roberdeau, your friend and sevt.,

J. Q. ADAMS.

---

*Moll Thompson, her initials being M. T.—*empty.*

Some years afterwards, upon the death of her honored husband, Mrs. Adams, in reply to a letter of sympathy, wrote as follows:

TO SELINA AND SUSAN.

WASHINGTON, 11*th March*, '48.

Accept my most cordial thanks, my dearest friends, for your kindly sympathizing letter; and be assured that among all the kind testimonials which I have received, no one has proved more grateful to my sorrowing heart, than the affectionate tribute offered by you both, on my sad and melancholy bereavement.

The memory of your dear sister Mary, and of our former friendship, still abides warmly and affectionately, in joy or in grief, in the heart of

LOUISA CATHERINE ADAMS.

Lafayette, during his visit to Washington in 1825, as the nation's guest, was a frequent visitor at Colonel Roberdeau's house, and left many treasured mementos of his visits; some flowers that he gathered and kissed before presenting them to one of the daughters, &c. When about to return to France, the last house he was in in Georgetown, was Colonel Roberdeau's, where he lingered until the mayor came and told him the procession was waiting for him.

A year or two after, in a letter to Mrs. Bomford, of January 1, 1827, published in the *Historical Magazine for* 1859, *III.*, 297, he wishes to be remembered to Colonel Roberdeau.

And again, in a letter to his countryman, General Bernard, who conveyed the *remembrances* upon his card as follows:

"GENERAL BERNARD. To take leave, and present the family of Colonel Roberdeau with the *souvenirs* of General Lafayette."   .

This gentleman, it may be observed, when a refugee from his native land after the downfall of Napoleon, whose chief engineer he had been, took refuge in this country, entered our army, and became chief engineer. He designed all the principal fortifications on the Atlantic Coast—Fortress Monroe being his largest work. Upon the accession of Louis Phillippe to power, he was recalled and became his aid; and eventually, lieutenant-general and minister of war.

May-day was formerly celebrated in the circle of Colonel Roberdeau's acquaintances. In 1822, the daughter of the Attorney-General, William Wirt, was chosen Queen of May; and in his life, published by Hon. John P. Kennedy, may be found some lines written by that distinguished jurist for his daughter to repeat on the occasion. A year or two later, one of the Misses Roberdeau was chosen Queen of May; and on account of the weather, the ceremonies that were to have taken place on Mason's Island, were adjourned to the house of Mayor Cox of Georgetown, who fitted up a throne for the coronation.

Among those present, was Colonel Samuel Cooper, afterwards Adjutant-General of the army, and more recently, senior General of the Confederate Army; who composed the following lines upon the occasion. Some years after, he sent them to the Queen of May, with the endorsement on the back (December 7, 1858):

To the fair Queen of May, Greeting:

Recently discovered among some loose papers, and now sent to her Majesty, who will thereby be reminded that the coronation which was to have taken place under the canopy of Heaven, was by the inclemency of the weather, adjourned to the mansion of the Lord Mayor of Georgetown.

First of May, 18—.*

" But soft! what light through yonder window breaks? It is the east, and Juliet is the sun."—Romeo.

> Hail lovely Queen! thy glory shines afar,
> And dims the lustre of the eastern star.
> The sun, at thy resplendent beauty, shrouds
> His golden beams behind the weeping clouds.
> The silver moon, obedient to thy will,
> Sinks pale and sad behind the western hill.
> The stars are dim; their brightness fade away
> At thy approach, sweet blooming rose of May.
> Ev'n Queens† before thy footstool humbly bend,
> To hail thee sovereign-beauty, royal-friend.
> Tho' nature darkens at thy royal birth,
> And sighs and tears o'er spread the gloomy earth,
> The Orient shall with lustre beam again,
> And nature smile on thy immortal reign;
> The lark shall carol forth her morning lay,
> And rocks and woods shall echo "Queen of May."

*" Hung were the heavens, with black" on that day; i. e., the clouds dropped fatness.
†Former Queens of May.

Sir Stratford Canning, the British Minister, who was present, as he knelt to the Queen, remarked that it was not the first time he had knelt to royalty. It was on this occasion, or perhaps at a picnic, that General Macomb, after being busily engaged in decorating the rooms with evergreens, in his ready way gave the impromptu distich:

Honor to Farley, glory to Macomb,
One cut the bushes, the other swept the room.

Colonel Roberdeau was fond of mathematical studies, and had paid much attention to astronomy and its kindred sciences. On the ninth of December, 1826, he read a paper before the Columbian Institute, entitled "Observations on the Sea Coast of the United States," which shortly afterwards appeared in Peter Force's *National Journal*. It has also been published in pamphlet form. Col. Roberdeau also wrote a "Treatise upon a National Observatory," but the writer has not succeeded in finding a copy of which to speak more fully.

In the former, he recounts what had been done by Mr. Hassler some years before; and urges the necessity of a thorough and systematic survey of the coast; evincing a familiarity with the operations of other nations in this matter. He also shows the need of an observatory in connection with the Coast Survey; the refraction being one important fact to be ascertained, and its laws discovered. He also further shows the advantage of having army and naval officers employed in connection with this work.

What would he think now to see all these suggestions adopted?—the army and navy giving their greatest talent to the work;—the Observatory furnished with the largest refracting telescope in the world, and the whole coast accurately delineated!

Although Colonel Roberdeau held only the lineal rank of major, yet from the smallness of the army at that time, he had but few superiors. The army register one year before his death shows the general and field officers to be as follows: major-generals, 1; brigadier-generals, 3; colonels, 16; lieutenant-colonels, 12; majors, 23, of whom he was the second.

The above-quoted sketch of Colonel Roberdeau's life is from a manuscript found among his papers, apparently the copy of a letter. The manuscript is three pages closely written, and concludes as follows:

This is an outline of my pursuits in life ; the details of other matters are varied, long, and often distressing ; nor can the relation of them be of importance to any one. I have always endeavored faithfully and with industry to perform the duties required of me, and I hope that in these endeavors, success has not been wanting in gaining the confidence and approbation of my superiors,—the affection and respect of all others. If so, my acknowledgments are due to the superintendence of that kind Providence, on whose support I have ever relied; and who, through dangers and difficulties, seen and unseen, has hitherto borne me up, and placed me where I am. Should adverse fortunes be hereafter imposed on me, I hope and pray that my submission to the will of Him who rides upon the whirlwind and directs the storm, may be entire and cheerful.

Col. Roberdeau died at his residence in the city of Georgetown, January 15, 1829. The following notice, written by Colonel McKenney, his intimate friend, appeared in the *National Intelligencer* of the next day:

DEATH.—On the 15th inst., at his residence in Georgetown, in the 66th year of his age; Lieutenant-Colonel Isaac Roberdeau of the Topographical Engineers, and Chief of the Topographical Bureau in the Department of War, over which he has presided from its creation, with great zeal and fidelity. No man sustained a higher character for general benevolence than the deceased. So exact was he in discharging the relative duties of life, that to him may well be applied, with the accompanying admonition, Pope's celebrated lines,—

Go ! pilgrim, go ! pursue the path he trod,
"*An honest man's the noblest work of God.*"

The funeral will take place on Saturday, (to-morrow,) from the late residence of the deceased in Georgetown, at 12 o'clock m.

The officers of the army and navy, and marine corps, and friends of the deceased in general, are invited to attend without further notice.

This funeral was military, the large number of his friends attending, all the prominent officers of the government, including the President and Vice-President, made the procession one of the largest seen in Washington up to that time. The Colonel was interred in the old burial ground near Georgetown.

In firing the three volleys over his grave, a man's hand was injured; remarked by his friends as a singular occurrence, at the funeral of one who in his lifetime had never harmed a single person.

To show the high estimation in which he was held,

may be quoted the following, which appeared in the *National Intelligencer:*

EXTRACT OF A LETTER FROM A GENTLEMAN IN GEORGETOWN, D. C., TO HIS FRIEND.

Saturday, Jan., 17, 1829.

Our excellent friend, Col. Roberdeau, is no more. We have this moment returned from paying the last sad honors to his memory. The funeral was military. The general attendance of his friends, including the President of the United States and the Vice-President, demonstrated their respect for his worth, while living, and for his memory, when dead. How could it be otherwise? Did he ever wantonly wound the feelings of any thing living? Did he not love to cheer the afflicted, comfort the mourner, and impart happiness to all who came within the sphere of his actions? Was he the enemy of any man? Nay, was he not the friend of all men? He was, indeed, *goodness* personified. Such a heart as his, seldom beats, or ceases to beat. . . . .

The life of such a man could not be otherwise than happy; nor could he be otherwise than beloved. His memory will be long and fondly cherished; and with the most ardor by those who best knew him.

You are familiar with his scientific attainments—I need not enlarge here. You know he preferred astronomy. Those stars, and yon moon, and the sun, so often contemplated by him, and in which he so often felt the power of the Godhead to be displayed, are all now under his feet. He has risen into that blessed world where the light of the sun and the moon and the stars are not needed.

The family now made preparations for removing to Philadelphia; and before their departure, President and Mrs. Adams, among many others of their intimate friends, wrote some memento in Mary Roberdeau's album. Mr. Adams' contribution is original poetry, as follows:

TO MISS MARY E. ROBERDEAU.

Dear Mary, many a pleasant day,
  Cheer'd by thy converse, I have past;
And now, it grieves me sooth to say,
  This day, perchance, may be the last.

Ages, since first thy father's sire,
  And mine were faithful friends, have fled;
And still shall burn that sacred fire,
  Though both now slumber with the dead.

Thy father, too, at dawn of youth,
  My swelling bosom learned to prize:
His breast was Love!—his voice was Truth;
  (Unbidden tears suffuse my eyes.)

We part; but wheresoe'er thy lot
  Shall lead thee o'er this world of care,
Friendship shall consecrate the spot;
  My heart, in Memory, shall be there.

Poor are these numbers, dull they roll;
  The bell of Fiction best may chime—
Take the thought burning from the soul;
  'T is feeling too intense for rhyme.

JOHN QUINCY ADAMS.

MERIDIAN HILL, *April*, 1829.

In later years, when Miss Roberdeau was paying a visit to them at their home, Mr. Adams wrote another piece in the same album, a translation from the French, dated Quincy, 14 October, 1831.

Not only from those in their midst did expressions of sympathy come, but from afar; the aged Lafayette heard of Colonel Roberdeau's death, and sent the following beautiful expression of his feelings:

PARIS, *May* 28, 1829.

DEAR MADAM: It is with the deepest regret, that I have heard the heavy loss for which you are so unfortunately mourning. The opportunities I had to appreciate the Colonel's worth, my personal attachment to him, to you, dear madam, and to your amiable daughters, make me more affectionately share in your affliction. I beg you and them to accept the sympathies, regards, and best wishes, of

Your sincere friend,
LAFAYETTE.

To hear from you, and of everything
that relates to each of you, dear madam,
will be to me a source of gratification.

Mrs. ROBERDEAU.

Few men have had paid to them such tributes of respect and affection, and from persons more distinguished, than has Colonel Roberdeau. One of the most flattering was from the Roman Catholic priests in Washington whom he had known intimately. And although a strict Presbyterian, they notified Mrs. Roberdeau of their wish to have peformed for him a requiem mass, and desired to know whether it would be against her wishes. She replied, on the contrary, that she would consider it a great honor, and appreciate their kindness.

Colonel Roberdeau's appearance was dignified and commanding, standing over six feet in height, and of erect, military bearing, a bald head, and mouth denoting decision of character. He was said to bear some resemblance to the Duke of Wellington, and when in London at one time was approached by a stranger with much deference, saying, "Why, my lord, I thought your grace was on the continent." To which was replied, "Sir, I am Colonel Roberdeau, of the United States Army." An old resident of Washington lately remarked of the Colonel, "that he was as well known here then as the President."

Mrs. Roberdeau now removed to Philadelphia, where she resided until her death, October 28, 1843, at the good old age of seventy-two years and eight months.

Their children, all born in Germantown, near Philadelphia, are :—

    19. i. MARY ELIZABETH.
    20. ii. SUSAN SHIPPEN.
    21. iii. FRANCES SELINA (Mrs. Buchanan.)

6. MARY ROBERDEAU.—Born in Philadelphia, but died at an early age, of the hives, as her father's letter-book informs us. She was undoubtedly a favorite child, for her father caused a gold medal to be struck, with the following inscription : "Mary Roberdeau ; Nat., Aug. 24, 1765 ; Ob., Oct., 13, 1769. Memento Mori." Reverse : "Now I have found Him ; Now I am going."

7. ANN (ROBERDEAU) SWIFT.—Born in Philadelphia, December 3, 1767 ; baptized March 27, 1768. Removed to Alexandria, Virginia, with her father, where, on the 24th of September, 1785, she married Jonathan Swift, an importing merchant and man of means, who became a resident in that town before 1785, and for forty years was a prominent citizen. He was the uncle of the veteran General Joseph G. Swift, mentioned in these pages. Mr. Swift's fine place bore the unique name of Grasshopper Hall, but being afterwards purchased by one of the Mason family, is now known as Colross. Jonathan Swift was also consular or commercial agent for seven European nations. He was an intimate friend of General Washington, and had a portrait of him by Peale, which is the subject of the following letter:

GENEVA, 12 *June*, 1858.

JONATHAN T. PATTEN, Esq.

DEAR SIR: The portrait of Washington in your house has always appeared to me more natural than most of the attitudes of his that I have seen. The background in the painting is Princeton College, as it was in 1776. My Uncle Jonathan, whose property it was, used to say it was "more natural" than Stuart's, and was painted by the elder Peale before the surrender of Yorktown. In 1824, at the reception of Lafayette in Alexandria, this portrait was in the procession, as I was told, by loan of Aunt Nancy, and was recognized by Lafayette as a good likeness. At the museum he recognized the handwriting of Washington, "his early friend," in a note found on the wall, written to my uncle, Jonathan Swift, regretting, &c., "Mrs. Washington and his own dancing days were over." Cousin Nancy told me Rembrandt Peale recognized the portrait above mentioned as being from the pencil of his father.. Tell your children, the grandchildren of Jonathan Swift and Nancy Roberdeau, his wife, that I have heard Alexander Hamilton, and Chief Justice Marshall, General C. C. Pinkney, say that the vulgar report of Washington swearing at Lee at the battle of Monmouth was an idle tale, not true. His uniform language and deportment was ever grand and correct, tho' violent when provoked.

Your friend and hum. servt.,

J. G. SWIFT.

The note of General Washington to Mr. Swift and others, here referred to, was presented by him to the Museum of Alexandria Washington Lodge of Alexandria, which was burned a few years ago with all its contents; among which was this letter and some other valuables, placed there by Mr. Swift, including a saddle presented to the government by the Dey of Morocco, while Mr. Swift was his consul. A photograph of the letter was however taken a short time previously, a facsimile of which appeared in the *Chromotype* of July, 1873, published in New York. It is probably one of the last that General Washington ever wrote, being dated November 12, 1799, within a month of his decease. Jonathan Swift was a member of the Masonic Fraternity, having received his degrees in this lodge;—initiated and passed February 25, 1785; and raised to a Master Mason February 24, 1786. As a brother mason, Mr. Swift attended General Washington's funeral; and was the one who sprinkled the earth over the body during the services.

Mr. Swift was himself buried with masonic honors by the lodge.

Jonathan Swift's valuable papers were all lost at sea soon after the death of his son, William Roberdeau, while being sent to New York; an event much to be regretted.

Mrs. Ann Swift was present at the inauguration ball in honor of General Washington, and during the evening, was led out to dance by him. A lifelike miniature of her on ivory, at the age of twenty-two, is in possession of her daughter, Mrs. Patten; who has also an oil painting at the age of sixty.

Jonathan Swift died August 22, 1824, aged sixty-three, and his wife Ann, January 16, 1833, the former at Alexandria, the latter at Madison Court-House.

The arms of Jonathan Swift, as shown by an engraved book-mark, appear to be *Sable, three bucks trippant or;* Crest, *a demi-lion rampant or, holding between the paws a helmet of the first.* A watch-seal, SWIFT impaling ROBERDEAU, now in the possession of Mrs. Dr. Wheat, shows for SWIFT, *or a chevron vair, between three bucks at speed (proper?);* Crest as in the previous coat. The latter arms, save the crest, are the arms of the celebrated Dean Swift's family, who was a near relative of Mr. Jonathan Swift, the subject of this sketch.

Their children, all born in Alexandria, Virginia:—

	i.	THE ELDEST SON,	still-born Oct. 10, 1786.
22	ii.	WILLIAM ROBERDEAU,	b. Aug. 29, 1787.
	iii.	A SON,	b. Nov 12, 1789; d. Nov. 13, 1789.
	iv.	DANIEL ROBERDEAU,	b. Nov. 9, 1790; d. unm. Aug., 1825.
	v.	JONATHAN,	b. Dec. 2, 1792; d. July 1, 1793.
23	vi.	ISAAC BOSTWICK,	b. Feb. 2, 1795.
	vii.	ANN SELINA,	b. Feb. 18, 1797; bapt. May 28; d. July 18, 1798.
	viii.	GEORGE WASHINGTON,	b. Feb. 11, 1800; bapt. Feb. 22; d. unm. Sep. 19, 1819.
24	ix.	ANN FOSTER,	b. Oct. 11, 1802; (Mrs. Patten.)
25	x.	MARY SELINA,	b. Jan. 18, 1805; (Mrs. Allison.)
	xi.	WILLIAM TAYLOR,	b. Sept. 20, 1808; d. next day.
	xii.	FOSTER,	b. May 20, 1810; bapt. Apr. 15; d. unm. Sept., 1825.

8. DAVID BOSTWICK ROBERDEAU.—Born August 22, and died September 14, 1770. Daniel Roberdeau's letter-book thus refers to this child, under date September 24, 1770: "It has pleased the Lord to visit me with the most afflicting trials I was ever exercised with; for from the 6th of last month to the 20th instant,

the life of my dear wife has from time to time been in jeopardy, but blessed be his Holy Name, at length I have found deliverance; but my sister, Mrs. McDougall,* can satisfy my friends with further particulars, therefore I shall not take up more of your time on this head, than to inform you that He that gave has taken away the infant boy, and blessed be his Holy Name." A few days after, General Roberdeau writes in a similar strain to his friend, Dr. Franklin, then in Europe.

9. A DAUGHTER.—The name illegible in the Bible record; born in August, 1771, while her father was in England negotiating the sale of his Pelham's River plantation at St. Christopher's. Immediately upon his return, after an absence of four months, he thus writes to the purchaser, under date of October 13, 1771: "I left London the 2d of August, at 5 o'clock the next morning after I took my leave of you; sailed from Gravesend the 3d; arrived safe and well at New York the 25th of September, and the 27th at my own cot; from where I have now the honor of addressing, and the pleasure of informing you, that except the infant born to me in my absence, which God has taken to himself, I found all my little family well; so good and gracious has been my Benefactor, whose mercies endureth forever."

10. PHILADELPHIA ROBERDEAU.—Born July, 1772; died young. The name seems to have been a family name among Robert Cunyngham's descendants.

11. MARY (ROBERDEAU) PATTEN.—Born in Philadelphia, May 6, 1774; removed to Alexandria with her father, where she was married, November 14, 1793, at the early age of nineteen, to Thomas Patten of that place. He was the son of Thomas and Anna Patten, and was born in Roxbury, Mass., July 22, 1769, but removing to Alexandria, became a merchant there. (His father was born April 4, 1734; died January 31, 1805; his mother, born September 25, 1742, died January 5, 1800.)

A miniature of Mrs. Patten on ivory, taken about the time of her marriage, and said to be an excellent likeness, is a most beautiful picture. She was indeed most beautiful; her brother Isaac remarked that merely to look at her would win the hearts of many.

* A sister of Mrs. Roberdeau married General McDougall.

Her beauty has also been inherited by many of her descendants, both male and female, to the latest generations.

Mrs. Patten was called at the comparatively early age of thirty-four, and the estimation in which she was held, caused the publication of the sermon preached by Dr. Muir at her funeral; from which the following extracts are taken:

The loss of Mrs. Mary Patten had long been anticipated. . . . Her ancestors, both by the father and mother, were Israelites indeed. Her mother, the most amiable and pious of women, was the daughter of the Reverend David Bostwick of New York, whose pious labors have embalmed his memory, and given it an immortality in the church; her worthy father, General Roberdeau, you know to have been active in collecting and establishing the Presbyterian congregation in this place.

Mrs. Patten was indeed a daughter of Abraham, and the child of many prayers; her person was dignified, and her address engaging; she moved in a wide circle, and was dear to all her acquaintances; she possessed in a high degree the delicacy of manners and the charms of conversation, which in the female sex are altogether irresistible. . . . . .

It is remarkable, that in the day of prosperity, as well as of adversity, she maintained a great respect for religion, the consequences of a pious education, and a safe example. . . . She had been on a visit to Boston that the change might benefit her health; during which her mind underwent a great change, her thoughts being directed more to religion than they had been heretofore. "I always respected religion," said she, "but now I enjoy it;" and from this time religion continued to be her pleasure, her comfort.

She died on the 31st of October, 1808, of consumption, her last words being "My God, thou knowest that I love thee."

Soon after his wife's death, Mr. Patten, having failed in business by his ships being lost at sea, and other misfortunes beyond his control, went to Louisiana, taking his then eldest son, Joseph May, and became a planter. There he died on his plantation, called Monroe, of asthma, February 6, 1820, and is buried on the banks of the Washita.

On their mother's death the care of the children devolved upon the eldest daughter, Mary Ann, although but a child herself; and when she married, her husband became their guardian and adopted Selina. Upon the death of Mary Ann, Selina then had an opportunity of extending to her sister's children, the same care and guidance that their mother had shown to her; and did act the mother's part towards them, adopting the eldest, Mary de Neale, whom her own children looked up to as an elder sister.

Mrs. Patten's children, all born in Alexandria, Va.:—

26. i. MARY ANN, b. Ap. 5, 1795; (Mrs. Wolfe.)
27. ii. ISAAC ROBERDEAU, b. Sept. 20, 1796.
iii. SUSAN SHIPPEN, b. Dec. 13, 1797; bapt. May 6, 1798; d. scarlet fever, March, 1801, bur. on 17th.
28. iv. JOSEPH MAY, b. May 26, 1799.
v. ELIZABETH CATHERINE, b. Nov. 18, 1801; bapt. Mar. 18, 1802; d. teething, Dec. 11, 1802.
29. vi. HARRIET ROZIER, b. Nov. 12, 1803; (Mrs. Miller.)
30. vii. SELINA BLAIR, b. Sept. 12, 1805; (Mrs. Wheat.)
31. viii. THOMAS ROBERDEAU, b. Jan. 7, 1807.

12. SELINA (ROBERDEAU) NICKOLLS.—Born in Philadelphia, November 9, 1775; removed with her father to Alexandria, where, in August, 1793, at an early age, she married Scudamore Nickolls, Esq., a lawyer by profession—an Englishman of highly respected family—the youngest brother of the Rev. Robert Boucher Nickolls, chaplain to the Duke of Northumberland. The family afterwards moved to Norfolk, Va., where they resided three years; and after the birth of their eldest child, removed back to Alexandria, where the other children were born. In 1803, when their youngest daughter was two months old, Mr. Nickolls died, and was buried in Christ Church, Norfolk, leaving his family to the care of his brother, James Bruce Nickolls* of Alexandria, who having no children adopted them. There they remained until the taking of Washington by the British, in 1814, obliged them to flee, when they took refuge in Winchester, Va. Five years after, they moved to Lexington, but Mrs. Nickolls' health requiring a warmer climate, they removed to Petersburg, and thence to Richmond, where Mrs. Nickolls died, October 10, 1837, at the age of sixty-two, having outlived all her own sisters and brother Isaac. She is buried in Richmond. Her children are:—

32. i. MARTHA BOSTWICK, b. June 26, 1796.
33. ii. MARY CAROLINE, b. March 2 1799; (Mrs. Holderby.)
34. iii. SELINA ANN CATHERINE, b. March 27, 1801; (Mrs. Irvine.)
35. iv. ANNA BOUCHER, b. ——— 1803; (Mrs. Baxter.)

---

*His wife Mary, born in Liverpool, England, April 18, 1762, married in Philadelphia, March 17, 1784; died in Alexandria, August 5, 1827. The Nickolls family were all staunch members of the Church of England. Among their family portraits, was one of the Very Rev. Dean Boucher, in his robes.

13. A DAUGHTER.—Stillborn, buried with her mother, who died February 15, 1777, in the Presbyterian Church at Lancaster, Pennsylvania.

14. JEANY ROBERDEAU.—Born July 17, 1781, in Philadelphia; baptized August 5th, by Rev. James Sproat, as appears by the register of the Second Presbyterian Church in that city. Undoubtedly died before the birth of the next child, who bore a similar name.

15. JANE (ROBERDEAU) ANNAN.—Born January 22, 1783, in Philadelphia; baptized by Rev. James Sproat, March 30. Removed to Alexandria with her father, and thence to Winchester, where, in 1803, she married Dr. Daniel Annan, a physician, of that place. He was a native of New Jersey, of Scotch descent; whose family had been active in aiding the American Revolution. Mrs. Annan in a limited degree inherited her father's antipathy to a cat; which has also descended to one of her daughters.

Her husband died in Alexandria, Va., in 1836; and Mrs. Annan, in Winchester, Nov. 5, 1842; lies by the side of her father, in Mt. Hebron Cemetery, removed there some years ago from the church-yard, where her grave has the following inscription :

> SACRED
> to the memory of
> MRS. JANE ANNAN,
> wife of
> Daniel Annan, M. D.,
> and daughter of
> General Daniel Roberdeau,
> born, January 22, 1783;
> died, November 5, 1842.
> [Then follows a long quotation from Scripture.]

Her children are :—

36. i. ROBERDEAU.
37. ii. SARAH ANN ROBERDEAU, (Mrs. McCraw.)
38. iii. HERIOT ROBERDEAU.
39. iv. JANE MILLIGAN.
40. v. MARTHA C., (Mrs. Bent.)
41. vi. JAMES ROBERDEAU.
42. vii. JOSEPH ADDISON.

16. JAMES MILLIGAN ROBERDEAU.—Born in Alexandria, Va., April 12, 1785. Removed when a boy with his father to Winchester. At the age of sixteen,

he was sent to Princeton College, and after leaving there, went to the West Indies, to an uncle, John Milligan. After a while, he entered the British army, and attained the rank of major, but resigned his commission at the commencement of the war of 1812. In 1816, he returned to Winchester; but two years after, removed to Fairfax county, Va., where he was married, January 8, 1818, to Mildred Lancaster Denny, who died soon after giving birth to her third child. He was then married a second time, June 20, 1822, to Martha Lane Triplett, who survives him, living now upon her farm, called "Milford," near Centreville, Fairfax county, at the good old age of seventy-four, the only one of her generation now surviving.

She is the daughter of James Lane Triplett and Martha Jennings, his wife, who was daughter to Daniel Jennings, of Virginia, and ——— Linton.

Mr. Roberdeau died March 10, 1832, leaving a numerous family; all born in Centreville, Fairfax county, Va.

By his first wife:—

	i.	HOWARD,	b. Mar. 31, 1819; bapt. Nov. 1; d. unm., Sept. 23, 1830.
43.	ii.	JANE ELIZABETH,	b. May 16, 1820; (Mrs. Powell.)
	iii.	HERIOT,	b. Nov. 30, 1821; d. Dec. 30, 1821.

By his second wife:—

	iv.	HERIOT TRIPLETT,	b. Mar. 27, 1823; (Mrs. Richardson.)
44.	iv.	HERIOT TRIPLETT,	b. Mar. 27, 1823; (Mrs. Richardson.)
	v.	MARTHA JENNINGS,	b. June 24, 1824; d. July 25, 1825.
45.	vi.	MARTHA ANN,	b. Jan. 24, 1826; (Mrs. Allison.)
	vii.	FRANCIS MORRIS,	b. Apr. 25, 1827; d. Mar. 10, 1833.
46.	viii.	ELIZABETH HILL,	b. Aug. 25, 1828; (Mrs. Foote.)
47.	ix.	JAMES DANIEL,	b. Feb. 6, 1830.
	x.	MILDRED LANCASTER,	b. Nov. 12, 1831; d. June 25, 1833.

17. HERIOT (ROBERDEAU) CONRAD.—Born in 1788, in Alexandria, Va.; and removed to Winchester with her father while young, where she was married, Feb. 16, 1809, to Dr. Edward Conrad, an eminent physician of that place; of German descent, as the name denotes. He was for a short time in the army as surgeon of the 8th regiment of infantry, from July, 1799; disbanded in June, 1800. He died Dec. 25, 1821, at midnight, aged forty-eight. Mrs. Conrad survived him nearly half a century, dying April 17, 1867, at the advanced age of seventy-nine; and was buried by the side of her husband, father, and sister, in the old churchyard, Winchester, but subsequently removed to Mount

9

Hebron Cemetery. Her mental and physical faculties were active to the last, and she attained the greatest age of any of the family. Her last words were: "The blood of Christ cleanseth from all sin."

She left two children :—

48. i. JAMES ROBERDEAU.
49. ii. DANIEL.

ONLY CHILD OF ANN (ROBERDEAU) AND WILLIAM CLYMER. [4.]

18. DANIEL CUNYNGHAM CLYMER.—He was born in Philadelphia, April 6, 1748, and baptized in Christ Church, in that city, July 12, 1748. Losing his father at an early age, the care of his education devolved upon his uncle, General Roberdeau, who regarded his nephew with a warm affection, as evinced by the many allusions to him, to be found in the General's letter-book.

Daniel Clymer had the advantages of a good educa-tion. He entered the college of New Jersey, at Prince-ton, and graduated from there in 1766; began the study of law. General Roberdeau thus alludes to him in a letter (1768) to his own uncle, Daniel Cunyngham, of St. Christopher's, after whom his nephew was named: "My nephew, now out of town, is studying the law, having all the advantages of a good education; having obtained by a public examination in one of our seminaries the degree of Bachelor of Arts, promises fair for making, I hope, a tolerable figure in his profession." And again, two years later, regarding some legal matters, speaks of "having committed the affair to my nephew, Daniel C. Clymer, a young chancellor, lately set up in practice, and a most indefatigable creature, with a promise of five per cent. on all he should recover."

Mr. Clymer afterwards attained an enviable position in his profession.

In 1768, Mr. Clymer attended the Second Presbyterian Church, in Philadelphia.

When the Revolution was approaching, Daniel Clymer was one of the first who joined the Associators. It ap-pears by a list dated May 1, 1775, that he joined Captain John Little's company, of the 2d Battalion of Philadel-phia Militia. The company then numbered between 60 and 70 persons, from the "middle part" of the city, among whom were Daniel C. Clymer and Thomas Mc-Kean. Mr. Clymer was elected 1st lieutenant.

On the 22d of June, he was appointed by Congress one of the Signers of Bills of Credit for two millions of dollars; and again, March 9, 1776, for four millions.

This latter year, Mr. Clymer was appointed by the Assembly, to the command of the Rifle Battalion of the City and Liberties of Philadelphia, with the rank of lieutenant-colonel. His commission, bearing date April 8, 1776, and signed by John Morton, Speaker of the Assembly, and afterwards a Signer of the Declaration of Independence, has lately been photographed, making an interesting fac-simile of this "valued and ancient relic of the times."

Soon after his promotion, the Convention to choose two brigadier-generals for the Pennsylvania troops, was called, and Colonel Clymer was chosen one of the delegates to represent his battalion. Of this meeting, an account of which has already been given elsewhere, Colonel Clymer was chosen secretary. The journal of the proceedings kept by him, and now in possession of one of his grandsons, is a valuable record of those times, containing, besides other facts, a complete list of the delegates from the various battalions of the State Militia.

October 29, 1777. In Congress: "A letter from Daniel Clymer to Richard Bache, respecting the confinement of Mr. William Franklin, was laid before Congress and read. Referred to the Board of War." Col. Clymer being at this time Deputy Commissary-General of Prisoners, and the gentleman here referred to was the son of Benjamin Franklin, and late royalist governor of New Jersey, who had been arrested and imprisoned for his opposition to the Colonies.

During the Revolution, Colonel Clymer was Commissioner of Claims of the Treasury, 1777.

In the year 1779 an affair occurred in Philadelphia which created much excitement at the time, and in which Colonel Clymer bore a conspicuous part. A full account may be found in *Watson's Annals of Philadelphia; The Life of Joseph Reed; Hazard's Register*, I., 317, &c., &c.

James Wilson, an earnest patriot and Signer of the Declaration, gave offence to many of the citizens on account of his services as an attorney in behalf of two men executed as traitors; and a mob collected around his house, on the corner of Walnut and Third streets. His friends gathered at his house on the appearance of violence, among them being Morris Bond, George and Daniel Clymer, General Mifflin, &c. They were armed, but destitute of ammunition. In this extremity, while the mob was approaching, General Nichols and Daniel Clymer proceeded hastily to the arsenal at Carpenter's Hall, and filling their pockets with cartridges, returned before the mob had reached the house. The assailants numbered two hundred armed men, accompanied by drums and two pieces of cannon. They soon made an attack on the house, when their fire was returned by the garrison. While preparing to bring their guns to bear, General Joseph Reed, with a detachment of the City Troop, came to the relief of the beseiged. He soon dispersed the mob, but not before several had been killed and wounded on each side. The house which was the scene of this affray was ever afterwards popularly known as "Fort Wilson."

During the closing years of the Revolution, Colonel Clymer removed to Reading, and became one of the leading lawyers in Berks and the adjoining counties.

In October, 1782, Colonel Clymer took his seat in the Pennsylvania Assembly as a representative from Berks county, and was placed on the Committee on Ways and Means, and was again elected the succeeding year.— (*Minutes of Assembly.*)

While in Philadelphia at this time, Colonel Clymer resided in Market street, between Fourth and Fifth streets, as appears by a list of lawyers in that city soon after the peace of 1783, given in *Watson's Annals of Philadelphia.*

Colonel Clymer was married about the year 1782 to Mary Weidner, daughter of Peter and Susan Weidner, of Berks county, who died December 5, 1802, in her forty-sixth year. Colonel Clymer died in Reading, January 25, 1810, in his sixty-second year, leaving issue :—

50. i. ANN,   b. ——, 1782.
51. ii. WILLIAM,   b. March 28, 1788.
52. iii. EDWARD TILGHMAN, b. August 14, 1790.

FOURTH GENERATION.

————————•————————

CHILDREN OF COLONEL ISAAC ROBERDEAU. [5.]

19. MARY ELIZABETH ROBERDEAU.—Born in Germantown, Pennsylvania, March 30, 1795; baptized January 30, 1796. She was a person of the most attractive manners, of great conversational powers, and cultivated musical taste; an intimate friend of Mrs. John Quincy Adams, whose guest she frequently was at the Executive Mansion, and with whom she corresponded until her death. She died unmarried, in Philadelphia, November 15, 1833, and was buried in the burying-ground of the Tenth Presbyterian Church, Walnut street, but subsequently removed to Woodlands Cemetery.

20. SUSAN SHIPPEN ROBERDEAU.—After her mother's death in Philadelphia, removed to Brooklyn, New York, where her sister then resided, with whom she has since lived—in Brooklyn; Charlestown, Massachusetts; and latterly in Washington, D. C.

21. FRANCES SELINA (ROBERDEAU) BUCHANAN.—After her father's death was married in Philadelphia, July 1, 1834, to McKean Buchanan, a purser in the navy, the title being afterwards changed to paymaster.

Mr. Buchanan was born in Baltimore, Maryland, July 27, 1798, but removed young to Philadelphia, where his father soon after died. McKean entered the University of Pennsylvania, and after leaving college, was for a time in mercantile life in the house of Asaph Stone, Esq. He then became a clerk for three years in the Navy Department, while waiting for his commission in the navy; which he received from President Adams, August 21, 1826, and was immediately ordered to take passage in the frigate Brandywine to join the schooner Dolphin, in the Pacific. He subsequently joined the sloop-of-war Vincennes, and in her made a cruise round the world— the first American man-of-war that had done so. He returned to the United States in June, 1830, after an absence of four years. Subsequently Mr. Buchanan sailed in the Falmouth, in the Pacific, an account of which cruise was published by one of the officers, entitled *Three Years in the Pacific*. In 1839–42 he was again ordered to the Pacific, in the noted frigate Constitution. During this cruise Mr. Buchanan, whose duty it was every Sunday to muster the crew, knew every man by sight, and from memory called off the names of the whole four hundred in their proper order.

During the Mexican war Mr. Buchanan was again in the Pacific, on his *fourth* cruise, a very singular circumstance. At this time he was attached to the sloop-of-war Dale, and participated in the capture of Guaymas, where he was made collector of customs.

In 1854–5 he was attached to the steam frigate San Jacinto, carrying to Spain the Hon. Pierre Soulé, the United States Minister, and was, at the minister's request, detailed to escort him to Madrid during threatened troubles. In 1856–8, attached to the steam frigate Wabash, which took prisoners General Walker and fillibusters at San Juan del Norte, Nicaragua.

Paymaster Buchanan's last cruise was in the frigate Congress, during the late war, blockading the James river, and participating in the sanguinary engagement of March 8, 1862, in Hampton Roads, with the Confederate squadron headed by the Virginia, (formerly the Merrimac,) commanded by his own brother, Commodore, afterwards Admiral, Franklin Buchanan. In this battle, familiar to all, Paymaster Buchanan commanded the berth-deck division.

The Virginia, in the beginning of the action, passed the Congress and sank the Cumberland with her prow. The Congress, to avoid a like fate, ran herself aground, and the Virginia being, therefore, obliged to use her guns, took up a raking position astern, where the Congress could bring to bear but two guns. These being soon disabled in this unequal contest, the ship having been set on fire several times by hot shot, and with her captain and one-fourth of the crew killed, after an action of three hours, it was decided to surrender, in accordance with the maxim that where you cannot injure the enemy nor better your own condition, it is your duty to surrender, to avoid needless loss of life. The Congress was then boarded by an officer from one of the Confederate steamers, who announced the officers prisoners, and that the crew would be paroled. But when forty men had been taken on board the steamer for the purpose of landing them, she was driven off by the batteries on shore, which had still kept up their fire. The officers and remainder of the crew then came on shore in the ship's boats, and the Congress blew up at midnight with a terrific explosion.

After the Congress surrendered, Commodore Buchanan appeared outside of the Virginia's iron plating, where he was severely wounded in the thigh by a minie ball from on shore; and was in consequence not in command the next day, when the Virginia fought the Monitor.*

Probably no action ever presented such disproportion of killed and wounded. It was at too close quarters for a shot to wound—it killed. On the Congress alone, of 434 souls there were killed 94; wounded 29, of whom 8 or 10 died the next day; prisoners 40; unharmed 271. The other vessels of the squadron also engaged, but the Congress and Cumberland bore the brunt of the battle.

Thus, in this first day's fight, with fearful carnage was inaugurated a revolution in naval warfare—the first engagement of an iron-plated vessel.

A few months before this battle Paymaster Buchanan was placed on the retired list of the navy, in accordance with the act of Congress of December, 21, 1861, which retired all officers of the navy over sixty-two years of age, or who had been forty-five years in the service.

Besides the above-mentioned service, Paymaster Buchanan has been stationed at the several navy yards at Philadelphia, Pensacola, New York, (both navy yard and practice ship Savannah,) Boston, at the yard, receiving ship, and twice as inspector. After leaving the Boston navy yard in 1853 he made Charlestown his home.†

---

*Commodore Buchanan, after this battle, received the thanks of the Confederate Congress, and was promoted over the heads of his superiors to be Admiral, and senior officer of the Confederate Navy. He commanded the Confederate squadron at Mobile in the desperate encounter of August 5, 1864, and being overwhelmed by numbers, and again wounded, was taken prisoner. He wholly recovered from both these wounds, and died at his home in Maryland, May 11, 1874. He was a man of remarkable strength of mind and of body, and bore a high reputation in both navies as an accomplished officer.—(See the *N. E. Gen. and Hist. Register*, xxviii., 364.)

†The details may be found in Hamersly's *Living Officers of the U. S. Navy.*

Paymaster Buchanan's service may be divided into sea service, 16 years, 0 months; shore duty, 16 years, 6 months; on leave, 12 years, 1 month; and during this long official life he has sailed in nine vessels, served eight times at shore stations, made four cruises to the Pacific, passing once round the Cape of Good Hope and seven times round Cape Horn, and has taken part in two wars. He was on duty but a few months before his death; a short time previous to which Congress reorganized the staff corps of the navy, whereby he acquired the title of pay-director, with the rank of commodore, assimilated to that of brigadier-general in the army. He was a man of exceedingly large acquaintance, it being a frequent remark of his that he had met friends in every part of the world in which he had sailed. He was beloved and respected by all who knew him, prompt and accurate in the discharge of his duties and in accounting for the millions that have passed through his hands during nearly half a century. He died at Charlestown, Massachusetts, March 18, 1871, from the shock his system received during the late unhappy war, and is buried in Mount Auburn Cemetery.

Ancestry of Pay-Director Buchanan.—The chart herewith given, compiled from private sources, explains itself. Dr. George Buchanan, the first of the family in this country, was a Scotchman by birth, a descendant of the ancient clan Buchanan, of the Lenny branch,* his home in Scotland being called Auchentorlie. He married in this country, and thus came into possession of a large estate, which he called Druid Hill, and which was sold a few years since to the City of Baltimore for $500,000, and is now Druid Hill Park. The ancient family burying-ground within the park is retained as a reservation to the family.

Dr. George Buchanan, grandson of the first-named, delivered an oration upon slavery, July 4th, 1791, which has been considered so rare and valuable a pamphlet as to give rise to the publication by W. F. Poole, of his *Anti-Slavery Opinions Before the Year* 1800, in which is a fac-simile of the pamphlet.

---

*Many of the same name in the United States are descended from four brothers of the *Curbeth* branch, contemporaries of Dr. George Buchanan, who settled in Ireland, they or their children afterwards removing to America. The late President James Buchanan is descended from one of these brothers.

Ancestry of Pay-Director McKEAN BUCHANAN, who married F. Selina Roberdeau.

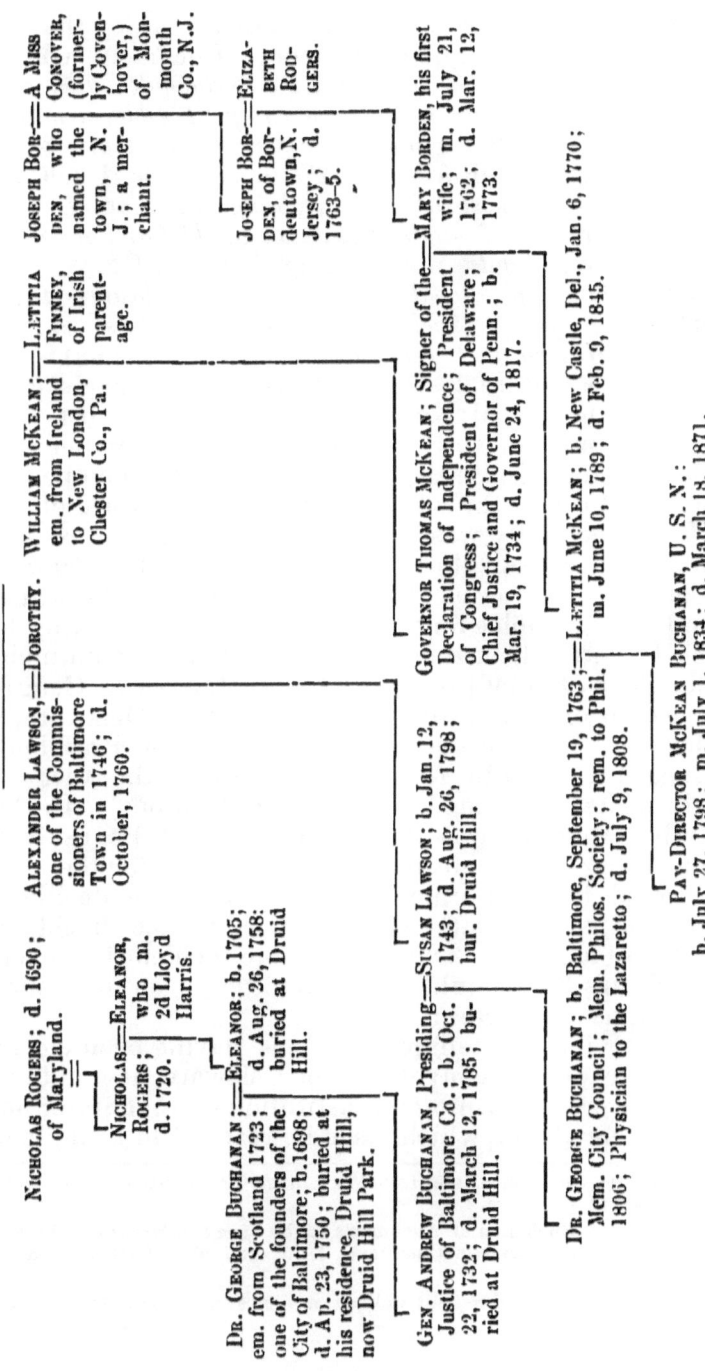

NICHOLAS ROGERS; d. 1690; of Maryland.

NICHOLAS=ELEANOR, ROGERS; d. 1720. | who m. 2d Lloyd Harris.

DR. GEORGE BUCHANAN; em. from Scotland 1723; one of the founders of the City of Baltimore; b. 1698; d. Ap. 23, 1750; buried at his residence, Druid Hill, now Druid Hill Park.=ELEANOR; b. 1705; d. Aug. 26, 1758; buried at Druid Hill.

ALEXANDER LAWSON,=DOROTHY. one of the Commissioners of Baltimore Town in 1746; d. October, 1760.

WILLIAM McKEAN;=LÆTITIA FINNEY, em. from Ireland to New London, Chester Co., Pa. | of Irish parentage.

JOSEPH BOR-=A MISS DEN, who named the town, N. J.; a merchant. | CONOVER, (formerly Covenhover,) of Monmouth Co., N.J.

JOSEPH BORDEN, of Bordentown, N. Jersey; d. 1763-5.=ELIZABETH RODGERS.

GEN. ANDREW BUCHANAN, Presiding=SUSAN LAWSON; b. Jan. 12, Justice of Baltimore Co.; b. Oct. 22, 1732; d. March 12, 1785; buried at Druid Hill. | 1743; d. Aug. 26, 1798; bur. Druid Hill.

GOVERNOR THOMAS McKEAN; Signer of the=MARY BORDEN, his first Declaration of Independence; President of Congress; President of Delaware; Chief Justice and (Governor of Penn.; b. Mar. 19, 1734; d. June 24, 1817. | wife; m. July 21, 1762; d. Mar. 12, 1773.

DR. GEORGE BUCHANAN; b. Baltimore, September 19, 1763;=LÆTITIA McKEAN; b. New Castle, Del., Jan. 6, 1770; Mem. City Council; Mem. Philos. Society; rem. to Phil. 1806; Physician to the Lazaretto; d. July 9, 1808. | m. June 10, 1789; d. Feb. 9, 1845.

PAY-DIRECTOR McKEAN BUCHANAN, U. S. N.: b. July 27, 1798; m. July 1, 1834; d. March 18, 1871.

The arms of the Buchanan family;* as by the book-plate of the last-named Dr. George Buchanan (who carried the arms *within a border, quarterly gules and argent, for difference*); are: *Or, a lion rampant sable, armed and langued gules, within a double tressure flowered and counter-flowered with fleur-de-lys of the second, for* BUCHANAN; *quartered with those of* LENNY, *being sable, on a chevron between three boars' heads erased, two in chief and one in base, argent, muzzled gules, a cinq-foil of the first.* CREST, *a hand coupé holding up a ducal cap, within a laurel branch disposed orlewise, proper. Ancient motto above the crest,* AUDACES JUVO. *Modern motto below the shield,* LEONIS NOBILIS IRA.†

On the maternal side, Paymaster Buchanan's grand-father, Thomas McKean,‡ was one of the most distinguished men of the Revolution. As a member of the Continental Congress, he was the only member who served through the whole term until the peace of 1783. He consequently was a Signer of the Declaration of Independence. At the time he represented *Delaware* in Congress, he was elected Chief Justice of *Pennsylvania,* and held the office for 22 years, both States claiming him. "When we reflect that at the time of his appointment to the office of chief justice, he was a Member of Congress, Speaker of the Assembly, President of Delaware, and that, in 1781, he occupied the station of President of Congress, one can form an estimate of the vast labor which he performed."—(*National Portraits.*) In 1799, Judge McKean was elected Governor of Pennsylvania, and being thrice elected, filled the office for the constitutional limit of nine years. In 1803, he declined to become a candidate for the office of Vice-President of the United States. One remarkable incident in Governor McKean's life, should not be omitted, even in so short a sketch as the present.

" Receiving intelligence of his having been elected a member of the convention in Delaware, assembled for the purpose of forming a constitution for that State; he departed for Dover, which place he reached in a single day.

---

* For the Buchanans, see *Griffith's Annals of Baltimore;* and *Scharf's Chronicles of Baltimore.*

† See, also, Buchanan of Auchmar's *Essay upon the Surname of Buchanan; Glasgow,* 1723; reprinted, Cincinnati, 1849; and, also, *Burke's Landed Gentry; &c., &c.*

‡ Pronounced, *McKane,* not McKeen, as almost universally but erroneously given.

Although excessively fatigued on his arrival, at the request of a committee of gentlemen of the convention, he retired to his room at the public inn, where he was employed the whole night in preparing a constitution for the future government of the State. *This he did without the least assistance, and even without the aid of a book.* At ten o'clock the next morning, it was presented to the convention, by whom it was unanimously adopted."— (Ibid. ; also *Goodrich's Lives of the Signers ; Sanderson's Lives.*)

One of Governor McKean's daughters, who "was considered a great beauty," married Senior Don Carlos Martenez, Marquis d'Yrujo, the Spanish Minister to this country. Her portrait (from the original, by Stuart, now in the possession of Henry Pratt McKean, Esq., of Philadelphia) is given in Griswold's *Republican Court.* Her son succeeded to his father's titles, and afterwards became the Duke of Sotomayor, *d. j. u.;* and grandee of the first class; and rose to high civil authority in Spain, having been ambassador to England, then prime minister, and at the time of his death, in 1856, *mayor domo* of the queen's palace.

After this digression, to return to the subject of this section :—Mrs. F. S. Buchanan, after her husband's death, removed the following year to Washington, D. C., where she now resides.

Her children are :—

53. i. ROBERDEAU, b. Nov. 22, 1839.
54. ii. LÆTITIA McKEAN, b. Dec. 24, 1842; (Mrs. Fife.)

CHILDREN OF ANN AND JONATHAN SWIFT. [7.]

22. WILLIAM ROBERDEAU SWIFT.—Born August 29, 1787, in Alexandria, Virginia, where he became a merchant. He was married, August 1, 1815, to Mary Donaldson, daughter of Edward Harper, of that place. At the dinner given to Lafayette, February 22, 1825, by Washington Alexandria Lodge of Freemasons, of which he was a member, he gave the toast, " Lafayette: one of the master workmen who assisted in fitting the keystone to the triumphal arch at Yorktown, when a victorious termination was effected, of our glorious struggle for freedom and independence." Mr. Swift afterwards removed to Baltimore, where he was a merchant for a

number of years, and thence to New York, and subse-
sequently to Washington, North Carolina, where he died
in October, 1833, leaving no children. His widow died
April 30, 1870, in her eighty-third year.

23. ISAAC BOSTWICK SWIFT.—Born February
2, 1795; died July 18, 1797. The church register, probably erroneously, gives the name Isaac *Roberdeau;* the
family record is as above.

24. ANN FOSTER (SWIFT) PATTEN.—Born October 11, 1802; baptized June 12, 1803; married January 13, 1829, by the Rev. Wm. S. Read, at Lynch-
burg, Virginia, to Jonathan T. Patten, afterwards a prosperous wholesale merchant in New York city, where they
still reside, both enjoying excellent health at their advanced years, Mr. Patten having passed his eighty-fourth
birthday October 18, 1875. Their children, all born in
New York, are:—

	i.	JULIA A.,	d. æ. 4 y. 7 mo.
55.	ii.	VIRGINIA,	(Mrs. Houghton.)
56.	iii.	MARY SWIFT,	(Mrs. Tinson.)
57.	iv.	WILLIAM SWIFT.	
58.	v.	JOSEPHINE,	(Mrs. Ward.)
59.	vi.	JAMES AUGUSTUS.	
	vii.	JULIA A.	
	viii.	ANN ROBERDEAU,	d. æ. 1 y. 7 mo.
	ix.	OCTAVIA,	d. æ. 3 y.

25. MARY SELINA (SWIFT) ALLISON.—Born
January 18, 1805, in Alexandria; baptized May 21; married while her mother lived at Petersburg, by the Rev.
B. Rice, August 8, 1826, to Henry Allison. He was
born in Stafford county, Virginia, December 28, 1793;
(and previous to this marriage had a first wife, Jane
Campbell Voss, married in Petersburg, August 19, 1819,
who died November 21, 1820.) They moved to Missouri,
where Mr. Allison died, December 26, 1871, in Smith-
ton, Pettis county, Mrs. Allison resides in Brownville,
Missouri. Their children:—

60.	i.	WILLIAM HENRY, b. April 24, 1828.
61.	ii.	ROBERDEAU, b. Jan. 29, 1830.
62.	iii.	JANE CAMPBELL, b. Jan. 9, 1832; (Mrs. Funkhouser; after-wards Mrs. Barry.)

CHILDREN OF MARY AND THOMAS M. PATTEN. [11.]

26. MARY ANN (PATTEN) WOLFE.—Born April
5, 1795; married May 14, 1816, to Dr. Thomas Wolfe,

a native of Winchester, Virginia. (By a previous marriage he had Alfred, Addison, Catherine, and Sidney. Catherine, now Mrs. William Russell, of Winchester, alone survives.)

He was educated in Edinburg, where he studied medicine, and afterwards graduated in London, where he was connected with the hospitals. He afterwards practiced in Philadelphia. They were married and resided in Winchester, but removed to Culpepper Court-House in 1818, where Mrs. Wolfe died August 23, 1822. Dr. Wolfe died December 25, 1825.

The following obituary was written upon the death of Mrs. Wolfe:

In the death of this estimable woman society is bereft of one of its brightest ornaments. . . . . Nature had cast Mrs. Wolfe in one of her fairest moulds, and endowed her with a mind of the first order, to which were united a polish and affability of manners and conversation, and a sweetness of disposition that could not fail to secure her the affection of all to whom she became known. She entered into the married state at a very early age, and at once assumed the responsibility of a mother to a family of children by a previous marriage. It was in this character,—a character calculated but too frequently to generate odious doubts and suspicions, that her virtues shone most preëminent. She was herself blessed with several children, but unto her, all were alike, all shared her affectionate and maternal care, and for the temporal of all did she evince equal solicitude. The deep interest manifested for her by her stepchildren during her long illness, and the grief with which they were overwhelmed on receiving information of her death, proved how near and how dear she was to them. In this character is Mrs. Wolfe a model well worthy of imitation by those similarly circumstanced. As a wife she was not less conspicuous—affectionate, politely attentive, prudent, and discreet, she entitled herself to the unlimited love and regard of her disconsolate husband. As a sister her memory will ever be cherished and revered by her orphan brothers and sisters whom she has left behind. They have, indeed, lost their best friend and faithful adviser. As a neighbor and friend she was obliging and sincere. Few women have died more regretted; none, perhaps, while living were more respected.

Her children:—

63.	i.	MARY DE NEALE,	b. May 17, 1817, (Mrs. Morgan, afterwards Mrs. Harmon.)
64.	ii.	THOMAS ROBERDEAU,	b. May 7, 1819.
65.	iii.	JOSEPH LEWIS,	b. Jan. 21, 1821; d. Nov. 11, 1833.
	iv.	JAMES EDWARD,	b. Jan. 22, 1822; d. in July, 1822.

27. ISAAC ROBERDEAU PATTEN.—Born September 20, 1796; baptized November 14; died of consumption, in Alexandria, December 7, 1814. During his illness he kept a diary, in which he frequently noted his thoughts and impressions of his coming end—unusual for one so young. He was buried from Colonel De Neale's house.

28. JOSEPH MAY PATTEN.—Born May 26, 1799; baptized September 5, 1800. Accompanied his father to Louisiana after his mother's death, where he settled and became a planter. He married, November 9, 1826, Ann M. Morehouse, of Washita Parish, La., who was born September 9, 1807. He died of consumption at his home, called Sherwood Plantation, June 23, 1841. (His widow, six years after, married Mr. May, who died in 1861.) She herself died August 6, 1872, and is buried by her first husband, Mr. Patten, in the little burial ground on their plantation. Joseph M. Patten's children, all born on the plantation :—

66. i.   SELINA ANN,   b. July 12, 1829, (Mrs. Kent.)
    ii. ELIZA CORNELIA,   b. Feb. 17, 1832; d. Sept. 20, 1837.
    iii. JOSEPH MAY,   b. Nov. 13, 1834; d. Nov. 9, 1837.
67. iv. NARCISSA MATILDA, b. Jan. 5, 1837, (Mrs. Williams.)
    v.   JOSEPHINE MAY,   b. Mar. 7, 1841; d. Sept. 30, 1842.

29. HARRIET ROZIER (PATTEN) MILLER.—Born November 12, 1803, in Alexandria; married January 29, 1819, at Williamsport, Maryland, to John W. Miller. (This family is German, descended from George Miller and Julia Ann Coolmenan, whose son, John Jacob, was born at Glenhausen, three leagues from Frankfort, July 31, 1731. Emigrated to North America in 1756, under General Abercrombie, and was afterwards a major in the American army; and married Catharine Spansaler, who was born in Lancaster, Pennsylvania, March 19, 1741, and died in Fredericktown, Maryland, December 21, 1811; he died November 25, 1810, leaving nine children, of whom John W. was one of the youngest, born in Fredericktown, August 11, 1783; and married, first, Julia Heiskell, who died in 1813, aged 19, leaving two children—Peter Jacob, who died aged 18, and Julia Heiskill, now Mrs. Doctor William Bailey of Tennessee. He married, secondly, Harriet R. Patten as above.) They lived in Winchester, Virginia, where all their children were born. They then

removed, in 1840, to Lake Providence, Louisiana, where both died of yellow fever in September, 1853, during the fearful prevalence of that epidemic, of which their daughter Selina also died the same month. Their eldest daughter Mary, Mrs. Dunn, after her parents' death, took her six small children, and brother and sister, the eldest being under ten years of age, and brought them safely up the river to her sister's plantation in Washington county, Mississippi. There she lost her husband of the same disease; and herself died of grief, a few weeks after.

Mrs. Harriet R. Miller's children, all born in Winchester, Virginia, are :—

	i.	WILLIAM SWIFT,	b. Dec. 15, 1820 ;	d. May 18, 1822.
68	ii.	MARY CATHERINE,	b. Apr. 24, 1823 ;	(Mrs. Dunn.)
	iii.	ELIZABETH MANTZ,	b. Feb. 3, 1825 ;	d. Aug. 25, 1825.
69	iv.	LAURA PATTEN,	b. June 4, 1826 ;	(Mrs Pierce.)
	v.	HARRIET ROBERDEAU,	b. Jan. 1, 1828 ;	d. Jan. 17, 1831.
	vi.	HARRIET ROBERDEAU,	b. Mar. 17, 1830 ;	d. Dec. 27, 1833.
70	vii.	JOSEPHINE WALTZ,	b. June 9, 1832 ;	(Mrs. Lancaster.)
71	viii.	ANNIE MARIA,	b. Aug. 29, 1834 ;	(Mrs. Mullins.)
	ix.	JOHN W., JR.,	b. Dec. 18, 1836 ;	d. Aug. 28, 1837.
	x.	SELINA MATILDA,	b. Dec. 24, 1837 ;	d. unm., of yellow fever, at Lake Providence, La., in Sept., 1853.
	xi.	THOMAS PATTEN,	b. Mch. 29, 1840 ;	d. Nov 5, 1840.
	xii.	ANNETTA JANE,	b. Sept. 30, 1841 ;	d. Sept. 1, 1842.
72	xiii.	FANNIE MORGAN,	b. Nov. 21, 1843 ;	(Mrs. Caldwell.)
73	xiv	ALBERT PATTEN,	b. Sept. 25, 1845.	

30. **SELINA BLAIR (PATTEN) WHEAT.**—Born in Alexandria, Virginia, September 12, 1805 ; baptized March 9, 1806, by Rev. Dr. Muir, and named after the wife of her uncle, Isaac. She was married, March 10, 1825, to the Rev. John Thomas Wheat, of Washington city. He was born November 15, 1801, and studied for the ministry under the Rev. Dr. Wilmer, of Alexandria. While studying, he also, at the age of twenty-one, instructed thirty youths in the higher branches ; under his good instruction and discipline, this school afterwards increased to eighty or ninety pupils, requiring two assistants. Mr. Wheat was then, in 1825, admitted to the diaconate of the Episcopal Church, by Bishop Moore, of Virginia, in Christ Church, Alexandria ; and a presbyter, in 1826, by Bishop Kemper, of Maryland, in St. Paul's Church, Baltimore. The next year, he took charge of a church in Wheeling, Virginia. From 1835–'8, was a rector of St. Paul's, New Orleans. In 1839–'49, in Nashville, Tennessee : leaving there to accept the chair of

Professor of Rhetoric, in the University of North Carolina, at Chapel Hill, where he remained till 1860. Then,
rector of Christ Church, Little Rock, Arkansas, 1860–'7.
During the war, in 1862, he was a chaplain in the Confederate Army. From July, 1867, rector of the Monu-
mental Church of St. Lazarus, at Memphis, Tennessee,
which he resigned, in July, 1873, after nearly half a century of clerical labor. The farewell services, on his taking leave of his congregation, were very impressive.
Previous to the opening of the regular services, Dr.
Carmichael, of a neighboring church, made an address,
in which he paid a just tribute to Dr. Wheat's high
standing and abilities, as showing the effect of his eloquence upon his hearers. "Sixteen years ago," says *The
Memphis Appeal,* " when the speaker was a young lawyer in Fredericksburg, Virginia, Dr. Wheat delivered an
address to the young men of that town. The fervid
eloquence, the lofty piety of the minister, and the great
and glorious truths he revealed that day, were not without their effect upon every one there; and at once induced him to resolve upon the study of the ministry.
This resolve was carried into effect, and it was owing to
the earnest efforts of Dr. Wheat on that day, that he (the
speaker) became a minister. His gratitude, his appre-
ciation for the good man who had induced him to espouse
the cause of the Lord, were deep and lasting." Besides
his clerical labors, Dr. Wheat has filled the honorable
position of a Delegate to the General Convention of the
Episcopal Church, during the triennial meetings of 1838
–'41,–'44,–'47,–'68,–'71.

In 1846, Dr. Wheat received the degree of Doctor of
Divinity, from the University of Nashville. In 1866, he
published a "*Preparation for the Holy Communion.*" In 1875,
this venerable couple celebrated their Golden Wedding,
on which occasion Dr. Wheat published a poem, dedicated to his wife, entitled "*Reminiscences of My Pre-Nuptial
Life,*" containing many interesting incidents.

Their children are :—

74. i.	CHATHAM ROBERDEAU,	b. April 9, 1826.
75. ii.	SELINA PATTEN,	b. June 12, 1827 ; (Mrs. Seay.)
iii.	A CHILD,	died at birth.
76. iv.	JOHN THOMAS,	b. Dec. 3, 1830.
77. v.	JOSEPHINE MAY,	b. Feb. 22, 1833 ; (Mrs. Shober.)
vi.	A CHILD,	died at birth.
vii.	REGINALD HEBER,	b. La., Jan.25, 1837; d. June, 7, 1839.
78. viii.	LEONIDAS POLK,	b. May 5, 1841.

31. THOMAS ROBERDEAU PATTEN.—Born in Alexandria, January 7, 1807; baptized August 9. After his mother's death, he left Alexandria at an early age, and went to sea. Three or four years after, he unexpectedly met his elder brother, on Red river, Louisiana, and in consequence, settled in that state; and in 1837, married Mrs. Matilda M. Childers, *née* McCraw. (She had, by her former marriage, a daughter, Narcissa, who died shortly before her father, aged about 16 years.) Mr. Patten died without issue, of consumption, on his plantation, October 27, 1850, and his widow followed him in 1862.

CHILDREN OF SELINA ROBERDEAU AND SCUDAMORE NICKOLLS. [12.]

32. MARTHA BOSTWICK NICKOLLS.—Born in Norfolk, Virginia, June 26, 1796. She never married, but lived with her sister, Mrs. Baxter, during her lifetime, and died in Harrisonburg, Virginia, August 30, 1863.

33. MARY CAROLINE (NICKOLLS) HOLDERBY. —Born in Alexandria, March 2, 1799; married in Petersburg, May 13, 1824, to Andrew S. Holderby. He was born in Brunswick county, Virginia, in 1800; but lived in Petersburg for a number of years, where he was a prominent bank officer; a man widely known and honored for his integrity and earnest piety. He was for thirty years a ruling elder of the Presbyterian Church, in that place; where he died, February 14, 1862. Mrs. Holderby survives her husband, and in 1866, removed to Alabama, with her son, with whom she has since resided. She is in the enjoyment of good health, and unusual activity of mind and body at her advanced age; and numbers more years than any other of the family.*

Her children, both born in Petersburg, Virginia, are:—

    79. i. ANDREW ROBERDEAU, b. Jan. 25, 1838.
       ii. SELINA FRANCES,   b. July 27, 1840.

34. SELINA ANN CATHARINE (NICKOLLS) IRVINE.—Born in Alexandria, March 27, 1801; mar-

---

* With the exception of one, who is connected by marriage.

ried November 3, 1822, in Lexington, to John Irvine of
Virginia. He was a commission merchant in Lexington,
Virginia; and at the time of his death, in April, 1833,
was in the iron business at Clifton Forge, Alleghany
county. His remains were removed to Lexington, and
there buried. Mrs. Irvine now lives in Richmond, Virginia, where both her children were born:—

   80. i. SELINA ROBERDEAU,   b. Oct 10, 1823; (Mrs. Sizer.)
      ii. LAFAYETTE,   b. May, 1825; d. Sept., 1825.

35. ANNA BOUCHER (NICKOLLS) BAXTER.—

Born in Alexandria, Virginia, in the year 1803, and was
married in Lexington, Rockbridge county, October 26,
1829, to Sidney Smith Baxter, Esq., second son of the
Rev. George A. Baxter,* (Rector of the Washington
Academy, and afterwards president of the same when
the academy was raised to the rank of college; and latterly, professor of Pastoral Theology in the Union Theo-
logical Seminary,) and of Annie Fleming, his wife,
daughter of Col. William Fleming, a Scotchman. Mr.
Baxter was born in Lexington, Virginia, November 18,
1802; graduated at Washington College in 1820; and
was licensed to plead law at the age of twenty-one years.
In early life he made a profession of religion, united with
the Presbyterian Church, and for many years was a ruling
elder. After his marriage as above, he continued to practice law in Rockbridge and the adjoining counties, until
December, 1834, when he was elected Attorney-General of
the State of Virginia, and removed his family to Richmond. He held this office for seventeen years, with
great honor to himself and satisfaction to the State.
While in Richmond, he sustained a heavy affliction—the
death of Mrs. Baxter from brain fever, September 2,
1846; being very pious, amiable, and energetic, her loss
was felt deeply, not only in her own family, but by a
large circle of friends. Judge Baxter—for so he was
styled by courtesy, in consideration of the high standing
he had acquired in his profession, although he never held
that position—Judge Baxter, then in 1852 or 3, removed
to Washington, where his legal abilities soon secured
him a large and profitable practice; while his social
qualities and general fund of knowledge, won him many

---

*See *Foote's Sketches in Virginia, Second Series,* for a long account of Dr.
Baxter and his professional labors.

friends, and made him a welcome and honored guest in the circles of the good and learned. He remained in Washington until 1861, when his sympathy for his native State led him to sacrifice all and return thither; where he held several offices under the Confederate government, devoting himself heartily to the cause he had espoused, although physically unable to take the field. Since then, he has been engaged in the practice of his profession in southwest Virginia, making Abingdon, Washington county, his residence.

Their children are :—

	i.	James Nickolls,	b. Lexington, 1831 : d. Lex., 1836.
81.	ii.	George Addison,	b. Lexington, Nov. 11, 1833.
82.	iii.	Mary Selina,	b. Lexington, Aug. 29, 1836; (Mrs. Coulling.)
	iv.	Sidney Smith, Jr.,	b. Richmond, 1837 ; d. P. Ed. co., 1839.
83.	v.	Martha Nickolls,	b. Richmond, Sept. 30, 1839 ; (Mrs. Spotts.)
84.	vi.	William Fleming.	b. Richmond, Oct. 15, 1841.
	vii.	Anna Lee,	b. Richmond, Aug. 29, 1844; d. Richmond, Aug. 27, 1846.

CHILDREN OF JANE (ROBERDEAU) AND DR. DANIEL ANNAN. [15.]

36. ROBERDEAU ANNAN.—Born March 31, 1804; married Helen McCormick of Virginia, and removed to St. Louis, where he was a merchant, and there died without issue, December 15, 1852. His widow survives him, living in that city.

37. SARAH ANN ROBERDEAU (ANNAN) McCRAW.—Born March 16, 1806; removed to Alabama and then to Louisiana. For a time she lived with her relative, Mr. Thomas R. Patten, in that state, at whose house she was married, March 6, 1843, to Samuel Dalton McCraw, (a nephew of Mrs. Matilda M. Patten,) a planter, who was born in Surrey county, Louisiana, December 10, 1810, and died March 6, 1849. Mrs. McCraw formerly resided in Monticello, at Lake Providence, and now in Midway, Richland Parish, Louisiana.

Her issue, one child :—

85. i. Sallie Jean, b. Feb. 27, 1845, Carroll Parish ; (Mrs. Cochran.)

38. HERIOT ROBERDEAU ANNAN.—Born in Winchester; now living in Leesburg, Va.

39. JANE MILLIGAN ANNAN.—Born in Winchester; now living in Western Virginia, with her brother Joseph.

40. MARTHA C. (ANNAN) BENT.—Born in Winchester; married, December 23, 1845, William L. Bent, of Winchester; who, before the late war, was secretary of an insurance company, and had charge of their valuables on their removal to Farmville. He is now an insurance agent and master commissioner in chancery in Winchester. They have no children.

41. JAMES ROBERDEAU ANNAN.—Born in Winchester, Virginia. He married Priscilla Isabella Perry, October 13, 1841, and lived in Cumberland, Maryland, where all his children where born. Mrs. Annan died March 19, 1859, and is buried in Cumberland. Mr. Annan removed from there during the late war and lives now in Baltimore, Maryland. Their children are:—

    86. i.　ROBERDEAU.
    87. ii.　ROGER PERRY.
    88. iii.　DANIEL.
        iv.　LUCY CALMES.
        v.　WILLIAM LEWIS.
        vi.　MARY ISABELLA, deceased.
        vii.　HERIOT JANE.

42. JOSEPH ADDISON ANNAN.—Born February 7, 1820, in Winchester. Removed to Cumberland, Maryland, and from thence, about the year 1841, to West Virginia; where he was married, November 20, 1845, to Sophia S., eldest daughter of Henry Hauser, of Preston county, (who was born February 27, 1825, at German Settlement, in that county.) They now reside in Rowlesburg, where Mr. Annan is in business as a merchant. Their children are:—

	i.	DANIEL HENRY,	b. Sept. 3, 1846, Green Glades, Md.; d. Jan 5, 1860, Rowlesburg, Va.
89.	ii.	WILLIAM BENT,	b. July 18, 1848, Green Glades.
	iii.	JAMES ATKINSON,	b. Aug. 1, 1851, at German Settlement.
	iv.	LAWRENCE HAUSER,	b. March 22, 1856, Rowlesburg; d. March 20, 1858, Rowlesburg.
	v.	OLIVER ABBOTT,	b. Ap. 12, 1858, Rowlesburg.
	vi.	VIRGINIA MAY,	b. May 9, 1860, Rowlesburg.

CHILDREN OF JAMES M. ROBERDEAU. [16.]

43. JANE ELIZABETH (ROBERDEAU) POWELL.—Born May 16, 1820; married, June 13, 1841, to

Walter Randolph Powell. Both are now living in Fairfax county, Virginia. Their children, all born there :—

  i.   JAMES ROBERDEAU.
  ii.   DALLAS MILLIGAN.
  iii.   WILLIAM BEVERLY, deceased.
  iv.   MILDRED LANCASTER.
  vi.   JOSEPH HOWARD.
  vii.   VIRGINIA ROBERDEAU.
  viii. MARTHA ELIZABETH.
  ix.   ELLA JONES.
  x.   WALTER RANDOLPH, JR.

44. HERIOT TRIPLETT (ROBERDEAU) RICH-ARDSON.—Born March 27, 1823; married, September 23, 1841, to Richard Alexander Richardson, at "Milford." She died April 13, 1853. Her husband survives and lives in Centreville, Fairfax county. Their children :—

        i.   ALICE MORRIS,   deceased.
  90.   ii.   JAMES WILLIAM, b. Ap. 26, 1845.
  91.   iii. HERIOT VIRGINIA, (Mrs. Triplett.)
        iv.   MARY ANNETTE.
        v.   MARTHA LINTON.

45. MARTHA ANN (ROBERDEAU) ALLISON.—Born January 24, 1826; married, October 14, 1858, to James Gordon Allison. He was a descendant of the Gordons of Aberdeen, and resided at Fairfax Court-House, until the commencement of the war, engaging in mercantile life. He then removed to Richmond, and subsequently to Orange Court-House, where Mrs. Allison continued to reside while her husband was in the Confederate Army. Mr. Allison died suddenly of camp fever, Nov. 17, 1864, near Richmond. After his death, his widow returned to her mother's farm at Centreville, where she lived until her death, January 20, 1873, and where her children now reside under the care of their grandmother. Their children :—

  i.   ELIZABETH GORDON,   died in Richmond about 1861.
  ii.   ELIZA CHATHAM.
  iii. JAMES GORDON ROBERDEAU.

46. ELIZABETH HILL (ROBERDEAU) FOOTE.—Born August 25, 1828; married by the Rev. L. Marders, July 29, 1845, at the early age of seventeen, to Stephen Daniel Foote. He was a resident of Fairfax county until 1858, when he removed his family to Texas and engaged prosperously in business. He died in Columbus, Texas, July 21, 1871, aged forty-three. His

widow and children then removed to East Bernard,
Wharton county, and subsequently to Quinan, Texas,
where they now reside.   Their children are :—

	i.	WILLIAM STEPHEN,	b. June 6, 1846, Fairfax co.; d. July 24, 1847.
92.	ii.	JULIA ANN,	b. Dec. 30, 1847 ; (Mrs. Spooner.)
	iii.	MARTHA JENNINGS,	b. May 19, 1850, Fairfax co.
	iv.	HENRY STEPHEN,	b. March 9, 1852, Fairfax co.
	v.	LILLIE DALE,	b. March 4, 1854, Fairfax co.
	vi.	ELIZABETH HILL,	b. Dec. 20, 1455, Fairfax co ; d. Dec. 18, 1857.
	vii.	JAMES ROBERDEAU,	b. Jan. 5, 1858, Fairfax co.
	viii.	BETTIE JEAN,	b. March 1, 1860, Colorado co., Texas.
	ix.	CORA HILL,	b. Dec. 10, 1861, Colorado co., Texas.
	x.	ALBERT HARRISON,	b. March 5. 1864, Colorado co., Texas.
	xi.	ALEXANDER,	b. Dec. 8, 1865. Colorado co., Texas.; d. June 20, 1866.
	xii.	EDWARD RANDALL,	b. Oct. 9, 1867, Galveston, Texas; d. Oct. 23, 1867.
	xiii.	STEPHEN ALEXANDER,	b. April 12, 1870, Bryan, Brazos co., Texas.

47. JAMES DANIEL ROBERDEAU, *the only head
of a family now bearing the surname.*—Born in Virginia,
February 6, 1830. He went to Texas about the year
1850, and engaged in mercantile life in Galveston. During the late war he entered the Confederate army and
was Captain of Company B, 5th Texas Regiment, of
General Hood's Texas Brigade. The brigade was ordered to Virginia, and participated in the battles of Seven
Pines, Gaines' Farm, Malvern Hill, Freeman's Ford, the
Second Manassas, South Mountain, Fredericksburg,
Gettysburg, &c. Then being ordered west, was engaged
at Chickamauga, Knoxville, Bean's Station, and Straw-
berry Plains. Again being ordered to Virginia, the
brigade was placed in General Longstreet's Corps, and
came up as the reserve at the battle of the Wilderness,
May 5, 1864. Captain Roberdeau was taken prisoner
and retained for many months in 1863–4. After the war
he resumed his mercantile business in Galveston, but removed in 1874 to Weimar, Colorado county. Captain
Roberdeau was married, November 30, 1865, to William
Sarepta McCormick, daughter of W. B. and Ann Virginia (Millan) McCormick, of Fairfax county, Virginia.
Their issue :—

i.	ELIZABETH BLACKISTON,	b. Nov. 28, 1866 ; d. Jan. 17, 1868.
ii.	ROGER COURTLAND,	b. Jan. 29, 1869.
iii.	ARCHER PELHAM,	b. July 23, 1871.
iv.	VIRGINIA,	b. Mar. 6, 1873 ; d. Oct. 22, 1874.
v.	NEY McCORMICK,	b. Ap. 19, 1875.

CHILDREN OF HERIOT (ROBERDEAU) AND DR. EDWARD CONRAD. [17.]

48. JAMES ROBERDEAU CONRAD.—Born in Winchester, Virginia, in 1810; and graduated as a physician, from the University of Pennsylvania, in 1831. He entered the army, August 21, 1838, as an assistant surgeon, and remained in the service until 1853. He has since resided in Winchester.

49. DANIEL CONRAD.—Born in Winchester, Virginia, in 1812; graduated, in 1842, from the University of Pennsylvania, as a physician; and practiced his profession in Winchester. In 1846, he married Sarah Jane, daughter of Mary and Alfred H. Powell, a lawyer of distinction in Virginia, and sister of Rear-Admiral Powell, U. S. Navy. Dr. Conrad died August 19, 1869, without issue; and his wife, August 17, 1863, aged fifty-three years; they both rest in Mt. Hebron Cemetery, Winchester.

CHILDREN OF DANIEL C. CLYMER. [18.]

50. ANN CLYMER.—Born in Reading, Berks county, Pennsylvania, in the year 1782, and died unmarried, at Morgantown, Pennsylvania, in August, 1852. She was a person of great force of character, and beloved by a large circle of acquaintances.

51. WILLIAM CLYMER.—Born in Reading, Berks county, Pennsylvania, March 28, 1788, at 9¼ P. M. He graduated at Yale College, and became a lawyer, in Reading; and was married, April 18, 1808, by the Rev. Dr. Muhlenberg, to Susan Rightmyer, of the same town, who was born March 15, 1790. He died there, October 10, 1845; and Mrs. Clymer, July 11, 1856.
Their children :—

		GEORGE,	b. July 21, 1809 ; d. unm., June 30, 1837.
	i.	DANIEL,	b. Nov. 26, 1810 ; d. unm., Aug. 13, 1838.
	ii.		
93.	iii.	HENRY,	b. Mar. 15, 1813.
	iv.	ELIZABETH,	b. June 15, 1815 ; d. an infant.
	v.	ELIZABETH,	b. Oct. 17, 1816 ; d. Nov. 11, 1818.
	vi.	WILLIAM,	b. May 2, 1818 ; d. May 6, 1818.
94.	vii.	MARY ANN,	b. Aug.15, 1822 ; (Mrs. Bonawitz.)
95.	viii.	WILLIAM,	b. Jan. 6, 1825.

52. EDWARD TILGHMAN CLYMER.—Born in Reading, Berks county, Pennsylvania, Saturday, Aug. 14, 1790, between 1 and 2 A. M. Educated at Princeton College, and excelled in Latin and Greek. He was married, June 11, 1818, to Maria Catharine, daughter of William Hiester, of Upper Bern township, Berks county, Pennsylvania; who was born March 14, 1793.

The Hiester family is of Silesian origin. Three brothers, Daniel, John, and Joseph, emigrated to Pennsylvania, early in the 18th century, and their descendants have been prominent in civil life. Daniel had several sons, viz: 1st, John, of Chester county, born 1746, Member of Congress, 1807–'8, resigned, and was succeeded by his son Daniel, 1809–'10; 2d, Daniel, of Montgomery county, born 1747, a Representative in Congress from Pennsylvania, 1789–'97, and from Maryland, 1801–'5; 3d, Gabriel, of Berks county, for thirty years in the State Legislature; 4th, William, the youngest son, for a short time in the Continental army, whose son, William, born 1791, of Lancaster county, was a Member of Congress in 1833–'5, and died October 15, 1853, and whose daughter, Maria C., married Edward T. Clymer, as above stated. The first-named, John, had a son, Joseph, a Member of the Convention to ratify the Constitution of the United States; repeatedly elected to the State Senate and House; Member of Congress, 1797–1807, and 1815–'21; Governor of Pennsylvania, 1819; died June 10, 1832. Besides the above offices, these gentlemen held many others, a full account of which may be found in *Rupp's Hist. of Berks and Lebanon Counties, Penn.*, and in *Lanman's Dictionary of Congress.*

To return: Mr. Clymer followed no profession, and died at his residence in the Conestoga Valley, near Morgantown, March 6, 1831. His wife followed him, March 24, 1845.

Their children :—

96.	i.	DANIEL ROBERDEAU,	b. March 31, 1819.
97.	ii.	WILLIAM HIESTER,	b. Octo'r 9, 1820.
98.	iii.	EDWARD MYERS.	
	iv.	WEIDNER,	b. May 12, 1824; d. July 16, 1824.
99.	v.	MARY HIESTER,	b. July 19, 1825.
100.	vi.	HIESTER,	b. Nov'm 3, 1827.
101.	vii.	GEORGE EDWARD,	b. Janu'y 8, 1830.

FIFTH GENERATION.

CHILDREN OF F. SELINA (ROBERDEAU) AND PAY-DIRECTOR McKEAN BUCHANAN. [21.]

53. ROBERDEAU BUCHANAN, *the compiler and writer of this Genealogy.*—Born in Philadelphia, November 22, 1839. Removed with the family, in 1841, to Brooklyn, New York, and from thence, in 1851, to Boston, Massachusetts, consequent upon his father's duties in the navy. Resided in Charlestown, where he was educated; and in 1861, graduated at the Lawrence Scientific School of Harvard University, as a Bachelor of Science, in the Department of Engineering. Engaged prosperously in the practice of his profession as a civil engineer, in Charlestown;—chiefly in the construction of water-works in the vicinity of Boston. But deafness from some unknown cause obliged him to relinquish his profession; and in 1872 he received an appointment in the Patent Office at Washington, D. C., in which city he now resides.

54. LÆTITIA McKEAN (BUCHANAN) FIFE.—Born in Brooklyn, New York, December 24, 1842; removed to Boston, Massachusetts, with the family in 1851; and was married in Charlestown, October 3, 1867, to G. S. Fife, an assistant surgeon in the navy. She died in Charlestown, July 20, 1871, and lies near her father in Mt. Auburn Cemetery. She was a person of pleasing presence, which made her a favorite among a large circle of friends. Her issue:—

    i. GEORGE WILLIAM BUCHANAN CAINS, b. Aug. 9, 1869; bapt. Sept. 21, by the Rev. Moses B. Chase, U. S. N., at the chapel in the navy-yard, Boston.

    ii. SELINA, b. July 18, 1871; d. the next day, and is buried with her mother.

CHILDREN OF ANN F. (SWIFT) AND JONATHAN T. PATTEN. [24.]

55. VIRGINIA (PATTEN) HOUGHTON.—Born in New York City; married by Rev. Dr. Hutton, May 11, 1851, to Royall Houghton, a broker of that city, who died March 22, 1873, at St. Augustine, Florida, where he had gone for his health. His widow resides in New York. Their children :—

   i. FRANK ROYALL,   b. March 2, 1852.
   ii. HERBERT RICHARDSON, b. June 26, 1853.
   iii. ELLA ISABEL,   b. Aug. 2, 1858; d. aged three years.

56. MARY SWIFT (PATTEN) TINSON.—Born in New York; married by Rev. Dr. Tyng, August 8, 1855, to Frederick Tinson, merchant of that city, where they reside. Their children :—

   i. TILLIE ROBINSON, b. Oct. 8, 1853.
   ii. ANNA SWIFT,   b. Oct. 19, 1857.

57. WILLIAM SWIFT PATTEN.—Born in New York City, where he became a merchant; married by the Rev. Dr. Shock, January 20, 1863, to Mary E. Hardmann, of that city. Their children :—

   i. WILLIAM H.,   b. Nov. 27, 1865.
   ii. MAY ELIZABETH, b. May 9, 1868.
   iii. JOSEPHINE WARD, b. Aug. 27, 1870.
   iv. GRACIE WARREN, b. March 28, 1873.

58. JOSEPHINE (PATTEN) WARD.—Born in New York City, and married by the Rev. Dr. Cox, June 8, 1864, to William P. Ward, a merchant of that city. Their issue :—

   i. ANNA PORTER, b. April 8, 1865.

59. JAMES AUGUSTUS PATTEN.—Born in New York City; married by Rev. Mr. Payson, March 1, 1870, to Laura N., daughter of Dr. Reaser, of that city. They reside on a farm at White Hall, Montour county, Pennsylvania. Their children :—

   i. FRANK EDWARD, b. March 28, 1873.
   ii. ROBERDEAU SWIFT, b. Sept. 17, 1874.

CHILDREN OF MARY S. (SWIFT) AND HENRY ALLISON. [25.]

60. WILLIAM HENRY ALLISON.—Born April 24, 1828. Resides on his farm in Lafayette county, Missouri. He was married twice: First, November 3, 1851, to Sarah Jane Miller, daughter of James Estell and Harriet

Miller, of Clark county, Kentucky, who died of consumption, December 23, 1856. And, secondly, December 27, 1857, to Rebecca Wade, daughter of William and Mary Pigg, of Clark county, Kentucky. His issue, all born in Missouri—

By the first wife:—

102. i. MARY SELINA, b. Boonville, Nov. 22, 1852; (Mrs. Norman.)
    ii. JAMES ESTELL, b. Pettis co., June 10, 1856.

By the second wife:—

    iii. WILLIAM HENRY, jr., b. Pettis co., July 11, 1859.
    iv. EMMA, b. Knob Noster. Johnson co., Ap. 30,1861.
    v. FREDERICK KEMPER, b. Boonville, July 14, 1864.
    vi. ELLA MAY, . b. Sedalia, Pettis co., May 14, 1868.
    vii. GRACIE GERTRUDE, b. Georgetown, Pettis co., Mar. 3, 1870.

61. ROBERDEAU ALLISON.—Born January 29, 1830; Married, August 26, 1851, Artemisia Rebecca Weedin, who was born December 15, 1830. Resides in Syracuse, Morgan county, Missouri, where he is principal of a flourishing high-school. Their issue, all born in Missouri:—

    i. KATE CAMPBELL, b. May 23, 1852.
    ii. HENRY ROBERDEAU, b. Nov. 3, 1854.
    iii. REBECCA SWIFT, b. Feb. 12, 1857.
    iv. BENJAMIN ESTELL, b. Feb. 3, 1867.
    v. WILLIE EUGENE, b. Sept. 13, 1869; d. March 27, 1872.

62. JANE CAMPBELL (ALLISON) FUNK-HOUSER, and lastly BARRY.—Born January 9, 1832, at Madison Court-House, Virginia. After her removal to Missouri with her mother she was married, at Boonville, December 11, 1852, to William Cross Funkhouser, who was in the commission and forwarding business. He went to California, and information was received that he died there in 1860. By this marriage there were five children. She was married a second time, January 27, 1865, to Robert L. Barry, a widower, by whom she has three children, and who died in Syracuse, Missouri, March 1, 1874. Her children—

By her first husband, W. C. Funkhouser:—

    i. MARY, b. Keokuk, I., June 12.1854; d. same day.
    ii. WILLIAM HENRY, b. Keokuk, I., May 15, 1855.
    iii. CHARLES FRANCISCO, b. Chicago, Ill., May 9, 1857.
    iv. MARY ANNA, b. St. Louis, Mo., Jan. 8, 1859.
    v. ROBERT PATTEN, b Boonville, Mo., June 26, 1861; d. March 20, 1862.

By her second husband, R. L. Barry:—

    vi. JULIA MAY, b. Syracuse, Mo., Nov. 9, 1867.
    vii. LILLY BELL, b. Syracuse, Mo., Aug. 15, 1870.
    viii. SUSAN KEMPER, b. Syracuse, Mo., Aug. 20, 1873.

CHILDREN OF MARY ANN (PATTEN) AND DR. THOMAS WOLFE. [26.]

63. MARY DeNEALE (WOLFE) MORGAN, and lastly HARMON.—Born May 17, 1817, in Winchester, and after her mother's death was adopted by her aunt, Mrs. Wheat. While in New Orleans, in 1836, was married to Judge Thomas Nicholson Morgan, of that place, and resided there until his death. The high estimation in which he was held may be seen from the following:

Nashville, Tennessee, 1844. Died of consumption, Thomas Nicholson Morgan, in the thirty-fifth year of his age—for the last ten years an associate judge of the city of New Orleans, Louisiana.

Judge Morgan was a native of Louisiana; his parents were from Philadelphia; his mother a daughter of Judge John Nicholson. He was graduated at Yale in 1831. Towards the end of his college life he became decidedly pious; and upon returning home, so firm and consistent was his religious profession in the communion of the Episcopal Church; that the strong current of worldliness and the countless temptations that assail a young man possessing all the means of self-indulgence in that gay capital, only served to show the beauty and strength of his Christian character. He took an active and leading part in all the great measures of reform which have so elevated the moral tone of that community; and gradually diffused through the wide circle of his own family and friends, the profoundest respect for his bright and winning example of that rare union of virtues—scrupulous strictness in his own case, and unbounded charity towards others.

The very high estimate in which he was held may be inferred from his having been appointed by the legislature to the office he held, over many powerful competitors, at the early age of *twenty-four*.

It was not only his high grade of scholarship and sound legal training which gained him this distinction, but the extraordinary weight of his moral and religious character.

He was junior warden of St. Paul's Church, New Orleans; and will be gratefully remembered by his pastor and people as one of the founders and most liberal supporters of that new parish.

By this husband Mrs. Morgan had four children, all born in New Orleans. In 1848, in New Orleans, she was married a second time, to John B. Harmon, Esq., son of Dr. John B. Harmon, of Ohio. In 1854 the family removed to California, where they have since resided, first in Sacramento, then in San Francisco, and latterly in Oakland, near San Francisco. Mr. Harmon is a lawyer of high standing, and enjoys a large and lucrative practice.

Her children by her first husband, Judge T. N. Morgan:—

103.	i.	THOMAS WOLFE,	b. New Orleans.		
	ii.	SARAH FRANCES,	b. "	"	dead.
	iii.	SELINA BLAIR,	b. "	"	dead.
	iv.	MARY ANN PATTEN,	b. "	"	dead.

By her second husband, John B. Harmon, Esq:—

104.	v.	DANA,	b. New Orleans.
	vi.	MARY WOLFE,	b. Warren, Ohio [while Mrs. H. was on a visit.]
105.	vii.	ROBERDEAU,	b. ——, Cal.
	viii.	KATE OGLE,	b. Sacramento, Mch., 1857; d. Oakland, April 1858.
	ix.	LAWRENCE PATTEN,	b. Oakland, June, 1859; d. Sacramento, February, 1861.

64. THOMAS ROBERDEAU WOLFE.—Born May 7, 1819, in Culpepper, Virginia.

He was married, July 25, 1843, to Maria Bernard Temple, of Fredericksburg, Virginia; and about the same time, removed to New Orleans, where he practiced law for thirteen years. He died of consumption, at Sharon Springs, New York, July 6, 1856. His high standing, in his profession, and the esteem in which he was held, may be seen from the following:

THE MEMBERS of the bar met in the Supreme Court room, yesterday morning, at ten o'clock, pursuant to a previous notice, to pay some tribute of respect to the memory of the late Thomas Roberdeau Wolfe.

A committee, consisting of Messrs. M. M. Cohen, R. H. Chilton, Rufus K. Waples, J. W. Duncan, and J. Q. Bradford, appointed by the chair, reported the following resolutions, which were unanimously adopted:

Inasmuch as it has pleased the Almighty Arbiter of Events to remove from our midst Thomas R. Wolfe, Esq.; and *inasmuch* as we, the members of the New Orleans bar, are deeply sensible of the loss sustained by his untimely death, cut down in the prime of life, and in the zenith of professional success; and *inasmuch* as the urbanity and simplicity of his manners, the purity of his character, his ability, and merited success as a lawyer, have won our affection and esteem; therefore—

Resolved, That in the death of Thomas R. Wolfe, Esq., the bar of New Orleans has sustained a loss irreparable.

Resolved, That in testimony of our regard for his professional talents, and for his many virtues, and as an expression of the sincere regret with which we have learned his death, we will wear the usual badge of mourning for thirty days.

(Signed)   CHRISTIAN ROSELINS,
                                                      Chairman.

After her husband's death, Mrs. Wolfe removed with her family to Baltimore, Maryland, where she now resides. Their children :—

	i.	ROBERT TEMPLE.	
106.	ii.	MARY PATTEN,	(Mrs. Ward.)
	iii.	ELSIE,	d. unmarried, Dec. 20, 1871.
	iv.	CHARLOTTE CARTER.	
	v.	MARIA TEMPLE.	
	vi.	ELLEN ROBERDEAU.	
	vii.	THOMAS ROBERDEAU, JR., d. Feb. 5, 1862; æ. 6 years.	

65. JOSEPH LEWIS WOLFE.—Born in Culpepper, Virginia, January 21, 1821. He died at his Uncle Joseph's house, in Louisiana, November 11, 1833. He had been ill, and was looking at the great meteoric shower of 1833, and " fell asleep," as all thought, but it was death, with a beautiful smile on his lips. He was buried in the bayou at Sherwood, Louisiana.

CHILDREN OF JOSEPH MAY PATTEN. [28.]

66. SELINA ANN (PATTEN) KENT.—Born in Louisiana, July 12, 1829; married in 1851, at New Orleans, Louisiana, to Isaac Newton Kent, formerly an editor, but now a planter in that State. She died there, November 30, 1853, leaving an only child. Mr. Kent has since married a second time.

Her issue :—

i. SELINA, b. 1853, La. ; d. Carroll Parish, 1867.

67. NARCISSA MATILDA (PATTEN) WILLIAMS.—Born January 5, 1837; married February 14, 1856, at Sherwood, her father's plantation, near Lake Providence, Louisiana, to John Branch Williams, a Floridian by birth, and grandson of Governor John Branch, of North Carolina, Secretary of the Navy under President Jackson. Mr. Williams was a planter, at Sherwood, where he died, July 29, 1873; Mrs. Williams still lives at the homestead, where, also, her children were born, viz:—

    i.   REBECCA BRANCH, b. Feb. 16, 1858.
    ii. JOSEPH PATTEN, b. May 21, 1859.
    iii. JOHN BRANCH, b. May 21, 1861.
    iv. ANNIE MAY, b. Dec. 23, 1863.
    v. ROBERT WHITE, b. Oct. 1, 1865, in Texas.
    vi. CHARLES ENGLISH, b. Sept. 24, 1868; d. Aug. —, 1873.
    vii. NARCISSA PATTEN, b. Jan. 16, 1872.

CHILDREN OF HARRIET ROZIER (PATTEN) AND JOHN W. MILLER. [29.]

68. MARY CATHARINE (MILLER) DUNN.— Born in Virginia, April 24, 1823. Removed with the family to Lake Providence, Louisiana, where she was married, in May, 1843, to Dr. Thomas Dunn, of that place, at the residence of her uncle, Thomas R. Patten. The family suffered severely from the yellow fever in 1853, as already related. Dr. Dunn died in October, at Greenville, in Washington county, Mississippi; and Mrs. Dunn died the following month, at the same place, from the effects of the same disease, and of a broken heart, having lost father, mother, sister, and husband, in the short space of one month. Her issue:—

107. i. BETTIE McALLISTER, b. L. Prov., Feb. 17, 1844; (Mrs. Dunn.)
108. ii. JOHN NELSON, b. Issaquena Co., Miss., Sept. 28, 1845.
109. iii. THOMAS WILSON, b. L. Prov., Nov. 14, 1847.
110. iv. CHAPIN HARRIS, b. " " Oct. 26, 1849.
111. v. SAMUEL REED, b. " " Feb. 7, 1851.
    vi. LOUIS FINLAY, b. " " in the spring of 1853; d. 1854.

69. LAURA PATTEN (MILLER) PIERCE.—Born June 4, 1826, in Wilmington, North Carolina; married, July 19, 1847, to Lewis H. Pierce, a stationer, whose family was originally from New England, but who was a native and resident of Wilmington, North Carolina, in which city he died, May 20, 1860. In September, 1862, partly on account of the yellow fever, then prevalent there, Mrs. Pierce removed her family to Clinton, North Carolina, where they now reside. Her children, all born in Wilmington, North Carolina:—

    i. IRENE, b. Sept. 4, 1848.
112. ii. MARY RIVERA, b. Oct. 10, 1850; (Mrs. Baker.)
    iii. ROBERDEAU EUSTIS, b. Jan. 31, 1853; d. Apr. 15, 1854.
113. iv. HARRIET ROZIER, b. Jan. 23, 1855; (Mrs. Barksdale.)
    v. LOUISE TALCOT, b. Jan. 18, 1857; d. Feb. 28, 1860.
    vi. LEWIS HENRY, b. May 25, 1860.

70. JOSEPHINE WALTZ (MILLER) LANCAS-
TER.—Born in Winchester, Virginia, June 9, 1832;
married in Greenville, Mississippi, April 19, 1853, to Dr.
Alonzo B. Lancaster of that place; she died in Madison
county, Mississippi, August 2, 1855.   Her only child:—

   i. SAMUEL TAYLOR, b. March 10, 1854, Greenville; d. 1859, in Boli-
      var county.

71. ANNIE MARIA (MILLER) MULLINS.—Born
August 29, 1834; married by Rev. William B. Hines,
in the Methodist Church, Greenville, Mississippi, October
22, 1857, to the Rev. Elisha Flowers Mullins.   He was
born in Copiah county, Mississippi, March 22, 1830,
united with the Methodist Episcopal Church in 1850, entered the ministry 1854.   They reside in Beauregard,
Mississippi, of which place Mr. Mullins has been the
mayor since 1870.   Their children:—

   i.   HORACE MILLER,   b. Greenville, Apr. 14, 1860.
   ii. ALBERT MILLER,   b. Wilkinson Co., July 21, 1863.
   iii. HARRIET TEMPERANCE, b. Copiah Co., May 29, 1870.
   iv. SERENA GRANBBERY, b. Beauregard, June 20, 1875.

72. FANNIE MORGAN (MILLER) CALDWELL.
—Born November 21, 1843, and after her mother's death,
lived for a time with her sister, Mrs. Pierce, and afterwards at Raleigh, North Carolina.   She was married
August 4, 1868, in St. Luke's Church, Salisbury, North
Carolina, to Julius A. Caldwell, M. D.   Dr. Caldwell is
a member of an excellent family;—the son of Judge
David F. and Fannie A. Caldwell, of Salisbury, where
he was born February 9, 1830; and where they now reside.   They have a family of beautiful little children, all
born in Salisbury:—

   i.   DAVID FRANKLIN,   b. May 13, 1869; d. June 22, 1870.
   ii. ARCHIBALD HENDERSON, b. Feb. 28, 1871.
   iii. FANNIE ALEXANDER,   b. Oct. 16, 1872.
   iv. ALICE LORRAINE,   b. Sept. 4, 1874.

73. ALBERT PATTEN MILLER.—Born Septem-
ber 25, 1845.   During the late war he was for a time
first sergeant in the Confederate Army, under General
Lee.   He has since the war resided in Winchester,
where, with his cousin, W. H. Baker, as partner, he carries on an extensive factory, giving employment to fifty
persons at the various machines.   He was married December 10, 1874, to Laura, youngest daughter of the late
Hon. Robert Fowler, of Baltimore county, Maryland.

CHILDREN OF SELINA B. (PATTEN) AND DR. J. T. WHEAT. [30.]

74. CHATHAM ROBERDEAU WHEAT.—If ever man was born a soldier, it is the subject of this sketch; —whose life was one of the most eventful;—having engaged in battles in the two hemispheres, under commanders world-renowned, and himself fought under six different flags!

He was born in Alexandria, Virginia, April 9, 1826, received an academic education, graduating from the University of Nashville, in 1845. The year before, having been chosen one of the representatives of a college society in the junior competitive exhibition of oratory, he departed from the established custom by making an extemporaneous address, and gave bright promise of the eloquence for which he was afterwards distinguished.

After graduating, he commenced the study of law at Memphis, and while thus engaged the war with Mexico broke out; whereupon he was the first to register his name as a volunteer, and was elected second lieutenant of the company of dragoons.* Upon the expiration of the twelve months for which the regiment had been enlisted, it was disbanded, in May, 1847, at Vera Cruz, most of the men returning home; but Lieutenant Wheat at once raised a company of one hundred men, of which he was chosen captain. The night before he left Vera Cruz he was seized with *romito*, an almost fatal form of yellow fever, and was carried in a hammock swung between two mules, and thus taken to Jalapa, where he arrived in an insensible condition. As soon as he was able, he reported to General Scott, and was detailed for special service, as captain commanding the body-guard of the commanding general.

Captain Wheat was several times honorably mentioned in General Scott's official reports "for important services and gallantry in the field." One instance deserves mention. At the battle of Resaca de la Palma his company had captured a number of prisoners, among whom was an elderly officer. To him Captain Wheat gave all the comforts his tent afforded, telling his orderly to bring coffee and to spread his folded cot for the prisoner. Not

---

*See *Gardner's Dictionary of the Army, Volunteers*, p. 544.

11

speaking our language, and unable to understand the generous act of his captor, the officer yielded reluctantly, almost fearing danger in such courtesy. For days he was thus treated, then released upon his parol, and his sword returned to him; and it was now that Captain Wheat learned that his prisoner was General La Vega, one of the most distinguished in the Mexican army. Asking an interpreter to be called, General La Vega handed Captain Wheat his sword, which was of great value, saying, "Take this in return for your kindness. You have treated me as a son more than your prisoner." General Scott then spoke: "Sir, this is a rare compliment for one so young, and a soldier, to receive. I am glad to be the medium of General La Vega to you." Captain Wheat, declining the sword for an act of mere civility, said, "It was the gray hairs on the General's head I honored, for I knew not the high rank of my prisoner. I was ever taught to honor old age." The General insisted upon his keeping the sword, which he finally did, and it is now in possession of his family.

After the taking of the City of Mexico, Captain Wheat was sent home to recruit his company, which he soon did in Nashville, Tennessee; where a flag was presented to them by the young ladies of Christ Church School. Returning to Mexico, Captain Wheat was stationed in Jalapa until the close of the war.

Peace being declared, Captain Wheat settled in New Orleans, resuming the study of law, and was admitted to the bar in 1847, at the age of twenty-two, and soon acquired considerable distinction as a criminal lawyer. His first effort resulted in the acquittal of one of his former command, after the senior counsel had given up the case as indefensible.

In 1848 Captain Wheat was elected one of the representatives of the city of New Orleans in the State Legislature. He also canvassed the State for the whig candidate pending the presidential election, and had no little success as a stump orator.

While in New Orleans he was frequently thrown into the society of General Lopez; through whose influence he soon evinced strong sympathies for the Cuban cause, and determined to join the expedition under Lopez, then preparing to start. He was by the Cuban Junta commissioned as colonel. To those who, opposing his determination, quoted the philosophic aphorism—"Who would be free, themselves must strike the blow"—Colonel Wheat replied: "Suppose a weak woman, gagged, manacled, dungeoned, completely in the power of a brutal force—would you hesitate a moment to attempt a rescue, even at the risk of your life? Every sentiment of manhood answers no! a thousand times, no!" With these feelings did he embark for Cuba. In mid-ocean the vessels were lashed together and the duty of acquainting the "emigrants" of their ulterior objects devolved upon Colonel Wheat; who addressed them in a stirring speech, during which the Cuban flag was hoisted. They then formed themselves into a skeleton regiment, to be filled up on landing. While the vessel, the Creole, was stopping for water, many of the men determined to abandon the enterprise, but Colonel Wheat dissuaded them, so great was his eloquence and the power he exercised over his men.

They were soon joined by Lopez, and a night attack made on Cardenas; which failed, for want of support. Col. Wheat was severely wounded, and on their return to the steamer, they narrowly escaped capture by the war steamer, Pizarro. Very providentially, Col. Wheat was prevented from accompanying Lopez in his second expedition; although much to his chagrin at the time.

It was not a mere restless spirit of adventure that led Colonel Wheat to join this expedition to Cuba; but a generous sympathy with the oppressed everywhere, the same which afterwards caused him to join Caravajal, in his efforts to put down the church party in Mexico, and give to that beauteous land our free institutions. And still later, when Generals Walker and Henningsen were in imminent peril of their lives, after their defeat at Rivas; it was pity for their respective families that prompted him to fit out an expedition at New York and hasten to their relief. Colonel Wheat had previously been tendered a high position by General Walker, while the prospects of the latter in Nicaragua were most promising; but after declining that flattering offer, and true to his characteristic self-sacrifice for the good of others, he hastened to their relief in the hour of adversity. In Nicaragua, he was made general, in command of an army corps.

While in Nicaragua, he met with the most wonderful of all his many escapes from death. By the explosion of

the boiler of a steamboat, he was blown from the hurri-
cane-deck into the river, so entirely without injury, that
he swam to the shore with ease, rescuing a wounded man
at the same time, whose life he thus saved. At this
time he weighed 260 pounds.

Having accomplished his mission in aid of General
Walker, General Wheat returned home. But soon
after, hearing that Alvarez had pronounced against
Santa Anna and the church party in Mexico, he accepted a commission in the patriot army; and was made
general of an artillery brigade, receiving from General
Alvarez, now President, official commendation and
thanks, with permanent rank and pay under his admin-
istration. When, however, by reason of age and its
infirmities, Alvarez resigned the presidency and retired
to his *hacienda*, General Wheat accompanied him, at
General Alvarez's earnest solicitation.

Being in the fullest flush of a matured manhood,
General Wheat could not be content with a life of in-
glorious ease; and as the world was beginning to
resound with the name and exploits of Garibaldi, who
urged him to join the Italian cause, he determined to
gratify a long-cherished wish to visit Europe; now
become doubly attractive by the rapid march of events
in the historic changes of governments. He landed in
England, and joined a party of congenial spirits going
to Italy; and if need be, to take part with Garibaldi.

General Wheat having known Garibaldi, in New
York, and afterwards receiving an earnest invitation to
join him in Italy, was received by him in most flattering
terms, being the leader of victorious armies fighting
for liberty. Promptly accepting the staff appointment
that was tendered to him, General Wheat engaged once
more in active service; and in the several engagements
which quickly followed, his dash and gallant courage
were the frequent theme of the army correspondents of
the British press. Besides the high rank which General
Wheat bore upon Garibaldi's staff—that of a general
officer—he was also the confidential friend of his commander, and was present when Garibaldi crowned Victor
Emanuel with a laurel wreath, as King of Italy.

The troubles arising at home gave another turn to
General Wheat's career. Proceeding to England, he
took the first steamer for New York; and upon his arri-

val, called to see General Scott, whom he called his military father, and for whom he had a great affection; as well as a reverence for the "old flag." General Scott, delighted to see him, promised him an eligible position in the Federal Army, but General Wheat, being a Southerner by birth and association, deemed it his duty to cast his lot with the Southern cause. He was actuated by the same feeling as was Robert E. Lee. Each acted from the most truly conscientious motives of what he *believed* to be right. For this reason, let those who differ in opinion, judge them charitably.

General Wheat proceeded to Montgomery and offered himself for duty, but, being a Whig, was not accepted. Remaining there but a few days, and hearing that his brother was in command of a battery at Pensacola, he said, "I will go and be a private in my brother's company. I fear he knows nothing of military tactics. I will teach him." He, however, first visited New Orleans, where General Twiggs sent for him and offered him a position to recruit near the city. But a number of Virginians, called the Old Dominion Guard, elected him their captain; at the same time a Louisiana company, called the Tigers, also petitioned to join his command, which was thus raised to a battalion, with Wheat as major. General Twiggs begged him to wait for a larger command, as the battalion could easily have been swelled into a regiment at least, but Wheat replied, "I fight not for rank, General, it is for my country—it is for Virginia that I go."

With this command, small indeed, for one who had commanded an army corps, Major Wheat left for Virginia; where he arrived just before the first battle of Manassas or Bull Run, in which his battalion, being assigned the extreme left, received the first attack. General Beauregard mentioned in very flattering terms that he won for himself and his command the proud boast of having fought the first hour, the battle of Manassas. Major Wheat was, however, most severely wounded. He was at the head of his command, having dismounted, with one hand holding the bridle of his horse, with the other his sword raised aloft to urge forward his men, his colossal frame being a conspicuous mark, a rifle-ball passed through his body, from side to side, piercing both lungs. He was carried from the field, when he was told that his wound must prove mortal, but he replied cheerfully, "I don't feel like dying." The surgeon said, "There is no case upon record of recovery from such a wound." "Well," responded the Major, "I will put my case on record." *And he did.* His recovery, the surgeon attributes to his resolute will.

General Beauregard, in his official report, says: "It is fit that I should in this way commend to mention the dauntless conduct and imperturbable coolness of Colonel Evans; and well indeed was he supported by Colonel Sloane and the officers of the 4th South Carolina regiment; as also by Major Wheat, than whom no one displayed more brilliant courage until carried from the field shot through the lungs, though happily not mortally stricken." Major Wheat was also conspicuously noticed by the Northern press, his death confidently asserted, and his biography published.

While he lay sick, a Federal officer who formerly had known him and was then a prisoner, requested permission to see him. The meeting was cordial on both sides. Major Wheat directed his orderly to give Colonel P—— his pocket-book and some under-clothing, saying "Colonel, you will need money while in prison."

The popular impression in and out of the army now was that Major Wheat should be promoted to the command of a regiment, if not to a brigade. As soon as he was able to walk without support, he went to Richmond to recruit his battalion, and on his way a brother officer said to him, "Wheat, I would give a thousand dollars to stand in your shoes to-day." To which Wheat at once demurely replied, "Orderly, give Captain B—— my shoes."

While waiting for promotion he joined his battalion, and was assigned to duty under General Stonewall Jackson, and accompanied him in his brilliant march down the Valley, pressing back the commands of Fremont, Shields, and Banks. The Southern newspapers seldom gave an account of a fight without his name being mentioned. At the battle of Port Republic, June 13, 1862, General Jackson, observing Wheat's horse killed under him, himself dismounted and sent his own to him. And after the battle was over, embraced him in his arms in admiration and gratitude to God that his life was spared.

After his wonderful escapes, Major Wheat, the hero of

many engagements, fell at last. It was in the battle of Gaines' Mills, near Cold Harbor, on the 27th of June, 1862, one of the seven days' fights before Richmond against McClellan's army.

In compliance with his request his body was interred near the spot where he fell. The next winter his remains were removed to Richmond and buried with full military honors in Hollywood Cemetery. *Promoted at last.* He has ascended to the great Captain of his salvation.

General Wheat's character and presence were such as are rarely met with; his noble bearing at once caught the eye; his eloquence and fluency of conversation, in several languages, charmed the ear; while the purity of his character and stainless honor won the admiration of the heart. He availed himself of none of the opportunities to enrich himself, so frequent in victorious armies; but returned to his own country as poor as he left it;— rich only in experience and observation. He daily read from a little book of devotions, sent to him by his mother; and the morning of the day upon which he was killed, finding the portion selected, to be particularly appropriate for men about to imperil their lives, he called his command around him in the grey light of early dawn; and reverently uncovering his head, the men following his example, he read to them the prayer "for a joyful resurrection." Then put the little volume in his pocket, where it was afterwards found.

General Wheat possessed the Roberdeau stature, standing full six feet four inches in height, and stout in proportion. He possessed the most unbounded influence over his men, who idolized him. He never asked his command to go where he himself would not lead; and after his death, no one could be found who could control the battalion, as did Major Wheat, and it was in consequence disbanded.

General Wheat's last words, "Bury me on the field, boys," have been made the theme of several pieces of poetry, published in the Southern papers of the day. General Wheat was unmarried.

75. SELINA PATTEN (WHEAT) SEAY.—Born June 12, 1827, in Maryland; married December 21,

1847, to Dr. John Seay, of Lake Providence, Louisiana, where she died November 8, 1872. Her children, all born at Lake Providence:—

114.	i.	John Thomas,	b. Sept. 27, 1848.
	ii.	Samuel,	b. Sept. 29, 1850; d. Dec. 20, 1859.
115.	iii.	Selina Wheat,	b. Mar. 19, 1852; (Mrs. Pilcher.)
116.	iv.	Mary De Neale,	b. Jan. 26, 1854; (Mrs. Brinton.)
117.	v.	George Wharton,	b. Sept. 7, 1855.
	vi.	Roberdeau Wheat,	b. June 24, 1857.
	vii.	Jane Wharton,	b. Apr. 13, 1859; d. Sept. 17, 1861.
	viii.	May Wheat,	b. Sept. 23, 1861.
	ix.	Leo Wheat,	b. Apr. 13, 1864; d. Apr. 25, 1864.
	x.	Leonore Wheat,	b. July 31, 1867.

76. JOHN THOMAS WHEAT, Jr.—Born in Alexandria, December 3, 1830. Resided in New Orleans, where he studied law and was admitted to the bar. He was elected secretary of the Louisiana convention, which in 1861 passed the ordinance of secession;—a prominent position for one so young; and attested the esteem in which he was held. Prior to the war, he was color-bearer of the battalion of Washington Artillery of New Orleans; but at the beginning of the war was elected one of the captains of the First Louisiana Infantry, and ordered to Pensacola, to General Bragg's command; where he remained, participating in the several bombardments with named distinction. Then ordered to Tennessee, he fell bravely fighting at the great battle of Shiloh, April 6, 1862. He was buried on the field, but afterwards removed to Nashville. He died unmarried.

77. JOSEPHINE MAY (WHEAT) SHOBER—Born in Wheeling, Virginia, February 22, 1833; married July 12, 1853, to the Hon. Francis E. Shober, of Salisbury, North Carolina. Mr. Shober was born in Salem, North Carolina, March 12, 1831; received an academic education both in his native State and in Pennsylvania; graduating at the University of North Carolina, in June 1851; studied law and was admitted to the bar in 1854. He was elected to the lower branch of the General Assembly of North Carolina in 1862–64, and to the State Senate in 1865. He was elected to represent the State in the Forty-first Congress, and reëlected to the Forty-second Congress, by a large majority.

Their children—the eldest born in Chapel Hill, the

others in Salisbury, North Carolina, where the family
now resides :—

  i. ANN MAY,   b. Apr. 12, 1854.
  ii. SELINA ROBERDEAU, b. Jan. 5, 1857.
  iii. FRANCIS EMANUEL, b. Oct. 24, 1860.
  iv. CHARLES ERNEST, b. Apr. 12, 1865.
  v. FRANCES WHEAT, b. Mch. 28, 1867.

78. LEONIDAS POLK WHEAT.—Born May 5,
1841, in Tennessee; married, January 16, 1872, to Florence Lyle Allen, youngest daughter of Joseph Allen and
Mary A. Stetson, of Richmond, where he now resides;
devoting himself to the study and practice of music, having studied for several years in Europe and attained
marked proficiency. Their children :—

  i. JOSEPH ALLEN, b. Jan. 22, 1873.
  ii. MAY,   b. July 31, 1874.
  iii. LEONIDAS,   b. Dec. 16, 1875.

CHILD OF MARY C. (NICKOLLS) AND ANDREW S. HOLDERBY. [33.]

79. ANDREW ROBERDEAU HOLDERBY.—Born
in Petersburg, Virginia, January 25, 1838. In July,
1864, he removed to Madison, Rockingham county,
North Carolina, where he was married, July 24, 1866,
to Hattie C. Smith, of Petersburg. Two months afterwards he removed to Mobile, and thence, in May, 1868,
to Tuskegee, Alabama. He was ordained a minister in
the Presbyterian Church in 1869, and now, besides the
charge of two churches, is superintendent of the Orphans'
Home of the Synod of Alabama, located at the latter
place. Their children :—

  i. ANDREW ROBERDEAU, jr., b. Mobile, May 11, 1867.
  ii. MARY MACLIN,   b. Tuskegee, Oct. 8, 1870.
  iii. MATTIE NICKOLLS, b. Tuskegee, Oct. 8, 1875.

CHILD OF SELINA ANN C. (NICKOLLS) AND JOHN IRVINE. [34.]

80. SELINA ROBERDEAU (IRVINE) SIZER.—
Born October 10, 1823; married in 1843 to William H.
Sizer, of Richmond, Virginia, for several years an officer
of the Farmers' Bank; and resided at the family homestead two miles from the city, where her children were
born. He died in 1856, much beloved by his friends.
His widow was married a second time, July 9, 1862, to
to S. M. Williamson, of Alabama, who, in 1864, removed

the family to Montgomery, and thence, in 1866, to Pollard, Alabama. Shortly before her death she was taken to Mobile, where she died, May 31, 1870. Her second husband, by whom she had no children,* was killed November 1 following, by being run over by a train of cars. Both are buried in Mobile.

Her children, all by her first husband, are:—

118.	i.	WILLIAM HENRY,	b. Nov. 14, 1844.
119.	ii.	JAMES IRVINE,	b. Nov. 1, 1846.
120.	iii.	ANNA BAXTER,	b. Dec. 12, 1848; (Mrs. Mayson.)
121.	iv.	SELINA ANN,	b. March 8, 1850; (Mrs. Drury.)
122.	v.	IRENE,	b. May 12, 1854; (Mrs. Bullock.)
	vi.	ROBERDEAU WHEAT,	b. Jan. 17, 1856.
	vii, viii, ix, x.	FOUR CHILDREN, died at birth or soon after; the dates not known, and of whom no authentic record can be found.	

CHILDREN OF ANNA B. (NICKOLLS) AND HON. S. S. BAXTER. [35.]

81. GEORGE ADDISON BAXTER.—Born in Lexington, Virginia, November 11, 1833; educated at Washington College, and the University of North Carolina, at Chapel Hill. He was for several years engaged in civil engineering; then entered the profession of law, and removed to St. Joseph, Missouri, where he took a high stand in his profession. His genial manners and generous, noble heart made him a general favorite, and none could be long with him without loving and admiring his many excellent traits of character. Here he was married, in 1861, to Levace Keys.

At the commencement of the late war, in obedience to the call of his native State, he returned to cast his fortunes with hers, and nobly and faithfully did he serve her; entering the Loudon Cavalry, the 6th Virginia, as first lieutenant of company K. He was engaged in the first battle of Manassas, at Leesburg, and at Ball's Bluffs. At the latter he had command of the company. Col. W. H. Jenifer, his commander, says of him: "This officer was with me at the battle of Ball's Bluffs on the 21st of October, 1861, and behaved in the most gallant manner. With only ten men he charged on two companies

---

* One correspondent says she had one child still-born by her second husband, but can give no more definite information, the family record being destroyed during the war. This child may be one of her four last-mentioned children.

of the enemy's infantry, and rendered other efficient services during the day. Such gallant and dashing officers as the one referred to, we need for the cavalry service." Again, Colonel E. Hunter, of the 8th Virginia, says: " Lieutenant Baxter was, in the early part of the war, under my command at Leesburg, and rendered me the most efficient service. He was for a long time in command of an out-picket post, and his services as scout and picket were of the most valuable character. He is bold and fearless, and is a good officer." Such was the opinion of his superior officers. He was for some time commandant of the post in Culpepper, leaving there to join General Stuart a day or two before the battle of Front Royal, in which battle he fell, May 23, 1862, gallantly leading his men to the charge. He lived but fifteen minutes and only spoke once, to warn his men of dangers. His cousin, Major C. R. Wheat, hastened to him on learning that he had been wounded, but arrived only in time to see him expire. A portion of his company was detailed to escort his body to Richmond, where it now lies by the side of his mother and grandmother, awaiting the general resurrection. Thus early in this unhappy struggle fell one for whom Generals Stonewall Jackson, Stuart, and others, had predicted a bright future. His daring courage and nobleness of soul well fitted him to rank high, and his loved ones thought him to have possessed a charmed life. He died without issue, and his widow now resides in St. Joseph.

82. MARY SELINA (BAXTER) COULLING.— Born in Lexington, Virginia, August 29, 1836, and was married in Petersburg, August 29, 1858, to the Rev. James Duval Coulling, (son of James M. Coulling and Mary Duval, of Richmond,) a minister of the Methodist Episcopal Church South, who was born May 20, 1812, and who died at Murfreesboro, North Carolina, November 28, 1866. She then made her home in Jeffersonville, Tazewell county, with her only surviving child, until January, 1871, when, during a visit to her father at Abingdon, she died suddenly, February 17, 1871. Her only surviving child now lives with his father's relatives in Richmond. Her children :—

i.   WILLIAM HOLDERBY, b. Charlottesville, Va., May, 1859; d. 1859.
ii. SIDNEY M. BAXTER, b. Charlottesville, Feb. 22, 1860.
iii. ANNIE,   b. Richmond, 1863; d. a few weeks old.

83. MARTHA NICKOLLS (BAXTER) SPOTTS.
—Born in Richmond, Virginia, September 30, 1839,
and was married in Jeffersonville, November 2, 1870, to
Addison Augustus Spotts, of Tazewell county, son of
George Spotts and Elizabeth Campbell, of Wythe county,
who was born in Wythe county, April 25, 1810. His
mother was a member of a family very prominent during
the Revolutionary war. Mr. Spotts is a farmer and gra-
zier; they now reside in Abb's Valley, Tazewell county.

84. WILLIAM FLEMING BAXTER.—Born in
Richmond, October 15, 1841. He entered Hampton
Sidney College, but on account of ill-health, was obliged
to leave before graduating. Ere he returned to college,
the war broke out, and he volunteered in the Petersburg
Rifles, where he continued until after the Seven Days' Battles before Richmond; when his health, always delicate,
again failed, and he was transferred to the cavalry, in
which he served faithfully, until prostrated by a severe
hemorrhage. He was then sent with dispatches to the Army
of the Trans-Mississippi; by which his health, being in a
measure improved, he returned to Virginia, traveling
over three hundred miles, on foot, to rejoin his battalion
(Col. White's). Soon after this, he was in 1864, taken
prisoner and sent to Washington, and thence to Elmira,
New York, where he contracted prison fever, from the
effects of which he never recovered. On being ex-
changed, he reached Richmond in February, and before
his health would admit of his again joining the army,
General Lee surrendered. But not to be deterred by
that, he proceeded south, intending to join the army
there. After peace was declared, he remained in Texas,
till August, 1867, when he returned to Virginia, his
health completely broken down, and died in Wytheville,
October 25, 1867, calmly and peacefully relying on his
Saviour. A more self-sacrificing and devoted patriot
never died in defence of his country. He was unmarried.

ONLY CHILD OF SARAH A. R. (ANNAN) AND S. D. McCRAW. [37.]

85. SALLIE JEAN (McCRAW) COCHRAN.—Born
February 27, 1845; married at Monticello, Carroll Parish, Louisiana, February 27, 1866, on the anniversary of
her birthday, to Thomas M. Cochran. His father, Wil-

liam Cochran, was from Virginia, but moved, at an early
date, to Warren county, Mississippi, where the son was
born, August 1, 1830.

Mr. Cochran was educated at Princeton College, New
Jersey. During the late war, he entered the Confederate Army, as 3d lieutenant of the 2d Arkansas Cavalry, of
which, at the close of the war, he had risen to be colonel.
"The regiment," he writes, "served in nineteen engagements, under Hindman; has joined many a charge with
old Bedford Forrest; heard the guns of Port Harrison;
and took a long, weary ride with old 'Pap Price'
through Arkansas, Missouri, Kansas, and the Indian
Nation. The bones of my regiment lie in Mississippi,
Kentucky, Tennessee, Alabama, Louisiana, Arkansas,
Missouri, and Kansas. 'Requiescat in pace,' says one of
the few survivors, to their ashes."

Col. and Mrs. Cochran, until recently, resided in Midway, Richland Parish, but now of Delhi, Louisiana.
Their children :—

    i. THOMAS STUART, b. Jan. 14, 1868; d. Aug. 2, 1873.
    ii. MARY EMMA,   b. Aug. 8, 1874.

CHILDREN OF JAMES ROBERDEAU ANNAN. [41.]

86. ROBERDEAU ANNAN.—Born in Maryland.
Was in the Confederate Army; severely wounded and
taken prisoner at the battle of Kernstown, Virginia,
which occurred March 23, 1862. He is now in mercantile life, in Baltimore, Maryland.

87. ROGER PERRY ANNAN.—Born in Maryland;
married Adelaide Stonestreet Hall, of Virginia, and is
now connected with a commission house in St. Louis,
Missouri.

88. DANIEL ANNAN.—Born in Maryland, and
married Virginia Opie Butcher, of Virginia, and is now
cashier of the 2d National Bank, of Cumberland, Maryland. Has issue :—

    i. ROBERDEAU,   b. 1870.
    ii. VIRGINIA OPIE, b. ——; d. Sept., 1872.
    iii. DANIEL, JR.,   b. ——.

CHILD OF JOSEPH A. ANNAN. [42.]

89. WILLIAM BENT ANNAN.—Born July 18,
1848, at Green Glades, Alleghany county, Maryland;
now in business as a merchant, in Newberg, Preston

county, West Virginia. He was married, February 14, 1873, to Nellie Gaylord, only daughter of Dr. William M. Dent, of Newberg, Preston county, West Virginia.

Their son had the unusual pleasure of seeing, at one time, one great-grandfather, two great-grandmothers, four grand-parents, and his father and mother. Their issue :—

    i. WILLIAM DENT ROBERDEAU, b. June 20, 1874.

CHILDREN OF HERIOT T. (ROBERDEAU) AND RICHARD A. RICHARDSON. [44.]

90. JAMES WILLIAM RICHARDSON.—He was born in Fairfax county, Virginia, April 26, 1845. At the breaking out of the late war he was one of the first to volunteer, at the early age of sixteen, and was in the battle of Bull Run, and many others, in the 17th Virginia Volunteers, of General Longstreet's corps. The history of this regiment has since been published. His bravery under fire is attested by all who knew him. He fought and died a private, his youth and modesty preventing his accepting a commission. And having served during nearly the whole of the war, was killed April 16, 1865, near Appomattox Court-House, in a series of battles immediately preceding General Lee's surrender, on the 19th. His long service for one so young is remarkable.

91. HERIOT VIRGINIA (RICHARDSON) TRIPLETT.—Born in Fairfax county, Virginia ; married, January 3, 1872, to her relative, Hayward F. Triplett, a merchant, residing at Gainesville, Prince William county, Virginia. Their issue :—

    i. ROBERDEAU.
    ii. RODERICK.
    iii. HAYWARD.

CHILD OF ELIZABETH H. (ROBERDEAU) AND STEPHEN D. FOOTE. [46.]

92. JULIA ANN (FOOTE) SPOONER.—Born in Fairfax county, Virginia, December, 30, 1847 ; married, February 6, 1866, in Galveston, Texas, to Horatio N. Spooner, a merchant, and now residing at Peoria, Hill county, Texas. Their children :—

    i. ALICE VIRGINIA, b. June 6, 1867.
    ii. SARAH EDNA, b. Oct, 19, 1869.
    iii. HORATIO N., b. Jan. 9, 1872.
    iv. STEPHEN FOOTE, b. Oct 30. 1874.

CHILDREN OF WILLIAM CLYMER. [51.]

93. HENRY CLYMER.—Born in Reading, Pennsylvania, March 15, 1813, and resides on his farm near that city. He married Harriet Hill. They have no children.

94. MARY ANN (CLYMER) BONAWITZ.—Born in Reading, Pennsylvania, August 15, 1822, and was married, December 25, 1864, to John H. Bonawitz, of Pine Grove, Schuylkill county, a master of machinery. No children.

95. WILLIAM CLYMER.—Born in Reading, Pennsylvania, January 6, 1825, and was married, December 26, 1865, to Ann Elizabeth, daughter of Jacob Maurer, of Reading. They reside 'in Reading, where Mr. Clymer is a manufacturer. No children.

CHILDREN OF EDWARD T. CLYMER. [52.]

96. DANIEL ROBERDEAU CLYMER. — Born March 31, 1819, in Berks county, Pennsylvania, and was educated at Litiz Academy. He was married at Mercersburg, March 31, 1846, to Delia Pierson, daughter of Silas and Sarah Pierson, of Morristown, New Jersey, who was born January 8, 1824, and died June 14, 1861. They resided in Reading, where Mr. Clymer, in 1853, filled the office of mayor, and where he is now practicing law. Their children :—

i.	MARIA HIESTER,	b. June 2, 1847 ;	d. Jan 9, 1853.
123. ii.	ANNIE M. C.,	b. June 24, 1849 ;	(Mrs. Brooke.)
iii.	DELIA PIERSON,	b. May 28, 1851 ;	d. Nov. 7, 1873.
iv.	DANIEL ROBERDEAU, jr.,	b. Nov. 6, 1854 ;	d. Dec. 7, 1858.
v.	HIESTER GEORGE,	b. Oct. 21, 1856 ;	d. Nov. 21, 1858.

97. WILLIAM HIESTER CLYMER.—Born in Conestoga Valley, near Morgantown, Berks county, Pennsylvania, October 9, 1820. In early life, he engaged in mercantile business, but in 1846, with his brother, Edward M., purchased the charcoal furnace at Mt. Laurel, Berks county, where he has since resided ; and has continued very prosperously in that business. In 1853, with others, he built and started an anthracite furnace, at Leesburg, and seven years after, with his brother, purchased the Old Oley charcoal furnace, which is now in

blast. In 1867–'8, they built the Temple anthracite furnace, at Temple Station.

Mr. Clymer was married, June 12, 1855, at Joanna Furnace, Berks county, to Valeria, daughter of Levi B. Smith. She was born in Reading Hall, Chester county, March 14, 1828. Their children, all now alive, are:—

i. EMILY SMITH,   b. July 16, 1856.
ii. EDWARD TILGHMAN, b. Aug.   8, 1857.
iii. WILLIAM HIESTER, b. March 21, 1860.
iv. LEVI SMITH,   b. April   2, 1863.
v. VALERIA ELIZABETH, b. April 29, 1865.
vi. FREDERICK HIESTER, b. May   2, 1869.

98. EDWARD MYERS CLYMER.—Born in Berks county, Pennsylvania; graduated in 1845, at the Law School of Havard University, and practiced law with success for ten years, in Reading. But gave it up on being chosen President of the East Pennsylvania Railroad; which required all his time to build and make the enterprise a success. This office he still holds. He was married, January 27, 1864, to Ella Maria Dietz, daughter of William H. Dietz, of New York City. They reside in Reading, and have one child:—

i. EDWARD MYERS, JR., born May 6, 1869.

99. MARY HIESTER (CLYMER) CLYMER.— Born in Berks county, Pennsylvania, July 19, 1825; and was married, August 10, 1852, in Christ Church, Reading, by the Rev. Milton Lightner, rector, to her cousin, William Bingham Clymer, the eldest son of Henry, and grandson of George Clymer, one of the Signers of the Declaration of Independence.—(See this family in the *Lloyd and Carpenter Genealogy*, by C. P. Smith, Esq.) Mr. Clymer was born at the homestead, near Trenton, Bucks county, Pennsylvania; his mother being Mary Willing. He received a liberal education, graduating with credit at Princeton College; and studied law, but never practiced. When quite young, he assumed the management of the Bingham estate. In 1842, was appointed General Agent for the Northern Counties of Pennsylvania, and in 1845, established the general office of the estate at Wellsboro. His management of this large property was highly successful, so that in 1867, he was appointed a trustee. He ever carefully considered the rights and interests of all; and enjoyed the confidence of the trustees; while his courtesy, kindness, and

perfect integrity commanded the respect of the tenants and others, on the estate. Mr. and Mrs. Clymer resided since their marriage, at Wellsboro, Tioga county, where all their children were born, with the exception of the third, who was born in Philadelphia. In July, 1869, they sailed for Europe, taking all their children, for the advantages of education ; and while abroad, on the 28th of May, 1873, Mr. Clymer died of apoplexy, in Florence, Italy. The family then returned to Philadelphia, in the autumn. Mr. Clymer's remains were sent home, and are interred in Charles Evans Cemetery, near Reading.

Their children, all baptized by Rev. Mr. Marple, rector of Christ Church, Wellsboro, are :—

     i. HENRY,   born June 10, 1853 ; d. Nov. 2, 1854.
     ii. MARY,   "   Dec. 13, 1854.
     iii. ELLEN S.,   "   Dec. 9, 1856 ; d. Mar. 30, 1858.
     iv. RICHARD WILLING,   "   Apr. 10, 1858.
     v. MARIA HIESTER,   "   Feb. 11, 1862.
     vi. ROSA NICOLLS,   "   Sep. 19, 1865.

100.   HON. HIESTER CLYMER.—Born in Berks county, Pennsylvania, November 3, 1827. He received a liberal education, graduating from the College of New Jersey, at Princeton, in 1847 ; and taking up the study of law ; after which he practiced in Reading and Pottsville. He was a delegate to the Democratic Convention at Charleston, in 1860 ; and the same year was a member of the Board of Revenue Commissioners. Served as State senator, 1860–6. Became the Democratic candidate for governor in the latter year, but was defeated by Governor Geary. In 1870 he was appointed by the governor a member of the Board of Public Charities, then just organized. In 1873 he was elected a representative to the XLIII. Congress, from Berks county, as a Democrat, and served on the committees on the Revision of the Laws, on Public Lands, and on the Library. He was re-elected to the XLIV. Congress, and was placed on the committees on Expenditures of the War Department, and the Joint Standing Committee on the Library. He was married, April 3, 1856, to Elizabeth M., daughter of Matthew Brooke, of Birdsboro. They resided in Reading, where their children were born ; and where Mrs. Clymer died, October 9, 1870. Their issue :—

     i. ELIZABETH M.,   b. Jan. 20, 1857 ; d. Jan. 12, 1865.
     ii. EDWARD BROOKE, b. Mch. 18, 1859 ; d. Jan, 24, 1861.

12

101. GEORGE EDWARD CLYMER.—Born January 8, 1830, and after graduating from Princeton College in 1849, became associated in 1854 with his brothers in the iron business in Pennsylvania. He spent the greater part of the year 1858 in Mexico, in connection with a party surveying the route for a railroad from Vera Cruz to the City of Mexico. In the summer of 1861 he raised a company of cavalry attached to the 6th Pennsylvania Regiment, Colonel R. II. Rush; of which he was made major, in March, 1862, but resigned the next year on account of business engagements. From 1865–8, Major Clymer was occupied in mining in Nevada and Chihuahua. In 1870 he severed his business connection with his brothers in Temple, Pennsylvania, and removed from thence to Cincinnati, Ohio, where he became interested in the Swift Iron and Steel Works, of Newport, Kentucky, of which his father-in-law is president. He himself was elected vice-president in 1874, and removed to Newport for convenience to the works.

Major Clymer was married, June 29, 1868, to Alice Cary Swift, daughter of Alexander and Susan Cary Swift, of Cincinnati. She was born March 24, 1844, and died in Jacksonville, Florida, February 14, 1873.

Their children :—

    i. EDWIN SWIFT,   b. June 16, 1871.
    ii. GEORGE ALEXANDER, b. July 25, 1872; d. May 1, 1873.

SIXTH GENERATION.

————•-•————

CHILD OF WILLIAM II. ALLISON. [60.]

102.   MARY SELINA (ALLISON) NORMAN.—
Born in Boonville, Missouri, November 22, 1852; and
was married, July 4, 1875, to George Norman, of Vernon
county, Missouri.

CHILD OF MARY DeNEALE (WOLFE) AND JUDGE TH. N. MORGAN. [63.]

103.   THOMAS WOLFE MORGAN.—Born in New
Orleans in 1837; removed in 1854 to California, with
the others of the family; and was married at Santa Cruz,
Christmas, 1865, to Christine Ross, a lady of Scotch
parentage.   He is a civil engineer by profession, the
family now residing in Oakland, near San Francisco.
Their children :—

 i.   Ross.
 ii.   MARY DeNEALE.
 iii.   JANET HARMON.
 iv.   THOMAS WOLFE, JR., b. Aug. 22, 1875.

CHILDREN OF MARY DeNEALE (WOLFE) AND JOHN B. HARMON. [63.]

104.   DANA HARMON.—Born in New Orleans;
graduated at Yale College in 1872, and is now reading
law with his father, in Oakland, California.

105.   ROBERDEAU HARMON.—Born in Califor-
nia, and is now about graduating from the University of
California.

CHILD OF THOMAS ROBERDEAU WOLFE. [64.]

106.   MARY PATTEN (WOLFE) WARD.—Born
in New Orleans; married, April 25, 1867, to Frank X.
Ward, of Baltimore, a lawyer, and died in Baltimore,
March 1, 1871, without issue.

CHILDREN OF MARY C. (MILLER) AND DR. THOMAS DUNN. [68.]

107.   BETTIE McALLISTER (DUNN) DUNN.—
Born at Lake Providence, Louisiana, February 17, 1844;
married, May 31, 1861, to her cousin, William Blanton
Dunn, of Greenville, Mississippi.   He was a planter at
the time, the war having previously interrupted his
studies in medicine.   He died at Greenville, August 3,
1861, leaving no children.

108.   JOHN NELSON DUNN.—Born in Issaquena,
Mississippi, September 28, 1845. He was married, Novem-
ber 14, 1872, at Memphis, Tennessee, to Mary Dee
Pickett, daughter of Edward B. and Laura Pickett, of
that place.   He is a merchant, now living in Greenville,
Mississippi.   Their children :

    i. BESSIE LEE,   } Twins, born { d. Oct. 24, 1873.
    ii. ADA,   } Oct. 3, 1873. { d. Nov. 21, 1873.

109.   THOMAS WILSON DUNN.—Born at Lake
Providence, Louisiana, November 14, 1847 ; a farmer
near Leota on the Mississippi river, Washington county,
Mississippi.

110.   CHAPIN HARRIS DUNN.—Born at Lake
Providence, Louisiana, October 26, 1849. In mercantile
life at Greenville, Mississippi.

111.   SAMUEL REED DUNN.—Born at Lake Providence, Louisiana, February 7, 1851 ; now in mercantile
life at Greenville, Mississippi.

CHILD OF LAURA P. AND LEWIS H. PIERCE. [69.]

112.   MARY RIVERA (PIERCE) BAKER.—Born
in Wilmington, North Carolina, October 10, 1850. Resided, until recently, with her aunt, Mrs. Thompson, at
Annapolis Junction, Maryland ; where she was married,
May 27; 1874, to her cousin, (through the Miller family,)
William Hartman Baker, the business partner of her
uncle, Albert P. Miller, of Winchester, Virginia, where
they now reside.   Their issue :—

    i. SARAH RIVERA, b. July 6, 1875.

113. HARRIET ROZIER (PIERCE) BARKSDALE.
—Born in Wilmington, North Carolina, January 23, 1855; and married, December 23, 1874, to Sherod Barksdale, a farmer in Clinton, Sampson county, North Carolina. Their issue:—

   i. LAURA PIERCE, b. Jan. 7, 1876.

CHILDREN OF SELINA P. (WHEAT) AND DR. JOHN SEAY. [75.]

114. JOHN THOMAS SEAY.—Born at Lake Providence, Louisiana, September 27, 1848. He went to Honduras in April, 1869, and is engaged in sugar planting in Manatee District, twenty-four miles from Belize, British Honduras.

115. SELINA WHEAT (SEAY) PILCHER.—Born at Lake Providence, Louisiana, March 19, 1852; married, April 5, 1874, to Charles Morehouse Pilcher, of Carroll Parish, a native of Tennessee. His mother was a sister of Mrs. Joseph M. Patten. Mr. Pilcher is a promising lawyer at Lake Providence. Their child:—

   i. SELINA WHEAT, b. July 27, 1875.

116. MARY DeNEALE (SEAY) BRINTON.—Born January 26, 1854, at Lake Providence, Louisiana; married, October 11, 1874, to C. H. Brinton.

117. GEORGE WHARTON SEAY.—Born at Lake Providence, Louisiana, September 7, 1855, and was married in July, 1873, to Mary Grebbeau, both being at an early age. Their issue:—

   i. SELINA WHEAT, b. 1874.

CHILDREN OF SELINA R. (IRVINE) AND WILLIAM H. SIZER. [80.]

118. WILLIAM HENRY SIZER.—Born in Richmond, Virginia, November 14, 1844. During the late war he lived in Alabama; but for the past four or five years had been in business in Richmond, where he died unmarried, June 22, 1875.

119. JAMES IRVINE SIZER.—Born in Richmond, Virginia, November 1, 1846. He saw considerable service in the late war; having been in Crenshaw's Battery of Artillery, commanded by Colonel Pegram, and was in the battles of the Wilderness, Cold Harbor, Petersburg, and Five Forks; and was finally taken prisoner at New Stone, Virginia, and sent to Fortress Monroe. He was lately engaged on the Mobile and Montgomery Railroad, but now lives in Pollard, Alabama. He was married at Fort Deposit, Alabama, March 18, 1869, to Green Annie Majors, daughter of Samuel and Mrs. Polly Majors, of Twiggs county, Georgia. She was born in Athens, Butter county, November 29, 1845, and died December 9, 1869, having had issue:—

   i. A CHILD, b. dead two weeks before its mother's death.

120. ANNA BAXTER (SIZER) MAYSON.—Born in Richmond, Virginia, December 12, 1848; married at Pollard, Alabama, February 11, 1868, to Francis Ramsey Mayson, of Pensacola, Florida, her sister being also married at the same time and place. They recently resided at Pensacola Junction, but now at Mobile, where Mr. Mayson is connected with the Mobile & Montgomery Railroad. Their children:—

   i. A DAUGHTER,   b. March 8, 1869; d. the same day.
   ii. CHARLIE BULL,   b. Nov. 6, 1870.
   iii. WILLIAM FRANCISCO, b. March 5, 1873.
   iv. ALBERT ROBERDEAU, b. May 20, 1876. The youngest member of
                          the Roberdeau family.

121. SELINA ANN (SIZER) DRURY.—Born in Richmond, Virginia, March 8, 1850; married at Pollard, Alabama, February 11, 1868, to John Francis Drury, who was born June 10, 1846, in the latter city, where they now reside. Their children:—

   i. A CHILD,   d. at birth.
   ii. SUSAN IRVINE, b. Apr. 9, 1871; d. Aug. 21, 1873.
   iii. JOHN HENRY, b. May 20, 1874.

122. IRENE (SIZER) BULLOCK—Born in Richmond, May 12, 1854; married at Bayminette, Baldwin county, Alabama, March 7, 1872, to John W. Bullock, (a native of Loundes county, March 23, 1851.) They now reside in Milton, Florida. Their children:—

   i. MARY SELINA, b. Feb. 22, 1873, Milton, Fla.
   ii. IRENE ADELLA, b. May 26, 1875, Letohatchee, Lowndes Co.

CHILD OF DANIEL R. CLYMER. [96.]

123. ANNIE M. C. (CLYMER) BROOKE.—Born in Reading, Pennsylvania, June 24, 1849, and married, June 22, 1868, to Edward Brooke, iron-master, of Birdsboro, Pennsylvania. Their issue:—

i. ANNIE CLYMER,   b. March 28, 1870.
ii. ROBERT EDWARD,   b. July 7, 1872.
iii. GEORGE CLYMER,   b. June 5, 1875.

CONCLUSION.

Our family lies scattered over fifteen States, and one member lives abroad, in Central America. It is believed that the above genealogy is COMPLETE down to the time of publication; containing a record of every descendant of the Cunyngham and Roberdeau families in this country. The only omissions possible, (and none are known of,) being infants in some of the earlier generations, either born dead or who died soon after birth; particular inquiry having been made for the names of *all* children. Contrary to the usual labors of genealogists, all of the older members of the family were in this case known, requiring the search to be downward for the later generations, in which the writer has been aided very materially by three members of the family; Mrs. Dr. Wheat, and a gentleman, whose name, at his desire, is withheld, to whom the whole of one branch of the family seems to have been known; and also to Edward M. Clymer, Esq., for the other branch.

Nor must the writer omit to mention the great assistance he has received from the voluminous manuscripts left by his grandfather, Colonel Isaac Roberdeau; consisting of letters, copies, official papers, and above all, including Robert Cunyngham's manuscript, which the Colonel had continued down to his own family, thus helping us over that most difficult step to American Genealogists—tracing the connection between their progenitor and parent family abroad. Colonel Roberdeau's papers have been quoted in almost every portion of this book.

A marked peculiarity in this genealogy must already have been noticed; and that is, the few who bear the

surname of Roberdeau. Of the 458 names forming the
genealogy, but 42 bear the surname; of this number,
7 gained it by marriage. There are now living, 3 who
have lost the surname by marriage, 2 who have in that
manner gained it, *and only five who bear it by birth!* Verily,
this genealogy is "like the tragedy of Hamlet, the
character of the Prince of Denmark being left out."

The name ROBERDEAU is thus seen to be exceedingly
rare, there being none in the country who bear it, either
as a christian or surname, other than those here enumerated, with the exception of two or three individuals who
were named in honor of some member of the family.*
The directories of the large cities may be searched for it
in vain. This name has, however, been preserved in the
family as a christian name, generally of a male. It has
been so borne by 39 persons.† Next as a favorite comes
the name *Selina*, borne by 22;‡ then *Heriot*, from our
ancestor, James Heriot, has been given as a female name
to 6 of the family.‖

Another peculiarity, and growing out of the former,
may have been observed; namely, the large number of
other surnames that appear; and which is accounted
for by the small number of males in proportion to females
who marry, and the still smaller proportion of those who

---

*William Roberdeau Swift, twin son of Lawrence Hill, born November, 1825;
baptized, 1st Presbyterian Church, Alexandria, Virginia, March 2, 1826. Mr.
Campbell, Colonel I. Roberdeau's partner at Oxford Furnace, named a son
Roberdeau after the latter. A brother of Col. J. G. Reynolds, U. S. M. C.,
was also named after him. Walter Whaley, of Fairfax county, Virginia, has
a son named Benjamin Roberdeau. Col. Roberdeau walking one day in
Alexandria, heard a boy call "Roberdeau" in addressing a companion; his
surname is unknown.

†H. R. Allison,[6] J. R. Allison,[5] R. Allison,[5] Heriot R. Annan,[4] J. R. An-
nan,[4] R. Annan,[4] R. Annan,[5] R. Annan,[6] W. D. R. Annan,[6] R. Buchanan,[5]
D. R. Clymer,[5] D. R. Clymer, Jr.,[6] J. R. Conrad,[4] J. R. Foote,[5] R. Harmon,[6]
A. R. Holderby,[5] A. R. Holderby, Jr.,[6] A. R. Mayson,[7] Harriet R. Miller,[5]
Harriet R. Miller,[5] Mrs. S. A. R. McCraw,[4] Ann R. Patten,[5] I. R. Patten,[4]
R. S. Patten,[6] T. R. Patten,[4] R. E. Pierce,[6] J. R. Powell,[5] Virginia R. Powell,[5]
R. W. Seay,[6] Selina R. Shober,[6] R. W. Sizer,[6] Mrs. Selina R. Sizer,[5] D. R.
Swift,[4] W. R. Swift,[4] R. Triplett,[6] C. R. Wheat,[5] Ellen R. Wolfe,[6] T. R.
Wolfe,[5] T. R. Wolfe, Jr.[6]

‡Mrs. M. S. Allison,[4] M. S. Allison,[6] Mrs. F. S. Buchanan,[4] M. S. Bullock,[7]
Mrs. M. S. Coulling,[5] Mrs. S. A. Drury,[6] S. Fife,[6] S. F. Holderby,[5] Mrs. S.
A. C. Irvine,[4] S. Kent,[6] S. A. Kent,[5] S. M. Miller,[5] S. B. Morgan,[6] Mrs. S.
Nickolls,[3] Mrs. S. W. Pilcher,[6] S. W. Pilcher,[7] Mrs. S. P. Seay,[5] S. W. Seay,[7]
S. Roberdeau Shober,[6] Mrs. S. Roberdeau Sizer,[5] Ann S. Swift,[4] Mrs. S. B.
Wheat.[4]

‖H. J. Annan,[6] H. R. Annan,[4] Mrs. H. Conrad,[3] Mrs. H. V. Triplett,[5] H.
Roberdeau,[4] Mrs. H. T. Richardson.[4]

have issue. These facts, with others, may be seen from the annexed Statistical Tables, made up from the names in this genealogy.

It is here seen, that contrary to usual statistics, the males born are in a deficiency; being nearly as 7 males to 8 females (1 : 1.12.) Those who marry are in the proportion of 2 to 3 (1 : 1.53); while those having issue are as 4 to 7 (1 : 1.75.) Among General Roberdeau's descendants, this disproportion is still more striking. Those who marry are as 1 to 2 (1 : 2.00); and those having issue are nearly as 2 to 5 (1 : 2.35.) As a consequence, three out of every four marriages bring in new surnames; hence, the variety observable.

A word about family traits. The family likeness, judging from a few individuals, seems to be a large stature, inclined to stoutness, the head broad, with prominently marked lips, erect forehead, and nose such as Napoleon would have liked!

It is a matter of regret that the expense should have prevented the insertion of family likenesses, and of engravings of the various old portraits.

Many of the family seem to write a peculiar back-hand. But the most noticeable of all is the clannish feeling existing between the members, which possibly came down from our Scottish forefathers. It shows itself as a veneration for our ancestors, and affection for our relatives, both distant and near. No further proof of this could be given, than the willingness, and in many cases enthusiasm, with which *all* have responded to the writer's applications for information regarding their particular branches. Their letters all evincing the warmth of relationship.

And to those who have followed him through these pages, the writer now wishes an affectionate adieu.

* Statistical Tables of the Roberdeau Family.

Generations.	Whole Number of Names.			Those Now Alive.			Lineal Descendants.		
	Males.	Fem.	Total.	Males.	Fem.	Total.	Males.	Fem.	Total.
1	2	1	3	......	......	......	......	1	1
2	2	4	6	......	......	......	1	2	3
3	9	14	23	......	1	1	4	10	14
4	36	38	74	10	16	26	21	28	49
5	86	80	166	48	50	98	60	60	120
6	86	77	163	64	56	120	75	73	148
7	9	14	23	8	9	17	9	14	23
Total.	230	228	458	130	132	262	170	188	358

Generations.	Those Who Have Married.			Added to the Family by Marriage.			Those Who Have Issue.		
	Males.	Fem.	Total.	Males.	Fem.	Total.	Males.	Fem.	Total.
1	......	1	1	2	......	2	......	1	1
2	1	1	2	1	2	3	1	1	2
3	3	5	8	5	4	9	3	5	8
4	10	15	25	15	10	25	6	14	20
5	19	23	42	26	20	46	14	21	35
6	4	11	15	11	4	15	4	7	11
7	......	......	......	......	......	......	......	......	......
Total.	37	56	93	60	40	100	28	49	77

```
First and second generations............................  ..............................      9
Daniel Roberdeau's children who died young............................       6
    Isaac Roberdeau's descendants..............................................   11
    Ann Swift,           "      ...................................................   72
    Mary Patten,         "      ...................................................  142
    Selina Nickolls,     "      ...................................................   56
    Jane Annan,          "      ...................................................   38
    James M. Roberdeau,  "      ...................................................   62
    Heriot Conrad,       "      ...................................................    5
                                                                                  ——
                                                                                  386
Ann Clymer's descendants: D. C. Clymer, only child...................   57
                                                                                  ——
                                                                                  458
```

Average number of children to a family, (exclusive of 16 *sine prole*,) 4.65.

* These statistics are compiled from a *complete* list of the descendants of one person, including also those added by marriage.

INDEX OF NAMES.—I.

BEING THOSE COMPRISING THE GENEALOGY, PART II., AND
INCLUDING THOSE CONNECTED BY MARRIAGE.

The exponents show the generation.

Females are entered under both their married and maiden names.
Both should be looked for.

————— ►••◄ —————

INDEX OF NAMES.—II.

BEING THOSE INCIDENTALLY MENTIONED, OR REMOTELY
CONNECTED WITH THE FAMILY; THE LATTER
IN SMALL CAPITALS.

13

ERRATA.

Page 13, note 13, add: The title Earl of Carrick is now borne by the Prince of Wales as heir apparent to the Scottish throne.

Page 18, note 19, for *Wennebald*, read *Wernebald*.

Page 36, line 10, and page 56, line 15 from bottom, for *Huntington*, read *Huntingdon*.

Page 45, line 10 from bottom, for *Griffitts*, read *Griffiths*.

Page 54, lines 23, 27, 31, for *Davis*, read *Davies*.

Page 97, line 14 from bottom, omit the fifth word.

Page 107, line 27, for *Rogers*, read *Rodgers*.

Page 108. The Gross family: Mr. Balch says that the Hon. Robert C. Winthrop, of Boston, has papers to the effect that the Gross family was Huguenot, originally writing the name Le Gros.

Page 123, line 10 from bottom, for *Chromotype*, read *Chronotype*.

Page 129, vii. child, for *Francis*, read *Frances*.

139, line 18, for *Sotomayer*, read *Sotomayor*.